Praise for Sheryl Nantus and the Blood of the Pride series

"Rebecca Desjardin rivals Sue Grafton's Kinsey Millhone as an interesting female P.I. Recommended for both fans of the genre and newbies to paranormal romance."
—*Library Journal* on *Claws Bared*

"If you're a fan of strong female characters and mysteries with a paranormal twist, this is a real winner."
—*Reflections on Reading Romance* on *Blood of the Pride*

"Sheryl Nantus' *Blood of the Pride* is a tale of murder mingled with mystery in a secret feline society that will scratch that itch for romance."
—*Love Romances & More*

"A really good read that kept me guessing till the end. I loved the romance between Rebecca and Brandon."
—*www.BookLiaison.com* on *Claws Bared*

"Well-written urban fantasy with a strong, appealing heroine."
—Nicole Luiken, author, on *Blood of the Pride*

"This is a shifter series that I will definitely be following."
—*TomeTender.blogspot.com* on *Claws Bared*

Also available from Sheryl Nantus and Carina Press

Blood of the Pride
Claws Bared
Battle Scars

SHERYL NANTUS

FAMILY PRIDE

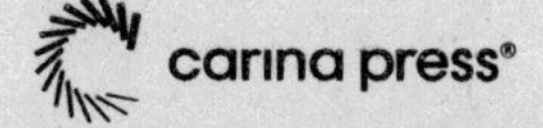

Recycling programs for this product may not exist in your area.

ISBN-13: 978-0-373-00217-7

FAMILY PRIDE

This edition published by arrangement with Harlequin Books S.A.

www.CarinaPress.com

Printed in U.S.A.

Dear Reader,

There's an old joke—you can choose your friends but you can't choose your family.

Having family brings into your life a number of burdens and responsibilities, some willingly accepted and some that are just too darned annoying for words. The drunk uncle who persists on falling asleep/ passing out on the couch overnight for every holiday. The younger sister or brother who is determined to carry the title of black sheep and carry it proudly no matter the consequences to anyone else. The cousin who gets away with everything and always has the full support of the family, despite the consequences.

But there's an even more traumatizing moment—when you introduce your new love to your family. That terrifying moment when you sit down with your potential in-laws and wonder what they think of you and your relationship—whether they'll approve or not.

Rebecca Desjardin may be Felis but she's like every other woman when it comes to meeting the family—and needless to say Brandon Hanover's family might just rival her Felis one when it comes to duplicity and internal politics.

And when it comes down to it she might have to choose one family over the other....

Sheryl Nantus

For my husband,
who never let me give up on myself, AD for
never letting me do anything less than my best
and for Jazz—still missed and loved dearly.

FAMILY PRIDE

ONE

"MY PARENTS WANT to meet you."

I dropped the thick ceramic mug in the sink. It bounced once before landing in the inch-deep soapy water. The clanging sound bounced around my skull, settling behind my left eye and throbbing.

"Your parents are dead." I turned and leaned against the counter. "Are we attending a séance?"

Bran bit his lower lip. He hadn't bothered to put a shirt on, choosing to pad around my house barefoot in a pair of jeans that fit perfectly in all the right places. We'd finally dragged ourselves out of bed for lunch, ordering in pizza because we had run out of groceries.

His dark eyes met mine, apologetic and pleading.

"They're not, ah, dead. They're sort of alive."

I picked up the mug and contemplated how much strength it would take to smash it. "Your parents are zombies?"

"My parents are alive and well and very much human."

I weighed the mug in my palm, letting him watch my fingers curl around the cool clay. "You lied to me. Four months ago you lied to my face."

"Maybe." Bran put out his hand, pointing at the mug. "Please put that down."

I glared at him.

"Okay, I lied. A bit." His hand didn't move, still outstretched toward the mug. "I told you my parents were dead but that was right after we'd met and we were on opposite sides of the case." Bran smiled. "And I didn't know how good we could be together."

I didn't blink.

"Cut me a break, Reb. You've got your own family secrets." He shifted to one side with a grin, showing off his newest scratches on one shoulder. "And I can make you purr."

Damned redhead had a point. We'd both kept things from each other back then. I hadn't exactly been forthcoming about the fact that I wasn't human, but when Bran had come face-to-face with my Felis heritage I hadn't lied and denied.

I still didn't have to like it. "Who are they and why did you lie?"

He didn't move. My gaze traveled over his bare

chest, resting on the fresh scars across his midsection courtesy of our latest work trip to Penscotta, Pennsylvania. He'd fought another Felis for his life and, in his own way, for me.

The least I could do was hear him out before throwing the mother of all temper tantrums.

"My father is Michael Hanover." Bran paused. "Of Hanover Investments."

I nearly dropped the mug.

"Hanover Investments. As in, they make more money in ten minutes than I'll ever see in my lifetime?" I croaked. I'd flipped through a few business articles over the past few years when I was supposed to be reading a paper and instead using it for surveillance. The business section guarantees you won't be distracted by the articles.

"Yeah. Them." He sounded almost apologetic. "It's a family business. Three generations."

"You're related to *those* Hanovers?"

"Michael and Bernadette Hanover are my parents." He reached out and took the mug from my numb fingers. "The reason I lied was because it'd become an instinctive reaction to explain away my wealth. Easier to say trust fund than explain my dysfunctional relationship with my parents." He shook his head, a sad smile on his lips. "You'd be surprised how many gold diggers are out there looking to snag a rich man. Or his son."

I tried to get my breathing under control. "Those Hanovers."

"We'd just met," Bran repeated. He placed the mug out of my reach and returned to stand in front of me, both hands up. "And I used the same line I use with everyone to explain my wealth. It was automatic."

I closed my eyes and drew what I hoped was a deep calming breath. "And when were you planning to divulge this little bit of information?"

It came out as a hiss between clenched teeth.

"I was waiting for the right time. I know it sounds silly but it's not exactly a topic to drop into casual conversation," Bran answered. He shuffled forward and put his hands on my shoulders, his heated skin scorching through the thin T-shirt I wore. "I'm sorry."

"This—" I shook my head "—this is a major thing. I could understand lying about your university marks or former lovers or something like that—but lying about your parents being alive?" I wasn't going to let him off so easily despite the heat surging down my spine at his touch. "What else have you forgotten to tell me?"

"Nothing else, Reb. I swear, nothing else."

His right hand moved to rub over the still-healing scars on his stomach. “I’d never want to hurt you on purpose.”

The cold grip on my heart shifted and melted. “Damn it, Bran…”

“I’m sorry.” He moved in and laid down a line of kisses from the edge of my mouth to my earlobe. “So sorry. So damned sorry.”

“Okay, they’re alive. And they want to meet me. They’re not going to like me,” I murmured, fighting to stay afloat on the emotional waves battering my defenses. “I’m not a purebred.” I couldn’t help grinning. “Sort of a nasty bitch when I think about it.”

Bran replied with a light tug on my earlobe with his teeth, enough to urge a gasp out of me. “They’re going to be fine. I’m a grown man, and I can make my own decisions about who to date.” Another soft kiss. “Mate.”

This time I couldn’t hold off the shivers running over my skin. In the month since we’d gotten back from Pennsylvania we’d taken another step forward in our relationship and it had been interesting, to say the least.

The definition of interesting included scratches, bruises, one sprained wrist (his) and one wrenched shoulder (mine).

We'd started off a few months ago, drawn together to find a killer, and moved into a relationship with little problem. The breaking point came three months later when I'd been forced to face my inner Felis and deal with my feelings about dating a human. We were a ferociously devoted species when it came to our mates and I didn't know if Bran could handle the emotional and physical commitment. Felis didn't do casual long-term relationships, and even though I had been cast out of the family as a teenager, neither did I. We mated for life, something I knew from working as a private investigator that a lot of humans couldn't handle.

Judging from the past few weeks we were doing fine.

"They're flying in today from London on the private jet. I told them we'd meet them for dinner." The heated whisper in my ear didn't do anything to dampen my flash of anger.

"London, England? Flew? Private what?" I tried to break away from his grip and failed miserably. "When? Where? Do I need to dress for this? I don't want to wear makeup. I don't have anything to wear. Why are you doing this to me?"

Bran chuckled. "Seven tonight. A small restaurant in Yorkville. If you have a dress it'd be nice—

anything but jeans will meet the dress code. And I love you." He dropped a kiss on the tip of my nose. "Chill, Rebecca. Chill."

I glanced around the kitchen. It was small, like the rest of the house. I'd bought it a decade ago and managed to finance thanks to one enthusiastic client demanding proof on a dozen possible suitors for his daughter. It served as home and office, saving me the expense of running a different place for my investigation business. The ground floor had my office/living room and kitchen with the upper floor holding my bedroom and a washroom. It wasn't fancy but it was mine.

But it was nothing compared to the top-level condominium Bran owned over at Yonge and King, a short drive out of Parkdale and a million dollars away. I couldn't imagine how his parents would react seeing their son with a woman who literally counted pennies.

I automatically checked the canning jar atop the fridge. Another few pennies and I'd be ready to roll them up and drop them at the bank before the damned coin got retired.

I somehow doubted the Hanovers counted pocket change.

Or if they did it was in solid gold doubloons.

The doorbell rang.

"I'm not expecting anyone today." I grabbed a dishtowel from the counter. "I haven't had a case since that car insurance scam and I sent out the paperwork yesterday. Be sweet if they're dropping off a check now."

Brandon stepped back. "Probably the paperboy. I'll take care of it." He walked out of the kitchen. I watched him leave, appreciating the view. He'd been naturally blessed with a tight, sweet butt that begged for biting or grabbing.

Good thing he enjoyed both.

Jazz hopped on the counter and lay down, a white carpet of relaxed catness.

I wagged a finger at her. "No. Get down."

She yawned, showing off one chipped fang, and curled up into a ball before falling asleep right next to the sugar bowl. One paw edged out to grip the corner of the counter, anchoring her in place.

"Hey, I tried," I told the linoleum before heading for the living room. "Bran, tell whoever's there to bugger off 'cause I don't have time…"

Two people stood by the secondhand couch I'd gotten from a store on Queen Street, talking to Bran. His hand brushed over a ripped corner I'd slapped duct tape on—the damage not from Jazz's claws but my own ineptness in getting it through the front door. I glanced around the room, assessing the rest of the furniture.

Nearby an oval dark wood stool held a stack of magazines, the concave shape of one leg showing Jazz's enthusiastic work in using it as a scratching post. A short hop from there sat my business desk, cluttered with old and new files as I put off buying another filing cabinet for as long as possible.

I'd never thought of my interior decorating skills as being lacking. Everything was functional and affordable, from the mismatched chairs to the generic nature prints on the wall. It wasn't fancy but it was home, comfortable and relaxed.

The two visitors looked like diamonds shining in a coal mine.

I winced and moved in closer.

The woman looked at me for a second before turning back to Bran. Her upper lip curled a fraction, so fast someone else would have missed it.

I didn't. Disdain. Contempt. Superiority. All in one expensive package glaring at me.

Blond hair, right out of a bottle, bounced around her shoulders. She wore a bright orange dress and enough bling to blind someone. Her matching purse hung limply from the crook of her elbow.

I turned my attention to the older man.

He had to be in his early sixties with a full head of red hair touched with a delicate gray around the temple. His three piece dark blue suit cost more than what I made in a month. The silk gray and white striped power tie screamed affluence.

I sniffed the air, afraid of what I'd find. The scents bounced back to me with a frightful speed and clarity, confirming what I'd suspected. And feared.

Everyone in this room was related to each other.

Except for me.

I forced a cheerful smile, feeling the jagged edge of panic digging into my belly.

Mom and Dad were early.

Bran looked at me. I could smell the fear radiating out from him as I advanced on them. Not for me—he was afraid of his parents. His shoulders slumped down and if he could have he would have been curled up on the floor in a fetal position—or worse, on his back in full submission mode.

He was scared shitless.

I felt a growl spiral up my throat, seeing the effect they had on him. This wasn't a healthy relationship. Not that I knew much about happy families, but this couldn't be what they looked like.

This was not going to go well.

The elder Hanover male smiled at me. "You

must be Rebecca Desjardin." He stuck out his hand, the finely manicured nails stabbing at me. "Michael Hanover. And this is my wife, Bernadette."

His grip was manlier than I'd expected, a quiet strength underlining the silk. A hunter and killer. This was not a man to be taken lightly.

I'd have expected no less from one of Canada's premiere wheelers and dealers in the business world. What I knew about investing could fill Jazz's food dish but I knew Michael Hanover made a lot of money for a lot of important people.

I couldn't connect the stern businessman in front of me with Bran. The truth about his parents still rankled—but looking at these two made me more sympathetic to his reasoning.

I imagined many a woman wilting under their inspection.

Bran gave me a halfhearted grin. "They caught an early flight. Since I wasn't at my condo they came here." His voice trailed off as the obvious question came to mind.

"How did you know to come here?" I let Michael's fingers slip free.

Bernadette took over. "We looked at the report we have on you. Address was right there on the front page. Took a few minutes to reroute the cab to this—" her nose wrinkled as she struggled to find a less insulting word than slum "—distinct neighborhood." She extended her hand. "Pleased to meet you."

It was like touching cold raw chicken. She pulled back as soon as manners allowed and gave me a big friendly smile.

"So," she murmured, "this is your home."

I felt the hairs on the back of my neck shoot straight up. I'd expected some resistance, sure—but this was like facing down a raging elephant with a potato gun. I resisted the urge to scurry around the room tidying up.

On the other hand I'd been busy lately hunting down murderers and renegades. They balanced each other out.

Bran cleared his throat. "Obviously we're not ready to go out yet. Why don't you two go home and have a bit of a rest? We'll meet you at the restaurant?"

"Of course," Michael replied. "We just wanted to stop on by and say hello." He stared at me, looking for a weakness.

He didn't find any.

His mother interrupted our mental duel. "We decided to change the restaurant. There's a charity event we have to make an appearance at before dinner. Sergio's instead. At eight o'clock."

"Of course. Eight. We'll be there," Bran answered.

Michael headed for the open door. Bernadette trotted out behind her husband, her high heels clattering along my hardwood floors with machine-gun precision.

I resisted the urge to flip them the bird.

A cool breeze rushed in the front door, smashing into my senses with even more scents. Fresh garbage from the street, dripping oil from a nearby car and…

And one I definitely did not want to find right now.

"Whuf." Bran shook his head. "That was…" He paused, seeing the expression on my face. "What the—"

I sprang past him and into the front yard, heart pounding with a combination of panic, fear and pride.

Jess dug the toe of her cowboy boot into one of the remaining green parts of my front lawn, having been confronted by the Hanovers. She shot me a deadly scowl as she faced the pair.

I had to give Bran's parents points for standing their ground. I'd seen lesser men and women shuffle to one side to give the Felis leader the right-of-way.

Bernadette moved behind Michael in a natural submissive move, using her husband as a human shield.

I sucked in my cheeks, holding the grin at bay. Sometimes fate had a wild sense of humor.

Michael cleared his throat, taking control of the situation. Or so he thought. "Jess Hammersmythe. I recognize you from the file. You're Rebecca's..." Michael let the sentence trail off, waiting for a response.

That sort of subtle fishing for information might have worked on someone else but not on Jess.

"Friend of the family." Jess didn't give an inch. Her one good eye studied the two Hanovers. I could see her assessing the pair and finding them wanting in most areas.

It wasn't personal. Jess plain didn't like humans.

Bernadette frowned. "An aunt, maybe? Her parents—" She cut off her words when her husband tugged on her arm.

"Really, dear. There's a time and a place for this sort of discussion and this isn't it." The elder Hanover gave Jess a gentle smile. "You'll have to forgive her. She's rather rabid about taking care of our son and wanting to know everything about the company he keeps."

A shadow passed over Jess's face. For a second she looked older than her years, the crow's feet around her eyes growing deeper and dragging the energy out of her. "I understand. All parents want to protect their young."

Michael pulled again at his wife's arm. "We'll see you for dinner, Brandon." He gave Jess a respectful nod as they slid past her.

Jess walked past me into the house, head held high as Bran's parents escaped the front yard with a clattering of heels and low mutterings. I noticed their expensive sedan sitting on the street and sent up a quiet prayer of thanks it hadn't been scratched up or worse, jacked and headed for the local chop shop.

Not that I'd know about such things.

"You go see what's up with her." Bran jerked a thumb at his retreating family. "I'll see them off." He shuffled off toward the car, sweat beading on his forehead. It was a case of the lesser of two evils—and I knew there'd be a reckoning on all fronts at some point for this.

I spun on my heel and headed inside, eager and terrified to find out why Jess had come here.

She didn't do social visits. The last two times she'd contacted me had been job offers from the family.

I didn't need any more distractions at the moment.

Jess was in the kitchen putting the kettle on for tea. Jazz, lying on the counter, looked at Jess and rolled onto her back, offering her pink tummy. I watched with a detached curiosity as Jess went through the motions of making tea, something she'd only do for an equal or a superior.

Which I definitely was not, being outcast from the Pride. Recent events had me bordering on legitimacy within the Felis family. Barely.

Not that I gave a damn. I hadn't cared for over two decades and that feeling wasn't going to change anytime soon. But this was something new, something different, and I knew there was trouble in the air.

The Felis had managed to stay hidden within human society for centuries, keeping our feline shape-shifting abilities hidden from those who would want to study us or destroy us. We worked in human society, played in human society and even married humans—but maintaining our secret was paramount, without exception.

Even I was sworn to stay hidden, outcast and crippled by my inability to Change on demand.

"Brandon's parents." Jess rubbed the white cat's belly.

"Yep." I watched Jazz slip into bliss, the tip of her tail fluttering.

"I thought they were dead." She looked at me sideways. "Didn't he tell you they were dead?"

"Not so much." I waggled my hand in the air. "Seems his family is loaded." I drew out the last word to eight syllables. "Natural reaction is to deny any connection."

"Good survival technique." Jess dug under Jazz's jaw with her nails, encouraging even louder purring. "Looking at those two I can't blame him. I'd wish they were dead too."

"Jess." I shot her as much of a warning look as I dared. "I'm pissed off but I can understand why he did it." I repeated Bran's words. "We've got our own family secrets."

She pressed her lips together into a tight, straight line before responding. "I'm not sure if I'm willing to concede the high ground to him on this one."

"Well, you're not the one sleeping with him." It came out a bit sharper than I intended.

Jess's right eyebrow arched. "Down, girl. Wasn't

trying to add fuel to the fire. You've got enough on your plate as it is." She grunted. "No wonder he can keep secrets."

I didn't pursue that opening. Bran was one of the few humans who knew about the Felis and possibly the only one with actual status in the family. Beating down Carson in Pennsylvania had earned him respect from that Pride and it would have definitely made news on the Felis rumor mill.

"So now you're meeting the possible in-laws." Jess smirked. "Sort of terrifying, hmm?"

I didn't answer. I didn't have to—she'd raised two daughters and knew darned well what emotions were running wild. I pitied the poor men who'd tried wooing her girls—you'd have to have balls of steel to suggest a date, much less marriage. The two women had moved south to other Prides, away from their powerful mother.

"I'm not too worried about that." I waited, knowing what Jess was building up to.

"They have a *file* on you?"

I flinched at the unspoken reprimand. "I'll take care of it." I couldn't blame her for being upset. She'd worked hard to keep our existence secret.

She glared at me, the return of the iron lioness complete. "Do what you can, but realize if it gets out of control we'll have to take measures to stop this intrusion."

I didn't ask her to elaborate what would happen if I didn't put the Hanovers off that particular track.

I knew.

Bran came back into the kitchen at a run, rubbing his hands together. "Okay, parents are off and all's well. What's up?"

Jess's good eye twitched. "They have a file on Reb. They had her investigated."

I could hear her teeth grinding with each word.

"Standard procedure for every woman I date." A sheepish look replaced the panic. "My dad's worth, at last count, about five billion dollars. A lot of gold diggers out there figuring I'm worth a pretty penny."

Jess snorted. "You better be worth it."

Bran blew her a kiss. "Every penny." He struck a pose. "I got some mad moves from those boys down at the Cat's Meow." He swiveled his hips at Jess.

I felt my cheeks burn at the reference to the strip club down in Penscotta.

Jess looked like she was caught between laughing out loud and scowling at Bran's impudence.

She compromised by shaking her head and letting out a deep sigh.

"What did you come here for?" I deflected the conversation away from the topic at hand. "The Council need another favor? Another trip to clean up someone's dirty laundry."

Jess turned her full attention back on me. The scathing look sent me back a step, closer to Bran. "I was coming by to give you an update. Let you know the Penscotta Pride's being broken up into smaller pieces, based on current events. More of their children spreading out to other groups."

I nodded. It wasn't a surprise. When we'd left the Pennsylvania Pride the Felis had taken over the local town council. Good for business but bad for keeping the Felis secret—the more contact we had with humans the more likely someone would let something slip and our secret would be out.

Bran and I had discussed this many times, usually in bed. He couldn't see why we kept ourselves part of, but apart from human society. We were judges, lawyers, car lot owners and hot dog cart vendors—but we always kept to ourselves. We married other Felis from other Prides, rarely, if ever, taking human lovers, never mind human mates. A human husband or wife had to be kept out of the loop, never knowing their significant other kept deep secrets. For the Felis who married humans there'd always be the sense of loss, of separation from the family.

There weren't too many Felis who married humans.

"The Penscotta Board couldn't have been too happy." I glanced at Bran. He'd almost been killed by one of their overzealous members in an effort to keep another deep secret.

"A slight protest, more for show than anything else," Jess said. "But it's all for the best. We've got a few of them relocating up here, believe it or not."

"Not Trace," Bran growled.

"No." There was a touch of joviality in Jess's voice. "Don't worry—he knows his place."

"Far away from me. And Reb," Bran answered.

I felt a little rush of pride. It'd taken time, effort and bloodshed but Bran had finally won the grudging acceptance of the Felis and declared me his mate. He didn't have too many kind feelings for Trace, who had tried to convince me I'd be happier married to a Felis—specifically, him.

"You could have told me all this over the phone and avoided this entire situation," I said.

"I could have." Jess pulled an envelope out of her jacket pocket and laid it on the table. She turned the heat off under the screeching kettle and busied herself with filling the Brown Betty with hot water and fresh teabags. "I thought I'd stop on by and see how you were doing, given your new, ah, situation. Taking a human as a mate sounds… interesting." A tinge of red dyed her cheeks.

Bran gave her a wide grin. "I'm enjoying it."

She scowled at him but there was a trace of humor underlying her threat. "I'm talking to Reb. Don't want her breaking you in half."

Bran puffed his chest out and flexed his biceps. "I'm holding my own."

She dragged her eyes over him just slowly enough to make Bran flinch. "I've seen better."

I cleared my throat. "We're fine, thank you." I opened the package and flicked through the thick wad of twenty-dollar bills inside. "You already paid me."

Jess pulled down three mugs from the cupboard and poured out the tea. "The Penscotta Board decided to send up a bonus. They may be pissed at us but they appreciated your help." She added a dash of milk to two of them and passed one mug to me. "Seems you made quite the impression on them. The club is making the Pride a lot of money and it's helping relocate the wanderers along with boosting the local economy."

"I did my job." I spun the tea around in the

mug, watching the caramel-colored liquid swirl. "I did what you asked me to do. I found the killer."

Bran slipped by me to prepare his own tea, accepting the subtle snub.

Jess took a tentative sip from the mug. "You kept our secret in a rather dicey situation. That's more important."

I shrugged, not wanting to pursue an argument. I wasn't going to pass up free money. "Give them my thanks."

"I will." Jess gestured at the door. "The parents."

"I'll take care of it," I said. "Don't worry."

"It's my job to worry where you're involved." Jess looked at Bran. "You'd be best to remember that. Keep me informed on how this turns out." She put the tea down half-drunk and walked out of the kitchen.

I let out a breath I hadn't realized I'd been holding. "Damn. She still scares the shit out of me on the good days." I fondled the thick packet of money. "But I am looking forward to putting this in the bank. Saving for a rainy day and all that—it'll be nice not to worry about where my next paycheck is coming from for a bit."

Bran's expression turned solemn. "I am so damned sorry about this entire situation." He cradled the mug in both hands, leaning on the counter. "I'd forgotten what bastards they could be."

"I assume you're talking about your parents. Consider it payback for me inflicting Jess on you."

"Not equal by a long shot." He took a drink. "I'd put my money on my parents over Jess, any day." The fear returned to his voice. "I can't believe they pulled the file on you."

"They're looking out for their son. Understandable." I tried not to grit my teeth. "They're not going to find anything." I could hear the fear in my own words.

"Jess wasn't impressed they dug up her name." Bran finished off the tea in a gulp. "And neither am I. If they start digging too deep…" He bit down on his lower lip before continuing. "They use good investigators. Not too cheap and just pushy enough to get what they want. Scum."

I raised one eyebrow.

"Present company excepted."

"They can dig as much as they want as deep as they want. There's nothing to find." I poured out Jess's tea into the sink and added Bran's empty mug. "I went into the foster system at fifteen years old. I've got more documentation and paperwork out there on me than most people." It took a concentrated effort to still my trembling fingers as I grabbed my own drink. "Jess's people know their job. They won't find anything other than what we want them to find." I sipped the tea, relishing the warmth. "Better people have tried over the years and not succeeded. I doubt some overpaid punks are going to excavate anything worth worrying about."

Bran tilted his head to one side and smiled. "Are you trying to convince yourself or me?"

I sighed. "Whatever's needed to make this go away. We need it to go away." I bit down on the last two words.

"I can't believe they're still pulling this shit at my age." Bran huffed. "And now we're going to Sergio's for dinner. I am so bloody sorry about this."

I pulled away from my worries about the report and fell into predinner jitters. "What's wrong with Sergio's? I hear they've got nice food." In my mind I flipped through my wardrobe, trying to find something appropriate. The classic black dress would have to do—I didn't have anything else and there wasn't time to go shopping.

"Sergio's is where my father takes his business partners. It's a way for him to show off how much money he's got."

"So what's wrong with that?"

Bran grunted. "He never does anything without a reason. There's someone there he wants to impress, some point he wants to make, someone he wants to see us there. He doesn't go to Sergio's other than to see and be seen." He ran a hand through his red hair. "We should start getting ready. I have to go back to the condo and get a suit." He gestured down at his bare chest and jeans. "Definitely not getting in like this."

I moved in for a kiss, hoping to soothe his jangled nerves. "Good enough for me. And that's all that matters." I reached around and squeezed his ass. "I prefer you naked anyway."

"That's a dress code I can get with." He gave me a sheepish smile before pulling away. "I'll come by at seven. Give us plenty of time to panic and for you to change outfits three times before heading out."

I sighed. "You know me too well."

He snatched a quick kiss before heading upstairs to find his shirt and shoes. "Don't get stressed."

"'Don't get stressed' he says," I groused to Jazz, who had managed to cover even more counter space, almost falling into the sink. "Because we nosh at Sergio's every night."

Jazz yawned and chewed on one of her toes, leaving me with half a pot of tea and a full stomach of butterflies. What had started out as a lazy, dazy day was quickly turning into a crisis of epic proportions.

The little black dress still fit, thank God—after a few tugs and pulls in various places. I dug up a pair of matching shoes with a respectable heel that wouldn't cripple me. I wasn't worried about running from the scene of the crime but I didn't need to be wobbling like a newborn kitten.

The doorbell rang at seven exactly.

"I thought I gave you a key." I smiled as Bran stepped in. The dark blue suit was tailored to fit in all the right places, the white shirt spotless and freshly starched. The matching tie was a fraction crooked, enough to urge me to grab it and either fix it or rip it off.

"Yeah, but I didn't want to spook you." His stare started down at my feet and moved up, slowly and deliberately tearing the clothing off me with his gaze. "Haven't seen you in that outfit before."

"Ditto." I exhaled, feeling the familiar tingle down my spine. "Damn, you look hot."

"Not enough time." He held up a hand, a lustful grin spreading across his face. "Not enough time."

He was lying and I knew it. And he knew I knew it.

I glanced toward the couch and licked my lips. "Race ya."

WE ARRIVED AT Sergio's at five minutes to eight, tumbling out of a cab. I'd heard of the restaurant before—they had faboo seafood and steak and I'd never been able to afford to eat there. It was one of those places that scanned your wallet at the door and if you didn't have enough credit or cash on hand they'd toss your ass out on the street. You didn't eat there unless you were someone or you knew someone.

"Your tie is crooked." I reached over and fiddled with the silk strip, so recently draped over the back of the couch.

"Your panties are as well, if I recall correctly," Bran shot back. "Want me to fix those?"

I giggled. The smell of good sex was intoxicating and a small voice at the back of my mind reminded me about the importance of making a good impression on his parents, blah blah blah. We stumbled up to the front door and past the long line waiting for a chance to get a table and eat sometime in the next six hours. The thick-necked security guard nodded at us as if we were weekly visitors.

Michael Hanover waited in the small lobby, his wife on his arm. He wore a black suit and light blue shirt, impeccably fitted with a salmon-colored tie. Bernadette matched him in another black dress, much like mine but without the wrinkles.

Not to mention a nasty dark spot near my knee from a forgotten chocolate candy.

I had to clean that couch more often.

"Brandon. Rebecca," Michael said with a nod. "Glad you could join us."

I noticed heads turning and the whispering starting from nearby groups of socialites, more than a few women checking out Bran. I resisted the urge to bare my teeth and turned back to the waiting parents.

"Rebecca, you look lovely," Bernadette joined in, giving me a wide smile that screamed fake. The diamonds in her ears and around her throat were real, catching every bit of light in the room to shine like a dozen supernovas.

We were the center of attention.

I hate attention. When people notice you they tend to notice too much. They study you and make judgments, try to figure out what they can get from you and what they can use you for.

I liked staying in the shadows.

Bran squeezed my hand, bringing me out of my daze. He gave me a reassuring smile and a wink, reminding me this would last a few hours and then we'd be free of this stifling alternative universe where I was pretty sure no one collected pennies.

The maître d' scrambled to put us at a private table at the far end of the room, cut off from the rest of the diners with a three-paneled divider painted with images of Italian villas. I settled down behind a menu the size of my Jeep and tried not to look intimidated at the variety of food assaulting my senses.

There was no way to avoid the onrush of scents coming from the kitchen. Lobster, steak, scallops, shrimp, al dente pasta, grilled asparagus, fresh basil and thyme, red wine and whiskey. My head was swimming from trying to catalogue the delicious smells trampling over my tongue.

"Rebecca," Bernadette purred, "I recommend the steak. Kobe beef, flown in daily."

The comment came to me in a haze as I blinked, trying to put together the words and the sounds rushing in from around us. Kitchen natterings from the staff, mutterings from the nearest tables, the waiters rushing around and mumbling under their breath about cheap bastards and expensive whores.

As a Felis I'd been trained to be always be aware of my surroundings, sometimes painfully so. Over the years I'd learned how to dial down the signal, tamp the white noise around me to allow me to survive the overwhelming smells and sounds crashing through my mind's eye.

I was dangerously close to losing it. There was so much going on, so much to pay attention to and so many different scents vying for attention.

It didn't help that I was on edge, my nerves jingle-jangling at every strange sound and smell.

"Rebecca?" Bernadette repeated.

"Yes. That would be nice," I answered, fighting my way out of the mental cloud.

The waiter hovered nearby, pen waiting.

I fumbled my way through ordering the steak, baked potato and mixed vegetables. The waiter didn't flinch when I asked for the meat to be rare.

Bran gave me a curious look as he and his parents placed their orders. I rubbed the tip of my nose, hoping he'd catch on to the reason for my temporary confusion.

"Mom, tell me about this newest charity you're involved with. Something about prisons?" He took over the conversation as I sorted through the mental chaos and balanced myself again, taking short, sharp breaths to anchor myself.

Bran patted my hand as his mother leaped into a cheerful litany about her new love, another rehab program for ex-convicts. I couldn't complain about their efforts; I'd seen some good work come out of those organizations. Sure it was a way for the rich to dump money and get tax write-offs but a lot of men and women got a foot up into a new, clean life.

The food arrived. I tried not to drool over the fat slab of near-raw meat on my plate. A handful of vegetables scattered around the edges of the steak completed the picture.

"Do you deal with a lot of criminals, Rebecca?" Bernadette sliced an asparagus spear into tiny bite-sized pieces.

"Not as many as you'd think." I followed suit, making mine even smaller. "Most of my clients have marital problems." The green stalk held a bit of char from the grill. "You'd be surprised how many normal people have problems in their marriage."

Her cool eyes caught mine with the efficiency of a laser sight. "How sad. Are they mostly based on money or love?"

I popped the tip into my mouth and chewed slowly, buying time for my answer. Bran, caught up in a discussion with his father over the future of ebooks and investing in same, kept watching me for signs of distress.

"Usually one leads to the other." I speared a

thin slice of steak. The piece of meat sat at the end of my fork, dripping blood. "If you marry for money you're likely to leave when the money runs out. If you marry for love you'll stay together through thick and thin."

"I see," she replied. "And which do you prefer?"

I looked over at Bran, still mired in the conversation with his father. "Love. Because in the end everything else can be taken from you but love lasts forever."

Bernadette drew her fork over the china. "Well played."

"Excuse me?"

Her eyes met mine, sharp and piercing. "I've seen gold diggers before. You think you're the first to try and seduce my son, take control of the Hanover fortune?"

I resisted the urge to stab her with my fork.

It'd ruin the taste of the Kobe beef.

I leaned in and dropped my voice to a whisper. "If you've done your homework you'll know I'm no dumb blonde looking to score a rich man. I had no idea who your son was when I first met him and I didn't know you two existed until this morning."

Her eyes narrowed.

I continued. "You married into the Hanover fortune—why can't I accuse you of the same thing?"

I knew it wasn't the right thing to say if I wanted to suck up to his parents but I'd had it with the Hanovers at this point.

One edge of her mouth twisted upward. "Our marriage was arranged. Does that surprise you?"

I didn't reply.

She drew the fork tines across the plate again, creating a high-pitched squeal that ripped at my eardrums. "My parents owned one of the first companies Hanover Investments bought out. Instead of hating the Hanovers, my parents became fast friends with them and worked for Michael's father for the rest of their lives. Both families saw the importance of making sure Michael married a good woman, a strong woman who could take the social reins and keep the company running on that front. Go to the charity meetings, smile for the cameras and organize the dinner parties."

"What a wonderful life," I said.

The smile vanished. "It's not a perfect marriage but it works for us. And I'll not have Brandon jeopardizing the fortune his family's made on some woman he picked up in a bar. He deserves a woman who can handle this side of the business, not someone used to slinking around in the shadows and who doesn't know which fork to use at a formal dinner."

I smiled.

She gave me a confused look. This was a woman used to threatening and getting what she wanted.

Too bad.

"I guess we'll have to leave that up to Bran." I sliced off another piece of beef. "Last time I checked he was of legal age and able to do what he wanted. Besides—" I lifted the bloody chunk up to eye level "—if you check your file again you'll see I'm very capable of handling myself."

It was a threat and I intended it to be seen as such.

Bernadette's eyes widened before she regained control. "Enjoy the steak." She turned away and joined the conversation between the other two Hanovers, letting me dwell on the oddities of parents.

The small talk went from Bran's newest published article on the death of Mike Hancock, a fellow journalist, to general chat about the stock market trends to the number of charities the Hanovers nursed in one form or another. The entire time I watched the two elder Hanovers watch Bran watching me for any sign I was about to snap.

The chocolate mousse chosen for dessert was light and fluffy, melting in my mouth with only the memory of sweetness left behind. It took all I had to not lick the plate.

The delicious finish had me purring right up until Bran's father spoke with a low, powerful tone that reminded me he wasn't just a nice old man.

"I'm going outside for a smoke. Rebecca, would you like to join me?" He extended his hand.

"I don't smoke," I replied.

Bran cleared his throat to my left, just out of sight.

Michael ignored his son's discomfort and reached out, his hand hanging in the air over the remains of the mousse. "Humor an old man. Let's go have a chat—let Bran have a few minutes alone with his mother."

I let him lead me away from the table. This had less to do with giving Bran some private time and more about getting me away from Bran.

If Michael Hanover figured he'd be able to scare me out of a relationship with his son he was about to be very surprised. I'd been threatened with much worse for lesser crimes.

The scars on my back itched.

We stepped past the doorman and back outside onto King Street. The line of people waiting for a table hadn't gotten any shorter and more than a few eyes followed our stroll with a mixture of envy and curiosity.

Hanover led me to the doorway of a nearby building, putting one foot up on the stone steps as he surveyed the traffic around us.

King Street was one of the happening places in Toronto, expensive restaurants rubbing shoulders with high-priced stage productions and a slew of bars offering fancy drinks at high prices for the elite.

The theater crowd was getting out from the evening performance and people swarmed toward the pubs and the cafes to discuss the latest stage offering. A set of rickshaw drivers waited for business, the backs of their chariots advertising the next big musical.

"You're a private investigator, according to your file." The elder Hanover withdrew a silver cigarette case from the inside of his jacket. He flipped it open and chose a single death stick.

He didn't offer me one.

"Your men do good work. Of course they could have looked in the phone book." A stiff breeze smacked my bare arms, raising goose bumps.

The slim silver lighter shot out a pencil-thin beam of flame. "I'd like to hire you."

I had no smart-ass answer to that.

TWO

HE TOOK A deep draw on the cigarette, encouraging the orange-and-black char to continue up the death stick. "I know what you're thinking. I've got plenty of financial resources at my disposal—why would I want to hire some second-rate hack who's dating my son?"

I had an answer but bit it back for Bran's sake.

Michael puffed out a smoke ring. "I need someone outside of my professional circle. It's a delicate matter that requires discretion. I've studied your file. You know how to keep secrets." He looked at me, his eyes the same dark brown as Bran's. "Consider it a favor."

"I don't do illegal." I kept my voice intentionally low. "I won't break the law."

His eyebrows rose. "I wasn't asking you to." He flicked an inch of ash onto the sidewalk before taking another deep long drag. Smoke trickled out of his nose. "I have an associate, David

Brayton. He has a somewhat…delicate situation on his hands."

"Girlfriend or boyfriend?"

"You're fast."

"When I have to be." I glanced at the evening crowd walking past us. "I don't like to work for family or friends. Too complicated."

It was the truth.

The tip of the cigarette burned bright, almost lost in the middle of the neon circus around us.

"There's a few gaps in your life. Holes in your file my man couldn't find anything on. Darkness when it came to your family life, your relatives." He took another deep drag. "Secrets."

I put on my best poker face despite the ice slashing through my veins. "Don't we all have secrets?"

Michael shook his head. "Not like this. The investigator did a fast and dirty first pass on you but I can tell him to start digging and start digging deep." His eyes bored into mine. "Digging up whatever it is you're hiding."

I almost giggled.

I opened my mouth to tell him he couldn't blackmail me, that it'd be useless to even try, and the reality slapped me across the face.

If I refused to do this favor for Michael Hanover I'd be signing his death sentence.

The Pride and Jess wouldn't care who he was or who he fathered; they'd take out the investigator and everyone connected without hesitation if he got close to revealing our existence to the public. First rule of the Felis—keep our secret at all costs.

I knew how far they'd go to cover our tracks.

It'd be bad enough if I didn't know the man, but I loved his son. I couldn't be responsible for his death and possibly his wife's as well. It'd destroy Bran and I couldn't bear that cross and hope to keep building a life with him.

All I had to do was one little favor.

"I don't keep secrets from Bran. Whatever I do, he knows. He knows everything about me so you can't shock him with your dirty little guesses about me or my past."

"Whatever. I've been around a bit longer than you and I can tell you husbands keep secrets from their wives all the time and vice versa. It's the natural state of things." Michael studied the smoldering tobacco. "I'm not worried about my son. He can take care of himself." He dropped the half-smoked cigarette on the ground. "But my wife, well... She can be quite vocal if the situation arises. And she protects her family like a lioness.

I wouldn't advise you take her on. The pen might be mightier than the sword but my wife's voice carries a lot of weight on the society pages. She can make or break reputations with a single word."

I stayed silent.

"Bran might not mind if your secrets came to life but your future employers might. If there were any of them left. A few words placed in the wrong ear and I can guarantee your current drought when it comes to customers will turn into a parched desert, putting the Sinai to shame." Michael grinned, a self-satisfied smirk. "But it's your call, of course." His hand went inside the jacket again and retrieved a business card and pen. "Please visit him tomorrow at my offices. It's nothing much, just a negotiation we'd like to keep under wraps." He scribbled a name on the back in flowing, perfect script.

"And off the record." I took the business card.

"I can pay you if you want." Michael ground the cigarette remains into the sidewalk. "Would it make things easier?"

"No," I replied. "It'd make it worse." I turned and walked back into the restaurant.

Bran watched me as I sat down beside him, his forehead furrowed. His left hand snaked over to rest on my bare knee.

"You okay?" he whispered.

Michael slid in beside Bernadette, nattering about the crowded streets outside and how the government hated smokers.

"I'm fine." I knew the pasted-on smile wouldn't fool him. "Later."

The rest of the evening went by in a blur of coffee, tea and small talk. We went over my school days, Bran's school days, Bernadette and Michael's school days—the simplicity of it all making me want to tear my hair out, one long blond strand at a time.

"Do you get a lot of murder cases?" Bernadette mused, her fork whittling away on a piece of cheesecake the size of a thimble. "Like the private investigators on television?"

"Not in Toronto." I smiled. "I let the cops handle that. Too much paperwork."

Bran squeezed my knee under the table. We'd met over one murder case and bonded through another.

"That woman we met at your house. Jess." Michael drew a line in the white frosting on his untouched carrot cake. "Was she in some sort of accident? Looks like she got mauled by a lion and lost her eye. Nasty scar." He clucked his tongue.

"Not a whole lot of men like getting it from a crazed cyclops."

Bran leaped in before I could speak. "Dad, enough. You've been grilling Rebecca all night. Let it go." He folded his cloth napkin in a neat square and placed it next to the remains of his chocolate cream pie. "I'm not a kid anymore. I don't appreciate you having a background check done on her. I thought this was going to be a nice dinner to get to know each other, not a fucking interrogation."

Michael moved to speak but was silenced by Bernadette's hand on his forearm.

"Brandon," she started, "we understand you find it a violation of privacy." She gestured at me with one hand. "For both of you. But you have to see our point of view." The blond wave of hair bobbled with each word. "Your father has worked hard over the years to secure a sound financial future for all of us. Even with the stock market bouncing around he's kept his customers happy and kept us safe. We're not out to criticize you or your choices."

I held back a snarky response. This wasn't the time or place to bring up our previous conversation.

"If we were, we'd have raised hell when you got stupid after that story." Michael grunted.

Bran chewed on his lower lip. I knew she was referring to Bran's article, the one he'd written after running with the street kids for months, the one that made his journalistic reputation.

And broke his heart. When the news became more about him and his adventures than about the needy kids scrambling for protection from their own demons he walked away from the journalism world and dived into writing filler for tabloids.

"That's not the point." Bran grated the words out between clenched teeth.

I put my hand atop his. "It's okay." I looked at Michael. "We're good." The smile was forced and hurt but I should have seen this coming. For all the differences between Felis and humans some things never changed—the demands of family.

I stood up. "We should be going. I've got an early day tomorrow." The almost imperceptible nod from Michael made my skin crawl. "Thank you for dinner. I'm sure we'll talk again."

Bernadette chirped, Michael shook hands, awkward hugs were exchanged and we were out on the street a few minutes later.

The line of waiting diners had diminished by half but still stretched down the block. We pushed by them as quickly as possible, moving on to clear ground a few minutes later.

Bran let out a loud sigh and stuffed his hands in his pockets. His shoulders slumped as he shuffled forward. There were no taxis in sight—they were busy couriering the evening crowd home.

"Let's walk for a bit. I could use the exercise." I tugged at his sleeve and we walked along the near-empty street, the majority of theater-goers sequestered in pubs and cafes or struggling to get home via the subway.

"I'm sorry. I just get so..." His fingers curled up into fists. "They make me feel like such a little kid begging for permission to go play outside. It doesn't matter how old I am—it all comes back round to what looks best for the family, what looks good to the public." He looked up at the night sky. A few stars fought for control over the illuminated skyline. "I know my mother gave you the 'get out of Dodge' speech about how you weren't suitable for me and the Hanover fortune."

I blinked, holding back my shock. "How did you know?"

"She's been doing that since I was old enough to date." Bran sighed. "Let's just say you aren't the first to get the lecture."

I shrugged. "I'll survive. I think I scared her a bit, though."

He chuckled. "That's what she needs, a reality check. What did my father want to talk to you about?"

"Just more family stuff." The taste of bitter chocolate rushed back in a nasty burp. "The usual speech about not taking advantage of you. Guess he wanted to make sure all the bases were covered in case your mother left anything out."

I didn't say anything about the devil's deal I'd cut. Despite my previous brave speech to his dad I didn't want Bran to know anything about this side job. I'd go see this fellow and take care of his dirty little secret and be done with it.

Telling Bran would only make him more pissed off at his family and I didn't want to be the cause of even more friction. It'd be a few hours out of our lives and it'd be over and done with. Hanover would have his buddy taken care of and there'd be no further investigation into my life.

Win-win. It wasn't the best scenario but it sure beat the alternative.

"Nothing special," he repeated, taking my hand. I felt the quiver in his fingers, the curiosity growing.

"He asked if you still had those pajamas with the little teddy bears on them."

Bran grinned. "If I recall correctly Jazz pulled those out of the drawer and made a bed with them last time we left her in the condo. What did you tell him?"

"I told him I had no idea—you sleep naked. In fact you like walking around the house naked as much as possible. And we were considering taking a vacation at a BDSM resort because you like being tied up and spanked."

"You did not."

"You'll never know." I rolled my shoulders back and increased my stride, dragging him along. "They were quite nice. For parents."

Bran let out a hum of agreement. "I'm sorry I won't get to meet yours." He squeezed my hand. "I'd like to hope they'd approve of me."

I chuckled. "Probably not. You are a reporter, after all."

"And not family," he added drily.

I looked down where our fingers were entwined. "More so the reporter bit. You seem to have the biting and scratching bit down."

He smirked, lifting my hand to his lips, then laying a fat, wet kiss in my palm.

Bran let out a low whistle as we crossed the street. We could walk all the way home if we wanted.

I suspect we wanted.

"You ever wonder how much our parents dictate what and who we become?" Bran kicked at a lonely stone on the sidewalk. It skittered into an alley and clanged against something metal. "They choose what toys we play with, what schools we go to, what people we date." He cocked his head to one side and watched me. "Do you ever worry about what your parents would think of you, the woman you've become?"

"I am the way I am because of who I am." I felt the cold scars on my back begin to ache. "If they'd survived the crash I might still have my, ah, disability."

I didn't like this line of thinking. I'd gone through the what-ifs for years after being cast out at the tender age of fifteen. Too many nights spent trying to figure out why I couldn't Change, what reason there could be for my deficiency.

Too many tears.

I took a deep breath before answering. "I think we are who we choose to be because of, or despite, our parents."

"Good answer." Another gentle kiss on the back of my hand. "Ever the peacemaker."

A cool breeze came up from the lake, buffeting us. I stopped and slipped off my shoes. My toes cried with relief as I wriggled and flexed them on the cold sidewalk.

Bran lifted his hand to flag down a lone cab cruising down the street. We'd passed out of the chic section of Toronto and were edging into an industrial wasteland of warehouses and overpriced artist lofts.

"I'm good," I protested.

"No, you're not. Your feet are sore and I won't have you cutting your foot on broken glass because you don't want to put shoes back on." He pointed at the waiting taxi. "Get in."

I resisted the urge to growl at his commanding tone. Instead I slid in over the faux leather, holding my shoes in one hand.

"My place or yours?" He kneaded my bare leg, skimming his hand up to the hem of my black dress.

"Mine."

The ride back was fast and silent. Bran paid the driver off and led the way up to my front door before unlocking it with his key.

"Am I staying the night?" He smiled the same disarming grin I'd first seen in a dive bar months ago.

I feigned a yawn. We played this game every few days, pretending to try to avoid the inevitable. "I guess you can sleep on the couch. If you're too tired to go home. You'll have to share it with Jazz though."

He pursed his lips for a second, forehead furrowed with thought.

"Nah." Bran grinned, a lustful smile raising goose bumps on my skin. He shrugged his jacket off and tossed it on the couch. "No room."

Jazz looked up from her spot on the cushions and padded over to make a new nest atop the jacket.

Before I could react he swept me up into his arms and over his shoulder. One hand held my legs in place while the other pushed the door shut.

"Let's see how fast I can get you out of this dress."

"Again," I squeaked, dizzy from the combination of wine and the sudden movement.

"Practice makes perfect." He slapped my butt hard, enough to send my pulse racing. "I'm working on improving in some areas." His hand crept up under the black fabric.

I tugged at a wayward lock of red hair. "Only if I get to play with that tie again. I haven't practiced my knot tying for months."

That earned me a cough and a chuckle as he headed for the stairs.

THE CLOCK READ 6:30 a.m., an ungodly hour for the most part but even more when you're in bed with a hot, sexy man.

I rolled away from Bran, who was snoring lightly and buried in three out of four pillows, and headed for the shower. The faster I got out and did this "favor" the faster I could forget it ever happened.

Not to mention getting back in bed.

"Whattadoing?" The sleepy mumble came as I turned off the hot water and stepped out onto the shaggy blue bath mat.

"Got a quick job I need to do—checking a company's security system for flaws. Only be a few hours and a fast couple of bucks." I dried off quickly and tossed the bath towel into the corner of the bathroom. "Go back to sleep and I'll meet you for lunch."

Bran mumbled into the sheets as I dressed, stretching and flexing his limbs. He smacked his lips, tempting me to jump back into bed and ravish him while he was half-asleep and more open to certain suggestions. His bare back showed countless scratches, courtesy of yours truly.

I grabbed my running shoes and cursed under my breath. I needed to get this job done and over as soon as possible. I hated keeping secrets from

Bran but I hated morning fights even more, and if he figured out I was working for his father, there'd be hell to pay.

ACCORDING TO THE address on the card David Brayton worked in the middle of Toronto's financial district. Hanover Investments was ensconced on prime real estate at the intersections of King and Bay Street. I hopped the streetcar and rode in with the rest of the business commuters. I stuck out in my leather duster and jeans when everyone else had on power suits and power dresses.

My uniform was a bit more useful.

I sniffed the collar of the duster. It still held a trace of the Pennsylvanian forest, the rich earthy scent chasing away the gas fumes and cologne/perfume.

It didn't take much to push me back to the wilderness. If I closed my eyes I could see the lush forest near the farm where I'd gone on my first hunt. Another whiff of my duster and I envisioned the clearing where Bran faced down a wild Felis and declared his love for me.

A foul-smelling diesel truck rolled by, smearing black smoke over the streetcar windows. I wrinkled my nose and pulled back to the present. I got off at the next stop and walked the last block trying to purge my lungs of the oily pollution.

It didn't escape my attention that the first twenty floors of the building belonged to Hanover Investments. I stood on the sidewalk and watched worker drones rush in and out of the various business hives.

A long black limousine pulled up halfway down the block from me. Car after car came to a screeching stop with the one lane now clogged. A single horn bleated out its annoyance but fell silent as everyone noticed the reason for the delay.

I craned my neck to see who warranted blocking traffic on a major street in the middle of rush hour.

Michael and Bernadette Hanover exited the rear of the car, the driver tipping his cap as the couple strode toward the building in front of me. Michael was carrying a briefcase and wearing a black business suit while Bernadette trotted beside him with her own version of a briefcase, a large pink-and-purple purse that could have hidden a small child. Her light blue dress, tied at the waist with a flashy silver chain, clung to her as she tried to keep up with her husband. A few seconds later the limo drove off, followed by a long line of delayed and annoyed commuters.

I spun away before they could see me, ending up behind a hot dog cart strategically set up on the sidewalk to take advantage of starving travelers looking for a fast nitrate fix. The smell of grilling onions had me drooling even as I watched the pair exchange cheek kisses and split up, Michael heading into the main tower through the front revolving doors and Bernadette off through another door to a smaller, less congested part of the triple-armed complex.

The hot dog vendor waved a pair of tongs at me as I moved away from the cart and headed for the entrance. I made a mental note to grab a dog or two on the way out—there's nothing better than street food if you know where and when to buy it.

Security guards flanked me the second I got through the revolving doors, marking me as not one of the regulars. I nodded to the uniforms and headed for the marble front desk, where a thick-necked supervisor checked my investigator's license and pawed through my messenger bag to make sure I wasn't smuggling in a bomb.

"I didn't know we had PIs in Canada," he muttered, passing the bag back.

"You learn something new every day." I slung the oversized purse over my shoulder and signed in at the open ledger. "I'm here to see David Brayton."

The woman passed me a visitor's pass and gestured at the bank of elevators. "Twentieth floor." She fixed me with a death stare. "Report to the receptionist when you get off the elevator. Please do not deviate from your destination."

I resisted asking how they'd know. One of my side jobs involved testing company security and I knew how far a system like this would go. So far Hanover Investments rated a B grade—but that wasn't what I was here for.

A wink and a nod to the supervisor, and I headed for the masses waiting to be shot into the sky.

I rode the elevator up, exiting along with a half dozen other people who scattered into the maze of corridors, leaving me to face down a receptionist perched at a glass desk like a vulture looking for fresh prey.

The middle-aged woman glared at me over her glasses. "Couriers go to the third floor."

"Good thing I'm not a courier." I shot her my friendliest smile. "I'm here to see Mr. David Brayton."

Her nostrils flared. "Mr. Brayton."

"Yes." I dropped my business card on her desk, half hoping it'd drop through to the floor. "I'm expected."

After a few minutes of stare-down she picked up the phone and called Brayton. I sauntered around the lobby, staring at warped sculptures of bulls and bears.

David Brayton shot out of a hallway and charged at me like I was holding the heart transplant he desperately needed. I almost stepped to the side to see if he'd keep going through the glass window in the lobby and plummet to his death.

The bad black dye job didn't hide all of his white short hair and his belt needed life support to hold the ample belly at bay, the white starched shirt stretched to its limit with buttons bulging. The nervous twitch in his right eye told me he was about to bust something if we stood out in public any longer.

I took the initiative and stuck out my hand. "I'm so glad you can help me out with my inheritance. Danged if I know what to do with it and investing it looks like the best way to go."

The receptionist eyed me with newfound respect.

"Of course, of course." His head bounced up and down like a bobblehead traveling on a gravel road. "Please come into my office."

The sweaty financial advisor led me to a corner room—a spartan, emotionless square with a wonderful view of the office tower next to us. A generic wooden desk with two office chairs. It had all the personality of a blank greeting card.

He gestured at the chair as he moved around the desk and sat down.

I sat back in the plush leather and crossed my legs, balancing my elbows on my knees and touching my fingertips together.

Brayton cleared his throat. “It’s a mess.” He withdrew a snow-white handkerchief from an inside pocket and wiped his face. “I mean, thank you for agreeing to help out. Michael said he was going to find someone safe, someone outside of the office and, well—” he spread his hands with a weary smile “—here you are.”

“Michael Hanover’s a good friend,” I deadpanned.

“There’s this woman…” Brayton paused, a sheepish smile on his face. “I guess you’ve heard that phrase plenty of times.” He played with the gold wedding band on his finger, twisting it over red, irritated skin.

“A few.” I allowed myself a grin. “And she’s not your wife.”

“No.” Brayton shook his head. “No, she’s not. Her name is Molly, Molly Callendar. She, ah, used to be a temp here. A few days a week doing odd tasks for anyone who needed her."

I couldn't resist. "And you 'needed' her."

His cheeks turned scarlet. A little pink tongue flicked out to wet dry, chapped lips.

"I'm not here to judge you or your actions. That's not my job." I leaned in. "What do you need me to do for you?"

"There's a baby," he whispered. "A boy."

I sat back. This was familiar ground and I felt more comfortable, despite the circumstances. "I assume there's no question of paternity."

He frowned. "Molly wouldn't be unfaithful."

Unlike you. "Have you had a paternity test done?"

"No need to," Brayton said. "I accept the child as my own. She put my name on the birth certificate with my permission." He dabbed at his forehead again. "The, ah, affair was over before I found out she was pregnant. She showed up six months after quitting with the baby in her arms and told me it was mine." He drew a staggered breath. "I won't leave my wife and Molly knows that, accepts that. It's over between us but now there's a baby involved and I want to do what's right for him." Sweat beaded on his forehead. "I can't have my reputation ruined over this. I won't let it be ruined and Molly agrees this is what's best for all of us. That's why I want the paperwork done under the table, as quietly as possible. I don't want anyone to find out."

"Understood. And you want me to..." I pushed the conversation along. The faster I got the details the faster I could do this "favor" and the faster I could get out from under Hanover's fat thumb.

"I want to get a signed agreement from her regarding child support."

I sat back. "That's all?" The hairs on the back of my neck shot to attention.

Brayton wiped his face again. "It may not seem like much to you but it's something of major concern to both of us. She, ah, she's demanding a legal document. She says she trusts me right now in regards to our financial arrangements but is worried about the future—if I pass away before the child reaches maturity and the estate cuts off the payment plan we'd set up." The damp cloth sat on the desk in a muddled mess.

I shifted in my chair. I'd heard this tune before. Same dance, different partners. "What do you need from me?"

"I've drawn up this agreement with my lawyer. I need you to take it to her at her hotel and see if she'll accept it. Obviously she can't come to the office and we want to be as discreet as possible." His left hand slipped into a desk drawer. "I think the terms are agreeable. That's where you come in." The thick wad of paper slid toward me.

"I'm not a lawyer." I didn't touch the stack. "I'm not a paralegal. I can't advise her on any legal documents."

"True. But that's not what I need you for. I need a smart, quiet courier to go over there and wait, get it signed and come back." He grabbed the handkerchief again and folded it into a neat square. "She's a good woman, a sensible woman." Brayton tucked the wet handkerchief back in his pocket. "We both made a mistake but don't want our child to pay for it. I just need to get this signed and tucked away and it'll be over and done with."

I didn't say anything. He'd already distanced himself from the entire affair by refusing to use her name past the initial identification. In his mind the entire affair was already over and done with, papers filed and checks presigned and sent out.

"Why me?"

He blinked rapidly, sending out SOS messages. "What?"

I pointed at the wall and the unseen front desk. "You can get a bike courier there and back in the length of time we've been talking. Fast, quick and no questions. Why me?"

Brayton rubbed the back of his neck with the damp handkerchief. "Couriers need to be paid. Receipts are signed, tracked, recorded. I don't want any trace of this operation." He glanced at the shut door and lowered his voice. "There are people who might use this against me."

"And Molly."

He drew back as if touched with a live wire. "And her, as well. Michael told me you could keep it quiet, keep it under your hat."

"I'm good at keeping secrets." I tried not to choke on the words.

"Here's the address she's staying at." He scribbled a note on a piece of paper and shoved it across the desk. "It's a hotel. She gave up her apartment when she had the boy. I'm paying for it—when the agreement is finalized she'll be moving west. It's all for the best." He reached for a plain brown envelope and stuffed the folder inside.

I stood up and took the note and the envelope. "Does your wife suspect anything?"

"I hope not." His lower lip trembled. "I hope to God not."

I didn't tell him the odds were not in his favor. It'd been my experience that most women knew when their men were stepping out on them. My money was on a nasty divorce within the next year or so for David Brayton.

He swallowed loudly. “I need this done quickly and quietly.”

I stuffed the envelope into my messenger bag, trying not to feel dirty. “Let me get going. The faster I get there and back the faster we’re done.”

With Michael Hanover, my inner voice snapped.

I gestured at the phone on his desk. “Give me your business card. I’ll call if there’s any problems.” I tapped my pocket and the cell phone inside.

He handed over the gold-embossed card along with a couple of twenty-dollar bills. “For the cabs. Don’t worry about giving me any change back; keep what’s left.”

I looked at him with my best professional face on, the one I reserved for troublesome clients. “Let me point out that if I find you’ve coerced her into this, any part of this, in any way, I will not only advise her not to sign but I’ll help her find a good lawyer and rip you to pieces. Hanover might be purchasing my services but neither of you can afford my soul.”

It had to be said. I wasn’t going to be part of any

deal forcing this woman to do anything against her will.

I could deal with Hanover's blackmail.

I wouldn't be responsible for pushing an innocent woman down an unwanted path.

Another beaded line of sweat appeared on his forehead.

I walked out.

The receptionist gave me a respectful smile and nod as I passed her spotless desk.

A long line of cabs waited at the taxi stand, politely waiting to be called into service. I waved the first car over with a wave and watched the driver leap behind the wheel and drive toward me.

The hairs on the back of my neck tingled.

I turned back toward the crystal palaces surrounding me. Someone was watching me. It could have been a curious visitor staring out of a window waiting for his chance to dump more money into the investment game.

It was more likely Hanover making sure I was busy dancing to his perverse tune.

I resisted the urge to wave and got into the cab.

MUCH TO MY surprise the hotel wasn't one of the dives on Lakeshore Boulevard, selling rooms by the hour, but a clean respectable one off of

Yonge Street. Tucked between a movie theater and a pricey shoe shop, the hotel catered to tourists looking to stay right in the middle of the city's downtown action.

The doorman gripped the brass doorknob as I exited the cab. He touched the brim of his cap and smiled.

This wasn't any cheap dive. This was a luxury hotel catering to rich visitors.

"Welcome to the Belmont Arms." He swept his arm inward. "The front desk is right over there."

I almost tripped over the deep, luxurious scarlet carpet, anchoring a series of chairs and couches that definitely weren't from the secondhand store. The décor was typical tourist chic with framed pictures of Lake Ontario and other scenic Toronto highlights circling around on the walls while low classic music hummed out of invisible speakers. Two large groups clustered around the front desk, elderly tourists waiting for their guide. The harried clerk waved her arms in the air as she tried to herd one group to the side.

I bypassed the desk and headed for the elevator. Molly Callendar was on the second floor at the far end of the corridor, right by the emergency exit stairs.

A breakfast tray sat on the floor by the door, the

remains of stuffed French toast and coffee waiting to be removed.

My stomach growled, reminding me I'd rushed out before grabbing anything to eat. I made a mental note to stop by the hot dog vendor when this was all over.

I rapped on the door and waited. Darkness covered the spyhole and I knew she was there assessing whether to open the door to me.

After a few seconds the door opened.

"Hello. You must be the courier."

Molly Callendar wasn't anything like what I expected. Instead of a witless young woman who tripped into an office affair I saw a tall, slender woman close to my own age with short red hair brushing her shoulders. She smiled at me and stepped back to allow me to enter.

The harsh chemical smell told me she'd recently colored her hair. It made sense considering she was about to relocate and wanted to change her appearance. An oversized flowery blouse and blue jeans completed the image of harried mother.

"I'm Rebecca." I scanned the room behind her automatically. Standard hotel issue, including a kitchenette. A portable crib sat in the far corner. "You're Molly Callendar?"

"Yes. You must be from David's office." She

gestured me in with a nervous glance into the hallway. Molly closed and locked the door before moving to sit on the couch, motioning for me to join her.

I sat opposite her in an overstuffed dark red chair, then pulled the envelope out of my messenger bag. "I brought the agreement for you to look over. Before we get started I have to ask—are you being forced into this? Is he threatening you in any way? Are you or the baby afraid for your life?"

"No, not at all."

I heard the truth in her voice. My shoulder muscles eased up, the tension rushing out of them as I watched her.

"I have to ask, you understand." I passed over the envelope. "I want to make sure you're doing this of your own volition. If you think you're in danger I can take you to a shelter, someplace safe for you and the baby." I knew I sounded paranoid but I'd seen angry men lash out at anything, anyone vulnerable if they felt they weren't getting what they perceived as their fair part.

There was no one more vulnerable than a mother and her newborn.

She nodded. "Thank you. I'm sure there might be women who fall into that sort of situation but I'm not one of them." The wad of legal documents fell onto her lap from the overturned envelope. "David's a nice fellow but we both got…stupid." Molly shook her head. "Both of us were fools. I should have known better, taken more precautions. I knew he wasn't going to leave his wife but it was the right time and the right place." She glanced at the crib, a gentle smile replacing the sadness of talking about her ex-lover. "But I can't be too mad at the man. He did give me Liam."

I glanced over as she flipped through the pages. "Liam. Lovely name."

"Runs in my family. He'll be the third generation. My father has it as a middle name and my grandfather had it as a first." She picked up a pen from the table, monogrammed with the hotel's name, and turned her attention to the forms. "Excuse me."

"Take as long as you need." I sat back. "There's no rush. Make sure you read everything through and understand what's being proposed and agreed to. If you have any questions, ask. I'm not a lawyer but I might be able to help you decipher the legalspeak."

She chuckled. "I think I'll manage. If it's got to do with money I'm pretty hip." Her attention went to the agreement. Molly chewed on the end of the pen as she flipped pages back and forth.

I didn't say a word.

My cell phone buzzed against my hip. I snatched it up, giving Molly a quick look. She hadn't turned away from studying the papers.

The text message leaped out at me in blocky letters.

It was from Bran.

WHERE R U?

I chuckled. He'd easily forsworn basic English for the textspeak.

My fingers bounced across the tiny keyboard. I hadn't gotten all the bells and whistles of this fancy model figured out. It was easier to mangle simple sentences than compose odes like other people could.

I FINE. WORKIN

I heard Shakespeare spinning in his grave like a wind turbine in my mind.

The response shot back a minute later. Molly ignored me, her pen zipping across the pages as she initialed some sections and boldly stroked through others.

MISS U. BED COLD. COME BCK SOON. LUV U

The lump in my throat could have throttled T. rex. I'd become a pretty good liar over the years due to my profession but this wasn't trying to trick some guy into telling me about his mistress or digging at some bar floozy to see how often a client came in and drank away his paycheck before going home.

This was the man I loved.

Each letter singed my fingertips as if I were pounding on red-hot iron. I needed to get this done and done quickly.

BE BACK ASAP. LUV U 2

The response shot back within seconds.

XOXOXO. I CALL LATER MAYBE WE MEET FOR LNCH?

I closed the tiny keyboard and felt even worse, if it were possible.

Molly scribbled something in the margin on one of the pages. "I'm changing this from quarterly to monthly. I don't want to end up destitute 'cause David forgot to make a payment. Monthly I can at least budget for mistakes and hold it together until things are sorted out." She looked over. "I'm telling you because I know he's going to give a big sigh and say he wouldn't forget." Her thin lips twisted into a smile. "He forgets."

The baby stirred in the portable crib. A low burble started, rising in volume.

I got up and waved Molly back to studying the forms. "I'll get him."

She eyed me for a second, sizing me up, before nodding. "That would be great, thanks. I'll be done in a few minutes." She returned to reading and marking up the paperwork.

I walked over to the dark purple crib and leaned in to see Liam. The blue-eyed boy grinned at me. He didn't have much hair, the reddish fuzz on his head barely enough to cover the fair skin. Wrapped securely in a light blue blanket he cooed and gurgled at me, a little bundle of happiness.

"Aren't you a sweetie?" I purred. He flicked his little tongue out with a look of surprise, as if he'd just discovered it.

I leaned in and picked him up carefully, supporting his neck and back as I'd been taught by Ruth.

I sighed, missing my old friend. She'd been a

surrogate mother to me and dozens of other Felis kids, from changing our diapers to helping us on our first hunts. The wound of losing her was still raw.

Liam burbled at me. He blinked, trying to figure out who this stranger was.

I smiled back and took a deep whiff of baby powder, formula...

And something familiar.

Liam settled into the crook of my arm, smacking his lips in anticipation of a feeding. I drew in a deep breath before focusing all my senses on the baby in my arms.

I smelled Molly's scent on him, fresh and powerful.

A secondary smell lay under, a blending of his parents. It wasn't as reliable as DNA but for the Felis it was as important. I'd been able to identify a Felis's lost child once through the scent of the boy's fur, a combination of the two parents along with his own distinct trace.

I sniffed again, mentally eliminating Molly from the mix.

The father wasn't Brayton. My short time in the office had provided enough for me to remember his scent. His sweat had thickened the air around us—imperceptible to anyone unless they had enhanced senses.

Like a Felis. Like me.

I tried to calm my racing heart. If Brayton was willing to take in someone else's child as his own, who was I to interfere? The arrangement between the two adults was none of my business as long as there was nothing illegal going on.

There was something familiar about the smell, like a faint memory of a mother's cooking in the kitchen. I wrinkled my nose and mentally flipped through my files, trying to identify the father.

My knees went weak for a second as my mind finished processing the odor and spit out the result.

Michael Hanover.

I was holding Bran's half brother.

THREE

I TURNED BACK to Molly, who was poring over the documents. Liam squirmed for a second before settling down, his tiny eyes closing as he figured out I wasn't going to be feeding him.

"Liam..." I paused, trying to find the right phrasing. "Brayton is his father, right?"

She glared at me. "Of course." The pen slammed down on the table as she strode toward me and plucked the baby out of my arms. "What sort of woman do you think I am?"

Liam let out a soft whimper at the abrupt movement. He scrunched his tiny face, considering whether to cry.

I held my breath.

He sighed and fell asleep again, curling into his mother's touch.

I fumbled to find the right words, the brain freeze cutting out all coherent thought. There was no easy way to ask if she'd been screwing Bran's father.

Even worse, I couldn't prove anything without a paternity test. Last time I checked, Felis scent identification wasn't legal in court.

"I apologize. It's that I've found in some of these cases the supposed father demands a DNA test before paying up. I know Mr. Brayton's passed on it up to this point but you may want to get one to avoid future complications." I tried to sound as sympathetic as possible. "Believe me, I've seen men demand a test after paying years of support to try and get out of the commitment. The wife finds out and instead of the husband standing up to her he asks for a paternity test to buy time and, if it's not his child, to duck out on any prearranged payments." I shot her a wry smile. "You'd be surprised at how intense a woman's emotions can get when she feels slighted."

"I see where you're coming from." She turned her attention to the half-asleep baby in her arms. "But David's accepted Liam as his son. That's all that matters."

I held up my hands. "No problem. I understand." I picked up the documents and scanned them. "Good choices here."

She'd upped the numbers, as I expected. Everyone likes to lowball on the first estimate on anything, including child support. It wasn't a huge increase but enough to allow for cost of living and plain old life.

A smile replaced the frown. “I want to do what’s right for Liam.” She looked down at the sleeping baby. “David’s stepping up to support us and that’s all I wanted. Enough to start a new life out west and give us a chance to start over.”

“He’s a good man,” I said.

I wasn’t lying—it took a lot of guts to claim a child that wasn’t his. I wasn’t sure if Brayton was in the same situation as I was with Hanover blackmailing him, but regardless of the situation Brayton was stepping up to care for what wasn’t his.

Molly nodded. “Yes, he is.”

I put the papers back in the envelope and into my messenger bag. “Let me run these back to the office and have him approve them—it shouldn’t take more than a few hours for me to be back with signed copies. You give a final set of signatures, I give you your copy and you’ll be all set.”

She sat down on the couch and rubbed her face with one free hand. Liam smacked his lips but stayed silent. “Sorry for snapping at you before. I know no one cares these days about single mothers and paternity but…” She sighed. “I’m a bit old-school. Should have known better and all that.”

“At least the little one’s going to have a good

life." I headed for the door. "And that's all we can ask for, right?"

Molly shot me a wide grin. "He deserves the best. And I'm going to make sure he gets it."

I stepped outside into the corridor and yanked hard on the doorknob. It took me a few minutes to flag down a cab, during which my mind spun faster than a Ferris wheel on overdrive. I slipped into the backseat and barked the address before falling silent, trying to quell the confusion threatening to overwhelm me.

Nausea burned my belly. I'd thought this was going to be a quickie and I'd be able to meet Bran for lunch. In retrospect, not eating had been a good decision; the driver didn't need to worry about cleaning up a mess on his backseat.

The cab driver kept looking in the mirror as we headed back to the glass towers. It might have been because I kept putting my head between my knees, trying not to throw up.

There was no doubt in my mind this was Michael Hanover's kid. He'd slept with Molly Callendar and he'd asked David Brayton to take the fall for it, then financed the payoff to get her and Liam out of town.

The problem was there was nothing illegal here.

Immoral, possibly. It depended on your point

of view. But at least Hanover was taking care of the kid via Brayton. Callendar seemed happy with the arrangement; Brayton didn't mind playing surrogate daddy and Hanover got rid of his messy affair.

My mouth tasted like I'd swallowed a bucket of sour candies as I argued with myself.

This wasn't my business.

I was just a courier running papers back and forth so no one could connect Michael Hanover to Molly and Liam Callendar. My part was almost done and I'd secured the safety of all the Hanovers and my Felis family with a simple taxi trip.

Problem was, it became my business when Liam became Bran's little brother and not a faceless statistic in the unending list of bastard children fathered by ignorant men.

THE RECEPTIONIST OFFERED me a cup of coffee as I waited for Brayton. Her attitude had changed a hundred and eighty degrees from my visit an hour or so ago and part of me relished the star treatment. Brayton must have made it sound like Dad's inheritance was pretty substantial based on the way she fluttered around me like a moth dancing to my invisible flame.

"You're sure about the coffee? Tea? We have

some lovely herbals," she murmured in a soft tone. "Maybe some bottled water?"

"No, I'm fine." I returned to chewing on my lower lip, working through a thousand options and finding them all unacceptable.

If I told Bran he'd be sure to want to confront his father. Not that I was against it but it'd set in motion the exact events I had been trying to avert with this job. I had no doubt Michael Hanover would set his dogs on my past with horrible repercussions for all of us.

But I'd just lambasted Bran about keeping secrets. And this was a biggie.

David Brayton poked his head out of his office and gestured for me to come down the hall. I waved to the attentive receptionist and walked down the hall at a leisurely pace—winning me more time to weigh options.

He closed the door behind me and retreated to his desk. "Did she sign?" His voice went up an octave on the last word.

"She requested some changes." I plucked the envelope out of my bag and slid it over. "Seem reasonable enough to me."

"How much did you talk to her?"

I put up my hands. "Just enough to make sure she was comfortable with the deal. There's no point in the two of us going through this if she's going to call a lawyer tomorrow and try and have the entire deal rewritten."

Brayton grunted his approval. He pulled out the folder and scanned the pages, giving a non-committal snort at each pen-marked paragraph.

I waited, standing in front of the desk. There were no pictures of friends or family on the walls or on his desk. It could be anyone's office.

He closed the folder. "I agree. Let me initial these changes and get it finalized. Make another set and we'll finish this up."

I watched him scribble on the pages, pondering my next move. I couldn't come out and call him a liar. I wasn't sure if he was even a victim—maybe Hanover had offered him something he wanted or needed to have him take responsibility for Liam. I couldn't assume he was in the same place as I was, blackmailed into staying silent.

"Molly and I spoke while she was going over the documents. She seems like quite a nice woman." I ventured forth, choosing my words carefully.

Brayton smiled as his black pen leaped across the pages. "She's a gem. I have no doubt she'll be a fantastic mother." I could hear the honesty in his words. He knew Molly, if not in the biblical sense.

I shifted my feet against the gray shag carpet. “How much does Michael Hanover know about all this? Does he know Molly?”

Brayton didn’t miss a beat. He shook his head. “He might have seen her on the floors—as I said, she worked here as a temp for a few months. I doubt he even knows her name. I only approached him when I found out she was pregnant and needed some, ah, neutral help.”

I didn’t have to be an investigator to pick out the lies in the statement. His body language screamed it loud and clear—the nervous tic in one cheek, the constant wetting of his lips. He was already fumbling the cover story, changing it from what he’d told me earlier.

I gave him my most comforting smile. “He’s a good friend. Someone you can count on.”

Brayton nodded, focused on the documents. “Fortunate for me and for Molly.” He closed the file folder. “Stay here for a few minutes, please. I’ll run this down to Legal, make copies, and you can head back to the hotel. I’d like to get this over and done with today.” His stare darted past me to the windows and the skyline, dotted with power towers. “I’m sure you’d like to get back to your other assignments as well.”

There was a note of curiosity in his voice that

hadn't been there before. He suspected I knew the depth of Michael Hanover's involvement in this situation but he wasn't going to ask and risk giving anything away.

I waved an invisible fly away. "I'm clear for the entire day. I'm here for as long as you need me." I stood up, feeling the coiled tension in my legs. I wanted to scream, to kick down a door, anything but sit here and play dumb. "How many people know about this situation?" I didn't say the word "baby"; I figured playing it safe was the best road to take for now.

He paused at the door, his hand on the doorknob. "As few as possible. Legal knows it's an arrangement for a client—they don't get to look at names, just numbers. We value the privacy we give our customers."

Brayton slipped into the hallway and out of sight.

I walked around the office, considering my options. They ranged from few to none. I couldn't confront Michael Hanover with the truth because it'd tick him off and he'd investigate me more, resulting in the Pride stepping in. I couldn't even tell him why I knew it was his baby and not Brayton's.

I had no idea what to tell Bran. It was one thing to run out and do a fast favor for his father but another to participate in a huge cover-up, something that directly affected Bran's life and his future. I didn't want to be there in twenty years when Liam came a-calling at Bran's door announcing his half brother status. Sure, it might not happen—but it could. And I'd be part of this horrible secret, an unwilling participant but guilty as hell of helping making it happen.

I couldn't keep this a secret from Bran, not with what we'd gone through in the past. We'd agreed to keep no secrets and this was about as bad as it could possibly get. From what I'd observed his relationship with his father was complicated, to say the least, and I didn't know what Bran's reaction would be. All I could do was be there and support him.

I didn't even want to start guessing about Bernadette and how she'd react. Maybe this was the latest in a long line of illegitimate children. Maybe Liam was the most recent half brother Bran did or didn't know about.

I just didn't know.

Brayton came back into the room. There was a lightness to his step, a definite change from the rapid stomp he'd left with. He smiled and handed me the folder.

"All cleaned up and ready to go. All you need

is to get her signature on the last page, initials on the changes and we're done. There's a second copy in there for her to keep—I've already signed off on both copies."

I tucked the papers into my bag. "Is this the first time you've covered for Michael? Do you owe him something or is he blackmailing you?"

He drew back as if I'd slapped him.

"I know it's his baby, not yours." I kept talking, trying to get it all out before he could stop me. "You're taking the hit for him and so is Molly—she's going along with the arrangement to make it easier for everyone. But the baby is Hanover's and sometime in the future Liam's going to figure out the truth and want to know where he came from, who's his real father. Did Hanover and you plan for that?"

A feral look came over him, replacing the weak and mellow man I'd been dealing with a few minutes ago.

"You have no idea what you're talking about. You are here to do a job, to do a simple courier job, and that's all you need to know or do. I don't want to tell Michael you've been more trouble than it's worth. Deliver the damned papers and get the fuck out of my business."

A growl started in my throat, threatening to

break free if I let go for a fraction of a second. I envisioned leaping over the desk and grabbing that scrawny tie. I wanted to snarl into this jackhole's face I wasn't one of his slaves, not one of the indentured souls who groveled for crumbs falling from his financial table.

Jess's voice snapped at the back of my mind, reminding me to keep control. Protect the Pride, protect our secret.

Protect my mate.

I took a step back and bowed my head a fraction of an inch, glaring at the carpet.

Some Felis traits worked just as well in the human world. Submission being one of them.

"I'm glad we understand each other. I appreciate your good intentions about the baby but there are some areas you shouldn't venture into." He cocked his head to one side, the sweaty skin slick and gleaming in the artificial lighting. "Thank you for your help."

I resisted the urge to slap the satisfied smile off his face. "I'll be back with the signed documents as soon as possible."

MY CELL PHONE hummed again on the elevator ride down.

FREE YET 4 LUNCH?

My fingers were shaking as I tapped on the minute keyboard. One of the businesswomen standing next to me moved closer to the sliding doors for a faster escape.

NO I B HOME SOON. YOU BUY STEAK DINNER

I'd need to tear into some raw meat after all this.

OK. LUV U

The cab ride wasn't long enough for me to list the various ways I wanted to kill Brayton.

Disembowelment was high on the list.

I flexed my fingers and studied the space between my knuckles. The wounds had healed over since the last time I'd been able to manifest my claws, albeit without control.

I really wished I had full control now.

I'd have loved to scratch up Brayton's expensive desk, scar the lovely varnished dark wood with the wonderful screech of destruction.

When we pulled up in front of the hotel, the doorman waited patiently as I hopped out, recognizing me from before.

"Wait here," I instructed the cab driver. "I'll be a few minutes."

The elderly man shrugged and tapped the meter. "Take as long as you want. She keep running." He grinned, showing off a pristine set of blinding white teeth. "I got no place to be." He waved at the doorman before parking off to one side of the long driveway.

The lobby was jammed with tourists, this latest swarming consisting of chattering teenagers out to take pictures of anything and everything Canadian. Cell phones bobbed above the crowd as the desk clerk attempted to translate from French to German and back again for the lone chaperone. I slipped by the commotion and headed for the stairs.

Different smells and sounds assaulted my senses as I walked down the hallway, more than on my previous trip. Wound up from my confrontation with Brayton, I felt more and more of my Felis senses coming out.

Especially the urge to kill.

A moan from behind a door, matched with a gasp. The sharp, almost acidic smell of sex.

Crying behind another. Sobbing, muffled with a pillow or clothing.

A childish giggle at the third. Boyish, high-pitched. Low whispering, another male.

By the time I got to the end of the corridor my senses were saturated, the virtual pool overflowing with what I could smell and hear. It took a concentrated effort to clamp down, get control and restrict my intake to what I wanted. I'd learned hard and fast the first day I'd landed in Toronto how to pick and choose what I wanted to experience. It'd proven to be an asset to my livelihood but still a sore point at times when I lost control.

I paused in front of the hotel door. There was no use in taking my anger out on Molly—whether I agreed or not with what she was doing she was Liam's mother.

A slow, deep exhalation brought me down to earth. All I needed was a set of signatures and this would all be over.

I rapped at Molly Callendar's door with short, sharp bursts.

The door shifted under my touch. I touched the white painted wood with my fingertips and pushed it open.

At first I didn't panic. The thick carpet in many hotel rooms made it hard to shut the door enough to have the lock catch. It looked closed but it only took a fraction of an inch to keep the lock from grabbing. It'd happened before when I'd left.

The coppery scent smashed into my mouth as I stepped inside. I knew the smell, knew it intimately.

Blood.

Another sharper, more pungent smell rose up. I didn't need to be Felis to recognize that one.

Feces and urine.

And not just what a baby would create.

I moved toward the couch, picking each step with care. If I was right the police would want to know exactly where I placed my feet.

Molly Callendar lay between the couch and the coffee table, dead. She lay facedown on the cheap industrial-issue carpet, her arms stretched out in front of her toward the crib. Blood seeped out from under her left side. She'd been shot in the chest.

The other bullet hole was at the back of her head. It'd taken part of her face off but I recognized her. Her short red hair was now dotted with bits of bone and brain.

I instinctively knelt down and pressed my fingers to her throat, hoping against hope to find a pulse. The odds were against it but miracles had happened before.

Not even a flutter under the skin. She was cold and clammy to my touch; she'd been dead for a while—not long after I'd left her.

My inner voice snapped she was past saving and I had another person to worry about, another life in this room of death.

The baby.

I sprang toward the portable crib, not caring where I stepped.

It was empty except for a small stuffed lion sitting in one corner, winking at me. No diaper bag, no bottles of formula.

No baby.

I closed my eyes and tried to pull up what little calm I had left. The situation had gone from bad to worse to horribly, horribly terrible beyond anything imaginable.

I retreated to the front door and dug my cell phone out. It took three tries to hit 911, my numb fingers refusing to work properly.

The cab driver wasn't going to like losing his return fare.

THE POLICE CAME, the cab driver left and the hotel owner was very, very unhappy.

The homicide detective who showed up flinched when I mentioned my friendship with one of his colleagues, Hank Attersley, and my intention to say nothing to anyone but Hank. A short phone call later, and I was off to the police station with an escort to see Hank while CSI processed the scene and the coroner dealt with the dead body.

It took over an hour to get washed and rinsed through the system, finally ending up sitting in an interrogation room waiting for Hank and in the early grip of a major migraine.

My cell phone had stayed mercifully silent. The last thing I needed right now was to try to explain to Bran why I was at the police station.

I looked around the room. The two-way mirror was scratched and bent in spots, showing physical contact. It smelled like sweat and fear and blood with a little trace of urine mixed in.

I fought not to gag. The walls were a drab gray and for a frantic second I thought they were closing in on me.

Being trapped is one of our greatest fears. We chafed at the bit doing office jobs and thrived outside—putting us in cages was akin to a death sentence.

I swallowed hard, forcing the ball of fear away. I had nothing to fear from the police.

Bran, however, was a whole other thing. I definitely wasn't making our lunch date.

The stainless-steel table had seen better days—the scrapes and dents on the surface held a thousand stories, none of which I wanted to hear or to add my testimony to. I shifted in the uncomfortable wooden chair and cleared my throat.

"Any chance of getting a bottle of water here?"

I knew there were people on the other side of the glass. I couldn't scent them but I knew they were there, studying me like a butterfly under glass.

"Please?"

The door opened, admitting Detective Hank Attersley.

He tossed a plastic water bottle at me as he closed the door.

I caught it with one hand and wrestled the cap off. The condensation dripped onto the table, forming a small puddle of water.

He threw a file folder on the table, sat opposite me and glared, a snarl curling his lips. The generic brown suit was tight across his shoulders, with the white shirt desperately trying to hold in an ample belly brought on by having a wife who loved to cook and cooked well.

Hank and I had a love-hate relationship.

He loved making a little money on the side by helping me out. I hated the fact he kept trying to set me up with his wife's nephew or worse, convince me to "go legal" and join the force.

He flipped the folder open but didn't look down at the pages.

A black-and-white picture of Molly Callendar was clipped to the top page. Smiling, vibrant, alive.

I knew the other photographs would be buried at the back under the autopsy report. Pictures no one other than the police needed to see.

"Fuck, Reb. What have you gotten yourself into this time?" He answered his own question. "Murder. Fucking murder."

I smiled, trying not to bounce in the chair. It was uncomfortable to sit still but jumping around would signal nervousness and I didn't want to be here a second longer than I needed to be. "Missed you too, Hank."

He rubbed his chin, the ever-present five o'clock shadow standing at attention. "Haven't heard from you for a few months. You still hanging with that fellow?" His lips turned up on the last word as if he'd stepped in dog poop.

"His name's Brandon Hanover. And yes, I'm still 'hanging'." He was making small talk, working his way up to the big event. “Still living in Parkdale and still paying my bills like a good little Canadian.” I tilted my head toward the world outside the closed door. “Let’s get down to business. Any idea what happened to Molly Callendar?”

His expression didn’t change. “That’s what I’m about to ask you.” He looked at the black-and-white photo before moving to the first typewritten page. “Girl, what the hell were you doing there in the first place?”

“I was running courier. I put everything in my statement.” I reached over and tapped the top page. “Delivering a legal document that needed to be signed by the victim. On my second trip I discovered the body and, as per the law, notified the authorities ASAP.” I tried not to sound bored. This was the third or fourth time I’d had to explain my presence and it was getting both annoying and upsetting.

Attersley grunted. “We’ve already spoke to Brayton. He confirms your temporary employment and your assignment.” He rapped his thick knuckles on the papers. “So how did you meet Brayton?”

The casual tone didn’t fool me. He wanted to know how a cheap PI ended up running papers for one of the biggest investment firms in the city.

I paused. If I told him about Michael Hanover I could be knocking over a whole nest of snakes. But if my answer didn't line up with Brayton's statement I'd be in Hank's gunsights for not giving a truthful statement.

I took a deep swig of water, buying myself a few more seconds to think.

The question was how much Brayton wanted to keep Hanover out of this situation. From what I'd seen, Brayton wanted to keep his buddy on the other side of the moon, if possible. Whatever Michael Hanover had on David Brayton was enough to make him claim a child who wasn't his and arrange a support agreement that would last decades—but was it enough to keep quiet about possible involvement in a murder?

I rolled the dice.

"His boss, Michael Hanover?" I allowed myself the biggest shit-eating grin ever. "Brandon's his son."

Hank's eyes widened. I heard a thump on the other side of the glass and imagined some low-level flunky being shredded by his superior for not making the connection. If they hadn't figured it out before, they knew now and I wasn't going to hide it.

"I met his parents yesterday. Daddy asked me

if I could do a favor for one of his employees—I don't know how much, if anything, he knew." I spread my hands. "Get on the family's good side and all that."

Hank sat back and crossed his arms. I knew he was giving me more time to talk and for the other detectives behind the one-way mirror to watch me for any signs of discomfort.

I drew a finger through the puddle. "I arrive this morning and Brayton tells me he needs a ghost runner. He didn't want to use anyone from the firm and risk being found out. Cash on the barrelhead, no paper trail and no one making the connection back from Callendar to Hanover Investments and David Brayton."

Hank slowly nodded like a tired bobblehead.

I licked my dry lips. "I don't have to tell you how much scandal this would cause if it hit the papers. Especially some trashy tabloid like the Toronto *Inquisitor*." I couldn't stop a sly smile. Bran had been working for the *Inquisitor* when we'd met and Hank'd warned me off the slick, silver-tongued reporter.

Hank didn't say anything.

He didn't have to.

"I figured it'd be a fast few hours of work and I'm in good with the parents."

That much was the honest truth.

Hank didn't respond. His left eyebrow rose a fraction of an inch.

I shut up. The line about anything you say being held against you isn't idle talk.

He broke eye contact and studied the file, flipping through the pages. "Do you know what the paperwork Brayton gave you to take to the hotel was in regards to?"

"Child support. The father wanted Molly to sign off on a deal. Told me she was going to move out west with the baby and start all over." I didn't add my theory about who the father was. "I saw the agreement. Nothing too complicated."

"She sent you packing."

"She didn't like the first draft. Couldn't blame her for wanting more money. I'd have done the same thing."

Hank glanced once to the mirror, then back down to the file. "So you went back to Brayton and returned to the hotel."

"The cab drivers can verify my trips and my times."

Now it was the detective's turn to nod. "We've already looked over their sheets. They verify your story."

I spread my hands. "So why am I sitting here?"

Hank snorted. "Because you were the last to see her alive other than the killer. And don't think you weren't a prime target for that title."

"Past tense," I replied. "Because I'm innocent."

"Because your alibi checks out. And you don't have any reason to kill a woman and run out with a newborn."

I flinched inwardly. The cold truth pricked me in all the wrong places.

"So I'm free to go?"

His expression didn't change. "We've got a dead woman lying on the floor of a hotel room. And a missing baby. Already got an AMBER Alert out on the little one." He glanced down again at my typed statement. "Although 'red fuzz' isn't much to go on. Too bad you couldn't give us any birthmarks or anything to identify him."

I resisted the urge to yell. "I only saw him for a few minutes bundled up in a blanket and Molly wasn't exactly keen on showing him off. She was focused on studying the agreement. Liam's a month old, maybe less. Find him and find him fast."

The note of panic that'd crept into my voice hadn't gone unnoticed. "What's up with the kid? You know something? He got some medical problems we should know about?"

There was no way I could tell him Liam was Hanover's baby. I had no proof other than my nose.

"Nope. I just don't like babies going missing. Not when the mother's been gunned down and he's probably headed for some damned adoption scam." The anger in my voice was genuine. There was an outside chance Molly had been in the wrong place at the wrong time, targeted because she had a newborn and seemed unprotected.

Stranger things had happened, sadly enough.

Hank studied me for a minute before giving a cautious nod. "We're talking to Brayton right now. We're checking out Callendar's history, see if anyone had a grudge against her." He gave me a thoughtful look. "What was your perception of the relationship between Callendar and Brayton?"

This wasn't Attersley the detective. This was Hank sharing a beer with me at the local bar after a rough week and tossing ideas back and forth on popular cases playing out in the media.

I rolled my shoulders back, feeling a bit of the tension easing out. This was familiar territory. "Couldn't give you a precise assessment since I just met them today. But if he was working out an arrangement and having papers drawn up it seems sort of back-asward to have her killed and steal the baby. It's not like he wouldn't automatically become a suspect, which he has."

Hank waved me on, encouraging me to keep talking. I knew he wasn't looking to trap me with my own words but to take advantage of my skills.

Hell, I wouldn't even send the police a bill.

I tapped my fingernails on the stainless-steel table. "It'd be a bad move on Brayton's part because he would know the murder would be discovered and tracked back to his front door. Sending any courier would be risky, but me? Why would he put me in the middle of this, knowing what I do for a living?"

Hank sat back and crossed his arms. "Why, indeed." He paused again, waiting to see if I would give him more.

I thought about whether I was prepared to give him Hanover as a possible suspect.

I decided against it. This could have nothing to do with Hanover and tossing his name out would bring down a shit storm of trouble on everyone—especially Bran and myself.

Hanover knew Brayton was sending me over and if he wanted Callendar dead he'd have more resources available to him, people who would be cleaner and faster. There was no doubt in my mind Michael Hanover was a very powerful man who got what he wanted. Why set his friend up as a possible suspect for the murder and bring me into the picture? He had to know I'd play pretty with the cops and wouldn't cover his trail where a murdered mother was involved. I loved his son but he was playing with some big balls if he figured I'd keep his murder of Molly Callendar as a dirty little family secret.

There was also the uncomfortable fact that if I pointed the finger at Hanover I'd have three pointed back at myself. A good prosecutor could make the case I'd killed Callendar because I was upset over Hanover's attempts to blackmail me. It wasn't much but I'd seen prosecutors file charges on a lot less in order to get a suspect in jail and under pressure.

I couldn't afford to spend time in a holding cell while the cops dug out the truth. Not to mention I couldn't afford the truth coming out about me, Hanover's attempted blackmail and the family.

Callendar's murder would be only the start in a long gory line of death. I didn't and couldn't imagine how many would fall prey to heart attacks, car accidents and accidental poisonings before the Felis felt safe again.

"Someone could have followed me to the hotel.

Takes out Callendar before taking the baby for ransom."

Hank sat back. "Possible but that's pretty hard-core, killing a mother and snatching a baby. Gotta have brass balls to look a woman in the face and gun her down." Hank shook his head. "Don't make sense. But then murder usually don't." He reached out and tapped my nose. "I see that look in your eyes. Don't you get wound up in this, Rebecca. You're already technically involved and I don't want to have to arrest your ass."

"Me?" I gave him an angelic smile.

"Oh, fuck," he moaned. "And it starts." He wagged a fat finger at me. "Don't get involved any more than you are, Desjardin. You're already on shaky ground. I'm going to have to answer why I'm not tossing your ass into a holding cell right now."

I held out my hands. "Go for it. She was killed sometime between my first visit and my return. I've got two cabbies who'll vouch I was in their cabs and a pissy receptionist who'll tell you I was in Brayton's office. I'll call Michael Hanover and he'll get a lawyer who'll run you and your crew to ground on a thousand little technicalities within the hour."

It was a bluff, one I hoped would work. I didn't

want to have to call Michael Hanover for anything, much less one of his lawyers. But I'd be a fool to pass up the opportunity to keep Hank's arrest-eager buddies at bay.

Hank scowled but I saw the underlying smile. "Get the fuck out of here before I toss you for being annoying."

As I turned to go he touched my arm, bringing me back. "Be careful, Reb. This isn't just about a dead woman. Whoever killed her took the baby and if you start rattling the wrong cages things could go south fast." His voice dropped to a whisper. "He could panic and kill the kid. He's already killed the mother—he's got nothing to lose. You put him in a corner and Molly's family might end up having a double funeral."

FOUR

THE LINE FOR the elevator included two foul-smelling transients and a trio of streetwalkers with dueling perfumes, so I decided to wait for the next one. Even without my hypersensitive sense of smell I'd have been throwing up the second the doors closed.

I leaned against the wall trying to find my balance. I'd dealt with a lot of strange cases over the years, up to and including child custody, but a kidnapping was way out of my league and experience.

More so when it was one of my own, in a manner of speaking. Bran was my mate and Liam my—what was he? Possible half brother-in-law? Could babies be in-law anything?

My head spun as I worked through the possible titles. It was easier than thinking about how to deal with Bran and find Liam.

"Rebecca."

I turned at the familiar voice.

Bernadette Hanover stared at me. She wore

dark blue slacks with a matching jacket. "What are you doing here?"

I resisted the urge to dig in my messenger bag, returned to me a few minutes ago, for my drug stash to fight the oncoming migraine. The last thing I needed was to give Bran's mother the impression I was an addict.

"I could ask the same," I shot back.

Her eyes narrowed. She wasn't used to being challenged by anyone, much less someone she viewed as far below her social status. "I'm here for a meeting about a new charity. We opened up a month ago and we're assessing the different programs." She nodded at a brightly colored poster on the bulletin board advertising yet another foundation aimed at helping ex-convicts to find meaningful employment.

She crossed her arms in front of her, building body armor. "And you?"

I flipped through the various stories I'd used in the past to cover an uncomfortable situation. I didn't know if she knew Brayton or not but I wasn't going to get her involved in this if at all possible. Not when there was an illegitimate Hanover baby out there somewhere.

The last thing I needed right now was to get

into another pissing match with Bernadette. I'd have plenty of opportunities for that in the future.

"I know one of the detectives." I waved at Attersley. He waved back, frowning at seeing me still in the police station and talking to someone far out of my social strata. He tilted his head to one side and watched us dance.

Bernadette crossed her arms. "I know you know some cop here. It was in your file."

I resisted the urge to snap her neck like the scrawny chicken she reminded me of. The last thing I needed was for Hank to overhear the word "file" and wonder what that was all about.

Her lower lip jutted out in a halfhearted pout. "What I want to know is why you are here, now." She gestured at the animated figures dashing in and out of offices. A missing baby set off all the bells and whistles and Attersley's people took their job seriously. "I understand your profession involves dealing with the police but I didn't expect to find you hanging out here."

I caught the disapproval in her voice mixed with curiosity. She'd likely gotten all of her knowledge about private investigation from bad crime novels and reruns of *Magnum P.I.* and I didn't fit into any of them.

Especially the cute mustache.

"I'm between cases right now." I figured the less she knew about my arrangement with her husband the better—I'd let him deal with the situation if and when it came up. "There's an AMBER Alert out for a missing child. I wanted to get a full description so I could pass the information on to my street sources. Any port in a storm and so forth." It was a half lie, one I could be comfortable with.

"Oh my." She glanced at the scrambling officers. "A missing child. That's awful." Bernadette turned her attention back to me. "Is it a random snatching or parental custody issue?"

I looked at her, startled by the logical question. Maybe there was more to this woman than seen at first glance. "Ah, we're not sure yet. At the least, a kidnapping."

"It wasn't a carjacking, was it?" She let out a plaintive sigh. "I work with one group who keeps reminding the public to not leave babies in the car, even for a few minutes while they rush into a store."

"No, no car here." I wasn't sure what to say or not to say, not knowing what or how much information had been released to the public. I didn't need Hank roaring down my neck for putting something out that hadn't been approved by The Powers That Be.

Bernadette shook her head. "Such a pity. I hope they find the little boy or girl. Awful business, especially where babies are involved."

She turned to go and I felt my heart begin beating again.

Bernadette suddenly stopped and spun on one tall stiletto heel to face me again. "We should have lunch sometime. I'll call you and we can chat about things away from the men. I'd like to hear about your mother." Her lips drew together into a tight line before moving again. "I'm sure it was quite traumatic when you lost her."

Suddenly I was ten years old again and curled up in Ruth's lap, crying and cursing with words I didn't even understand yet.

"Yeah. Have your people call my people and we'll do lunch," I croaked out.

She gave me a practiced smile. "We'll have a little girl time together since you're spending so much time with my son." The last two words came out almost as a curse, her lips curling around the syllables.

"Sure." I lifted a hand to give a halfhearted wave but she'd already disappeared down the hallway and into the stairwell, her blond locks bouncing around her shoulders.

A cool breeze wafted through courtesy of a

well-placed fan by an open window at the far end of the hallway and I drew in a deep breath, both gathering myself and enjoying the reprieve from the funky station house smell.

The wind also carried another scent, a variation of one I'd recently become familiar with.

I closed my eyes. This was part of the reason I could never become a cop. I couldn't handle this part of the job.

I opened them to look down the hall, zeroing in on a frail-looking couple being guided along the corridor by a pair of uniformed policemen.

The Callendars.

The older woman was this side of retirement, her gray hair pulled back into a tight bun. A white shawl hung on her narrow shoulders, draped over a black blouse and matching slacks.

Her husband had a handful of follicles left and had chosen to do a comb-over to try to keep some sense of having hair. He wore an oil-stained black T-shirt and jeans. His hands sat on her shoulders—calloused and leathered. Mr. Callendar was a man who worked with his hands and worked hard for a living.

They stopped outside one of the interrogation rooms. The uniforms muttered something and walked away, leaving the grieving parents alone to sit on a wooden bench and wait for the detectives to show up and brief them.

I moved over to the open window and looked out, tuning in to the bereaved couple. It didn't take much to zone in on the emotional whispers and lock out the grumblings and mutterings from the nearby cops. I felt my ears twitch as my natural radar zeroed in on the grieving parents.

"I can't believe this," Mrs. Callendar said between sobs. "Who would do this to her, right after she had the baby? Who?"

Her husband tightened his grip on her shoulders. "That bastard." His fingers trembled where they rested. "That bastard," he repeated.

She reached up and touched his hand. "Right now we have to focus on Liam. We need to find Liam."

"We'll find the bastard and make him pay," Mr. Callendar rumbled. The hardness in his words startled me. There was a lot of bite behind this bark. "We'll find him and the baby and do what's right." He shot an angry look at a uniformed cop. "We'll do right by her."

The distraught woman shook her head. "I wish she had stayed with Ian. He was such a nice boy..." Her sentence trailed off into a new outburst of tears.

Her husband shook his head. "You know it wouldn't have worked out, Julia. They grew up together but they weren't meant to be together no matter how much we all wanted it to work." He let out a snort. "I wish she had told us who Liam's father was. We'd have a place to start."

"You don't think it was Ian?" Julia Callendar pulled a tissue from her sleeve and dabbed at her eyes.

Mr. Callendar shrugged. "She said it wasn't him and I believe her. I don't know how I'm going to tell him." He sighed. "I'll call his dad on the construction site. Maybe that's the best way to go about this."

"Until they bring him in for questioning." His wife sniffled. "You know the police will want every detail, every ex."

"We'll give it to them. And let Harrison clear his own name," Mr. Callendar replied. "It was supposed to be a nice breakup, an amicable deal." He shook his head. "I'll kill the bastard." He swiped at a wayward tear making its way down his cheek. "I'm more worried about Liam. He's so young, so little—" He buried his face in his wife's shoulder.

The two wobbled back and forth, leaning on each other for support.

I couldn't watch anymore. I turned away, giving them their privacy.

I also had another lead in Molly's murder.

Attersley appeared at my side, startling me. "Who was that?"

"Who?" I blinked, trying to regain my focus. It was always hard to switch back to the present after using my Felis senses.

"The fancy lady bending your ear." He stabbed a thumb at the stairwell where Bernadette Hanover had gone. "Thought for a second you were about to jump out the window, you looked so terrified."

"Michael Hanover's wife." I tried to sound nonchalant. "Bran's mum."

Epic fail.

The pudgy detective let out a low whistle. "I think you'd be better off single than dealing with that barracuda."

I tilted my head and smiled. "You don't think I can handle her?"

"Sweetie." He gave me a sad smile. "My mother-in-law hates my guts. No man would ever be good enough for her daughter and in your case no woman would ever be good enough for her son. There's nothing you could do, outside of maybe saving the world, that would bring her over to your side."

"Thanks for the pep talk."

"No problem." He grinned. "Why are you still here?"

I jerked a thumb at the elevator. "Waiting for my ride." I couldn't help looking back at the Callendars.

He followed my glance toward the mourning parents and shook his head. "Don't screw with them, Reb. They're good folks who not only lost their daughter but now they're worried about having to bury a grandson."

I paused, weighing my options. I could, in all good faith, walk over and offer my services to help find Liam.

Hank seemed to be reading my mind. "Don't even think about it. You're mixed up in this enough as it is, you take those two on as clients and I'll have the higher-ups demanding I put you in a cage for interfering with an investigation." His hand landed on my arm—a light touch, more grandfatherly than official cop. "Let us do what we do best. Here." He shoved a page into my hand. "You want to help out go hit the streets and spread the word about the baby."

I looked at the information sheet. The color

photo showed Liam in all of his glory, his eyes barely open under the red fuzz covering his tiny head. It was a generic hospital photograph taken not long after his birth.

"Go save their world." Hank nodded at the Calendars.

The elevator doors slid open. I stepped inside, leaving him behind.

"I'll go get my cape," I replied as the steel shutters closed.

The new cell phone Bran had bought me had all the bells and whistles, including the ability to take photographs. I pressed the paper against the elevator wall and took the shot, making sure to keep the tiny baby face in focus.

It took a few seconds to send the photograph and a few more to dial the number myself.

The elevator doors opened as the connection came through.

"Rebecca. What a surprise." Jess wasn't lying, the shock evident in her words. "What's this picture?"

"I need a favor." It was like gargling bleach.

"Really." The curiosity overrode the lack of etiquette. "A favor. From me."

"You owe me after all the things I've done, all the help I've given you and the family." I took a deep breath, feeling the nervous flutters in my stomach threaten to break free. "I need you to call a hunt." I spoke quickly, afraid what would happen if I sat and thought about the words. "The picture is of Liam Callendar. He was stolen from a hotel room within the last few hours. Punk took the diaper bag and all the supplies but you know how fast babies go through stuff. People would notice a guy being awkward with a baby, unsure how to handle him. I need our people to be on the lookout for someone acting suspicious."

"What happened to the mother?" I heard tapping on the line—Jess texting to the Pride. The electronic alert was going out even as we spoke. She wasn't waiting for my reasons.

"Murdered. Shot in the back of the head." The image of Molly Callendar's shattered skull popped into my mind's eye, twisting my stomach into knots.

"And this is a *human* baby."

"Yes."

"Why are we helping you find him? The police have their own informants and systems for this. AMBER Alert and so forth. Children go missing every day and it breaks my heart but what's so special about this one?"

I drew a deep breath. "He's Bran's half brother."

The silence hung between us for a few seconds.

"I see. Consider it done," Jess replied in a calm, measured voice. "I'll be in touch as soon as we have something." The line went dead. I'd been expecting an interrogation or at least a reprimand for asking for Felis help in a purely human matter.

I wasn't sure what the price was going to be for asking Jess for this favor but I was willing to pay it.

The lobby was full of hustle and bustle, the usual perp walk of innocent criminals going in and out. But things were different with the news that a baby was missing, an added urgency infecting everyone. People walked faster, phones answered quicker.

Even the hookers looked concerned, one stopping to drag a bright red neon fingernail across the bottom of the brand-new poster of Liam stuck on the bulletin board. She shook her head and mumbled something to the man beside her, who thumped the floor with his walking stick.

It took a lot to piss off a pimp.

The cell phone vibrated against my hip.

I hesitated, not recognizing the number. At least it wasn't Bran—I wasn't sure I was up to dealing with him right now.

I hit the button and put it up to my ear. If I

was lucky it was a sighting of Liam by one of the family.

"Rebecca." I froze, recognizing Michael Hanover's voice.

So much for luck.

"I'm here." I didn't want to speak his name aloud. It was sort of like the Bloody Mary urban myth.

"Where are you?"

"About to step out of Division 14 after having a rousing game of canasta with the police."

Police and civilians flowed around me as I headed for the front doors. I fought against the tide until I got outside.

"We need to talk."

"No shit, Sherlock." I trotted down the front steps, free of the constraints of the police station. "Just tell me—did you try to set me up for Molly's death because I love your son? Because if you say yes I'm about to bring down the shit storm of all shit storms on your head."

"You can't talk to me like that."

I sat down on the concrete steps. "I can and I am. You're in a ton of trouble and I wouldn't count on Brayton going down on a murder charge to keep your name out of all this."

"I need you to come to my office. We need to

talk about this and I don't like doing it over the phone."

"I'm on my way." I cut the connection before he could respond.

The cell phone buzzed again before I could even think about putting it away.

WHERE R U?

Bran.

My fingers paused over the tiny keyboard. I had to tell Bran but I had no idea how to even start to approach the subject. Honey, I love you but I might have accidentally participated in the murder and cover-up of your father's secret lover and the kidnapping of your half brother.

Didn't roll off the tongue.

STILL WORKING. BE HOME SOON.

WHERE ARE U?

DOWNTOWN AT MTNG. GOT 2 GO. LUV YOU.

I wondered if there was a special confession rite for lying through text messages.

FIVE

IT TOOK ME a few minutes to flag down a cab and direct him to the Hanover Investments complex, after which I sat back and searched for Ian Hamilton, using the cell phone's built-in web browser.

I could get used to this sort of investigating.

A plethora of Ian Hamiltons popped up in the results page, thinned slightly by adding "construction" to the search criteria. It was a page long but it was a start.

As we stopped in front of the tall glass needles I saved the details and tossed the driver a twenty before heading for the front doors.

The security officers watched as I approached the desk for the second time, my messenger bag flapping against my hip. I signed in again and flashed my license to the same senior officer I'd seen on my first visit.

"I'm here to see Michael Hanover this time."

"Fifteenth floor." The supervisor checked his clipboard. "I don't have you on his list of appointments today." He eyed me over the clear plastic. "We need to call upstairs. Are you expected?" The tone in his voice told me he was used to turfing surprise visitors.

"No, but he'll see me." I looked at his clipboard. "You may want to call a few of those and tell them he'll be running late."

MICHAEL HANOVER HAD his own floor and private receptionist, both of which looked extensively reworked to look expensive. The young blonde woman smiled at me while offering Godiva chocolates and freshly brewed coffee or tea as I waited.

Interns rushed back and forth while I lounged on the black leather couch, stretched out and chomping on square after square of mouthwatering dark chocolate. I played with the wrappers, wishing I knew enough origami to turn them into tiny cranes or unicorns. I settled for a large foil ball.

It was after five in the afternoon, the usual quitting time for most of the world, but the floor showed no signs of clearing out. Instead it seemed to get even busier with more frantic interns dashing in and out of rooms with wild silent gestures to each other and nervous, sweaty faces.

"Rebecca." Michael waved me over, standing

in the doorway of his office. He sounded like he was about to order pizza.

Hanover had gone all out on the decorating, unlike Brayton. I felt like I'd stepped onto the bridge of a pirate ship.

The dark wooden panels covering the walls held picture after picture of Hanover with what I assumed to be important people. Shaking hands, cutting ribbons, digging a hole with a golden shovel.

There were no photographs of his family. Bernadette appeared in one or two in the background but there were none of Michael with Brandon catching fish or playing ball.

The oak desk was larger than most small cars, the polished surface covered with papers and folders, fat stone paperweights with fossils embedded in them holding down thick wads of reports. A tiny computer sat on a smaller desk with the screensaver running—a display of old tall ships ranging from the USS Constitution to the more recent ones used for racing.

He gestured to the two chairs in front of the desk while he wandered around to his luxury seat.

I sat down and crossed my legs.

"Rebecca," Michael started then caught himself. He leaned on the desk, his arms pushing aside file folders and piles of Post-it notes. "Believe me when I say I have nothing to do with this."

"On the contrary. You have everything to do with this."

Michael nodded. "True. I am sorry I pulled you into all this. I didn't foresee this being such a complicated affair."

"Death usually is." I pointed at the parade of photographs on the wall. "Is Molly Callendar in any of those? Might want to hide them when the cops come to visit."

Michael frowned, the tufts of white on his temples twitching. "Why would they be interested in me? I already spoke to Detective Attersley and explained I gave your name as a favor to Brayton. Aside from that I have nothing to add to this whole horrible affair."

Now it was my turn to lean forward. "You don't think Brayton is going to keep his mouth shut forever about this deal? That you're the one who had the affair with Molly, not him?"

He didn't flinch. No blinking, no emotional change of any kind.

I'd hate to face Michael Hanover across a poker table.

"What makes you say that?" The cold reply chilled my bones.

"I saw the baby." Time to roll the dice—but not to show all my cards. "He looks a hell of a lot like you. And Bran."

He dismissed me with a wave of his hand. "All babies look the same. Cute, adorable, blah blah blah. You haven't told the cops this insane theory, have you?"

I studied his face. So much like Bran's but with an inner hardness that would shatter diamonds. "And if I have?"

Michael leaned back, touching his fingertips together. "I think you haven't. Because there's no proof." He spread his hands. "Without proof, well…the police tend to nitpick about such things. And so do lawyers." He tilted his head to one side. "Have you shared your theories with Bran?"

I mentally squirmed.

He studied me for a second before continuing. "I see." Michael looked over at the photo gallery. "I'll make this brief because I have to get back to work. Brayton isn't going to say anything about me to the police because there's nothing to say. If you mention this wild theory I'll not only continue the investigation into your family and make it public, I'll make sure you never work in this town again."

I couldn't help smiling at the classic threatening phrase.

Michael frowned. "I'm not joking. As for your relationship with Bran, his mother and I will be having a discussion with him as regards his future in general and specifically with you. While I realize you played a part in his…rehabilitation, you have to understand the Hanover name stands for security and safety. Having a loose cannon spewing rumors and theories in the family wouldn't be good for us. Or you."

"You'd make him choose between me and you?" I smiled. "Really?"

"Bran has had the best of everything up to this point. Schooling, training, access to anything and anyone he's wanted." Michael touched his fingertips together. "True, he turned his back on honest journalism for a bit but he relied on the family name for his rent money. What do you think he'll do if I tell him to choose between staying with you and utter poverty?"

"He'd choose me." I had no doubt in my heart.

"Really." Michael smirked. "You might want to reconsider what you know about my son."

My cell phone buzzed. I ignored it.

"You may want to answer that," Michael said. The sly smile begged to be slapped off.

I grabbed at the slim technological wafer.

WHERE R U?

AT WORK. B HOME SOON.

NO.

I stared at the screen.

IM IN LOBBY WAITING 4 YOU. COME DOWN. NOW.

I closed the connection without replying and tucked the phone back into my pocket.

Michael stood up. "Perhaps my son can talk some more sense into you." One eyebrow rose. "Since you don't keep any secrets from him, right?"

THE ELEVATOR RIDE down was slow and agonizing. If I was lucky the cables would snap and send me down to the hell that waited for liars.

It didn't break.

I spotted him the second I stepped off the elevator despite a swarm of businessmen and women clotting the lobby.

Bran stood inside the front doors, waiting with arms crossed.

"I'm over in Yorkville at a little café, having a coffee with a magazine editor who wants a series of articles on Toronto street life, and I get interrupted by a message from my mother asking why my girlfriend was hanging out in a police station." The fury in his eyes could have torched half of Rome. "Especially when I thought you were doing a fast security system check for a client and there was no reason for you to be with the cops. So I have to explain to her about how I'm not your keeper and how there must be a good reason even though I can't think of one right now. And then I get a call from my father's office telling me to come pick you up here. So what is going on?"

I held up a hand. "Can we at least get home before you toss me over your knee? Let me get into the school girl outfit."

This earned us a guffaw from the security supervisor and curious looks from the other guards and bystanders.

Bran didn't smile. He crooked a finger at me and walked out. I gave a shrug to the audience and followed.

He was silent the entire way home in the back of the cab.

I shuffled my feet, not daring to make small talk. There was no way to be gentle about what I had to tell him, no way I could think of.

I'd have rather gone on a hunt against a rabid boar with a toothpick.

Bran paid off the cab driver and led the way up to my house and inside, using his own key to unlock the door. His leather duster flew onto the back of the couch.

I added my coat and messenger bag. The oversized purse slid onto the floor.

I didn't move to pick it up.

Jazz flew by us in a white blur heading for the stairs. Old girl could move it when she needed to and right now she sensed she needed to get as far away from these two humans as she could.

Bran sat down on the couch, shoving both coats aside. "Can you imagine how pissed off I am right now?" His hands flew back and forth, slicing the air in layers. "My mother, she doesn't need a reason to dislike you—all you needed was a vagina. Now you're slinking around police stations and lying to me and seeing my father in his office and—" He stopped for air. "Feel free to jump in anytime."

I looked at him and all I could see was Liam's sweet, innocent face. I broke into tears.

"What the..." He bounded off the couch and grabbed me in a bear hug. "What's going on?" His hands moved up and down over my shirt. "Are you hurt? Did someone attack you? Is that why you were at the police station?" In a flash his tone changed from demanding to protective.

"No, no. I'm fine." I buried my face in his shoulder. "It's bad. It's so damned bad." He smelled of coffee and nervous sweat. "God, I don't know where to start."

My stomach growled, the loud noise startling both of us.

"When was the last time you ate?" Bran asked.

I gave a shrug and shook my head.

"No wonder you're fucked up. You probably skipped brekka as well." He lowered me to the couch, kneeling down. "Let me get some dinner. Then we can talk about what's going on."

There was no room for negotiation.

Bran pulled off the afghan from the back of the couch and wrapped it around me. "I think there's some cold pizza in the fridge. Let me nuke it and get something for you to drink." He stood up. "I don't know what's going on here but I'm not going to have you get sick over it."

I nodded, not knowing what to say.

Jazz trilled from the top of the stairs before

coming to my feet. She hopped up and head-butted my hip. Whether we were related or not was an ongoing joke of Bran's but never let it be said a cat didn't know when someone needed comfort even at the risk of an angry mate.

Bran entered from the kitchen carrying two slices of pizza on a plate, and a can of soda. "Figured you'd need this." He offered the drink first. "Eat, drink and we'll talk."

I emptied half the can in a gulp as Bran sat down beside me with his own reheated slices and a can of soda. He ate quickly and efficiently with sideways glances at how I was doing.

There was no talking, just a lot of happy chewing.

The pizza was a classic pepperoni and mushroom from a small family business, the dough made fresh every day and almost tastier than the actual toppings.

"Right." He took the plate from me and placed it atop his own on the floor. Jazz immediately hopped off to investigate. "What's this all about?"

I rubbed my eyes with my palms. "Your father..." I stopped, unsure of where to go next.

"My father is an asshole. What did he say to you last night that got you into all this trouble today?"

"Your father asked me to do a favor for him."

Bran didn't flinch. "Bastard. Let me guess—you do a favor for him and he gives you the file about your family."

I squirmed. "In a way."

Bran waited. The man had the patience of a saint.

And the passion of a sinner.

The words rolled out in one breath. "Your father told me if I didn't do this favor for him he'd sic the dogs on us, send a full investigative team in to dig up everything on me and my family, everything about us." I bit my lower lip. "Bran, they'd have killed all of you."

I didn't have to elaborate who "they" were. He knew how far the Felis would go to keep secrets.

"Fuck." Bran ran a hand through his short red hair. "Stupid bastard. He should have known better—"

"No, he couldn't have. And he can't ever know." I rolled the can between my palms, letting the condensation drip onto the floor. "He asked me to go see a man named David Brayton. Works for your father downtown in one of those towers."

Bran's face was blank. "Can't say I know the man. But I don't know a lot of my father's associates." I saw his jaw tense. "I don't walk in those circles, haven't for a long time."

I pressed the wet metal against my forehead. "Brayton's just another financial flunky, far as I can tell. He asked me to do a courier run. He wanted no paperwork on this, a private job, which is why I got called in to keep it as secret as possible."

I needed another soda. Instead I swallowed hard and continued.

Bran didn't say anything.

"He wanted me to go to a hotel, meet a woman. The paperwork, it was a support agreement for her baby. Named Brayton as the father and arranged for her to get a sweet sum of cash for staying quiet and disappearing. She was going to move out of town, take the money and build a new life."

"I take it Brayton's married."

"Yes. He told me it was a mistake, the usual crap when men have affairs and don't want to admit they were thinking with the little head more than with the big head."

Bran grinned.

I shrugged, enjoying the brief moment of levity.

The mood vanished as I took a deep breath, knowing what I had to say but not finding the right words.

"I saw the baby." I chewed on my bottom lip, delaying for a few more seconds. "It wasn't Brayton's child."

Bran blinked. His eyebrows came together as he frowned.

"I—" I touched the tip of my nose. "I could tell he wasn't Brayton's because I recognized the scent from another male. Liam's real father."

I could see him putting the pieces together in a horrible, heartbreaking sequence. Our first case, the event that had brought us together and revealed my secret to him involved my ability to sniff a sample of Felis hair and determine a relationship between father and son. Each person had their own scent but there was always a trace of their parents in there, a family trait.

The baby wasn't Felis but the same rules applied.

If Brayton wasn't Liam's father someone else was, someone who I could identify by his scent and who would have reason to want the paternity kept secret.

Someone who would use blackmail to keep me quiet.

"My father." He said the words like a curse.

I dropped my head down. I couldn't say the words.

Bran pressed his hands against his knees, hard. The muscles on his arms went rigid as he stared at the floor. He drew short, rough breaths.

I didn't do anything. I didn't know what to do.

Everyone reacts differently to bad news. I've seen women break into the giggles when discovering their husbands are fooling around and grown men shrug off infidelity as if it were a bug bite.

I couldn't even begin to guess at what Bran would do.

I reached out to touch him, to somehow apologize for fracturing his reality. "Bran."

He stood up and swung at the lamp on the table beside us. It crashed against the wall. The black clay shattered, exposing the electrical wiring that lay limp on the floor. The black lamp shade bounced away behind the couch and out of sight.

"That bastard," he shouted. "A baby. A fucking baby."

Jazz disappeared in a white blur up the stairs to the relative safety of the bedroom. I wanted to join her but couldn't.

I'd brought the storm. Now I had to deal with it.

Bran brought his fists down on the cherrywood table. It didn't break but angry cracks spun out from the impact site through the varnish. The narrow legs wobbled in preparation of surrender.

I got up and stood there, hands at my side.

Another hammering and the side table gave way. It sank to the ground like a dead animal, the dark wooden legs splayed out in all directions. Chips of varnish flew around my feet and under the couch.

Bran drew a shuddering breath. He turned to me.

“Bastard.”

Blood trickled down his fingers.

I took a step back, fear curdling the pizza and soda in my stomach. He looked like a trapped animal, an angry wounded animal about to lash out at anyone in range.

I didn’t know what to do or say.

He stared at me and for a second I saw the little boy inside him, betrayed and hurt. Another blink and his expression flashed forward into the steely-eyed predator I’d encountered in the Pennsylvanian forest, unbroken and proud.

I couldn’t breathe. It was like I’d been punched in the chest so hard my heart couldn’t beat and I was dying.

“Reb?” Bran whispered. “Are you okay?” He looked down at his bleeding hands, then back at me. “Oh God. Are you afraid of me?”

I shook my head even as I stepped back a pace, my feet moving independently of my mind.

"You're trembling." He took a step closer. His scent washed over me, the thick musk filled with testosterone.

I froze like a deer caught in the headlights. My legs turned to rubber, threatening to drop me to the ground.

"Oh God." His arms went around me. "I'm so sorry. I didn't mean to scare you. I'd never hurt you, never." He pulled me to the ground, both of us kneeling on bloody splinters.

"It's okay." I felt the fear dissipate, washed away by a surge of emotion. "I just, I've never seen you like that."

"I've never been so mad. So fucking mad at my father." He tilted my face up so I could see him clearly. "But not mad at you."

"You were. A little bit."

"A little bit," he admitted. "But I can't stay mad at you. You're too damned good in bed."

"You know it." I took hold of his shoulders and stood up, a little shaky on my feet. "You're bleeding. Let's get you fixed up."

He followed me into the kitchen and shoved his hands in the sink. I turned on the cold water and let it wash away the blood.

"Bastard," Bran repeated. The anger in his voice was still there, tempered with sadness and acceptance.

I opened up the drawer and got the first aid kit. There was nothing to add.

"Tell me the whole story." The warning tone in his voice demanded honesty. "All of it."

It took the length of time for me to disinfect and clean his hands to go through the details, including calling Jess and asking for the Felis to help find Liam. The scratches weren't deep—I was more worried about splinters sneaking under the skin. He'd be sore and a bit bruised but he'd survive.

"A half brother," he whispered. "A half brother." Bran drew a deep breath. "What does he look like?"

"Cute. Adorable." I ruffled his hair, dropping a kiss on his forehead. "Red hair. Did I mention cute?"

Bran chuckled. "Family trait."

I waited. I couldn't even begin to figure out what to say and didn't want to try. This was far and away from anything I'd ever dealt with.

He chewed his lower lip before speaking. "Jess, your family—do you think they can find Liam?"

I smiled. "When we call a hunt it's a serious

thing. The cops might have their street connections but we've got a lot more people in a lot more locations looking for Liam. Whoever took him won't be able to stay underground for long."

"Thank you for asking. I know that must have been tough for you."

"Remember that when the bill comes due," I said. "Jess doesn't give away anything."

Bran nodded. "When it's time I'll be there for you, no matter what." He sighed. "My family, they're… They're complicated. They're all about appearances, on what looks best for them and the business. When I was ten years old we got a dog." He flexed his fingers, inspecting the thin bandages. "It was a small dog, a corgi. I was told he would be my responsibility."

I wasn't a big fan of dogs but this wasn't the right time to bring it up.

"I took care of him. Walks, grooming, feeding, the whole deal." Bran studied his palm. "One day I came home and Billy was gone."

"Gone?"

"My parents overheard someone in their social circle commenting on our having such a small dog. Seems at that time it wasn't fashionable to have anything other than monster hounds." He pulled his fingers into a fist, tightening the bandages. "The next day a Great Dane arrived and I was told this was my new dog. It was like Billy had never existed and now this new dog was supposed to slide into his place without me caring or changing a thing."

I didn't know what to say.

"That's how my parents roll. It's all about appearances and what people think of them. When I lost it and started working for the *Inquisitor*? They never called, never asked if I was okay. They told their friends I was doing some research for a new book. And the money kept flowing as long as I'd stay quiet and not embarrass them by coming to their parties."

I shifted my weight to one side, feeling the pull of the marred skin on my back.

I'd forgotten some scars weren't visible.

"My father's had affairs for years. I caught him once with my nanny." He chuckled. "He told me he was helping her shelve some books in his library and gave me money to go get some ice cream. I was seven and stupid, I didn't know any better. When I got older I knew. And I did nothing because I figured it was their business, between them." He shook his head. "And now the chickens have come home to roost, I guess."

"Did your mother know?" I felt like I'd swallowed a pound of sand.

"I never asked her but I'm sure she did. The way she looked at him at dinner when he showed up late or when he left for business trips. She knew what was expected of her when she married him because of the business, not because she loved him. But she loved the social status." Bran sighed. "The perils of being a successful businessman. Everyone wants something and they're willing to trade anything for it."

"Molly Callendar wanted nothing." I stepped into the danger zone. "She denied knowing your father."

"In the biblical sense," Bran joked. I heard the pain under the humor.

"Brayton was willing to take the fall. He must owe your father big-time." I wanted to shift the conversation away from the infidelity, the elephant in the room threatening to crush the life out of us.

"Enough to claim a baby that wasn't his? I guess." Bran poked at the gauze. "Major favor."

"Whoever killed Molly Callendar and kidnapped Liam had a reason." I took two cans of soda out of the fridge. "Right now the police are focusing on Brayton and the people who might have grudges against him."

"That's logical." He took one can from me and pressed it against the bandaged side of his hand. "My father might not even be involved with this." Bran sounded optimistic. "It might be as it seems—a pissed-off business associate out to get him."

"Or not." I hated to bring pain but it was my job. "But yes, that's where the cops are going to be focusing their attention." I opened my drink. "We can't write off an attack on Molly Callendar directly either. I heard her parents talk about Ian Hamilton, an ex-boyfriend. Could be he got ticked off when Molly took up with David Brayton and went to her one last time to get her to stay in town or something along those lines. He loses his temper and kills her, takes Liam and runs."

Bran nodded. "Sounds plausible."

"The cops are going to be hunting him down and checking him out. It's basic procedure," I added.

"So he's covered. Where do you want to hunt?"

I smiled at his phrasing despite the circumstances. "Our first priority is to find Liam. The police don't know your father's involved at all. Let them run down the Brayton and Callendar trail—we'll take the one less traveled."

Bran took a deep gulp of soda. "Who knows the baby is my father's?"

"At last count Molly Callendar, David Brayton and myself. Now you and Jess. I don't think Molly's parents knew. They'd be the first to toss your father under the bus and rightfully so. I got the impression she never told them who the father was, likely because it was part of the deal. Take the cash and go away but never speak of who the father is again."

"Or let people assume it was David Brayton." Bran drained his soda can in a pair of gulps. "The cops are missing a whole set of possible suspects." He gave me an odd look. "You scented Liam was related to me. Could you pick up the smell of the guy who took him? I know the CSI people have gone all over the room and tore it to bits but you're a Felis, you could pick up on something they've missed."

I drew in a deep breath over clenched teeth. "I might be able to pull him out but I can't track him outside of the room. I'm not that good."

"It's something. I have to do something, I can't sit here and watch everyone look for him." Bran slurred his words a fraction. Most people wouldn't have caught it but I did. His temper was rising again and he was eager for a fight.

"Let's go back to the hotel." His fists waved in the air. "I don't care if there's cops there or not. Fuck my father; it's time he stopped trying to run people's lives. And I sure as hell want to have a talk with him about this damned file. I will not have him threaten you or your family." The fire dimmed into smoking embers. "We need to find the baby first."

I covered his hands with my own, hoping my touch would help calm him down. "We're going to find Liam. Every Felis in the city is going to be looking out for a newborn with red hair. The cops have their system, we have ours." A note of pride crept into my voice. "And ours is better."

"I need to talk to my father." The strength in his voice startled me. "I need to find out what he has to do with this, if anything." His eyes met mine, soft and teary. "I need to know if he had her killed."

"I know—but not yet. Liam's the priority here. After that, your father."

He gave a weary sigh and nodded. "We need to find the baby and fast." Bran rubbed his nose. "Be honest—what do you think his odds are?"

I squeezed the bandaged hands. "If someone wanted him dead he'd be dead already. Whoever kidnapped him knows he's only valuable if kept alive." I paused for a second before going to the dark side. "It all depends on how much knowledge the kidnapper has about babies. If Liam gets sick this could turn from a kidnapping into a homicide real quick."

"Let's go." Bran moved toward the door, first stopping at the foot of the stairs. "Hey."

I watched Jazz slink down the steps, eying him cautiously.

He chuckled and put out one hand, palm-up. She nuzzled against the gauze and licked his fingers with a mother's urgency.

"Sorry, sweetie," he murmured. "Sometimes I've got a worse temper than your big sister."

"Sometimes?" I pointed at the kindling near the couch. "I'm not cleaning that mess up."

THE HOTEL LOBBY was filled with lines of people checking out, nattering among themselves to see what they could pick up on the gossip train about the dead woman. Bad news spread fast and despite the hotel's best efforts I knew the AMBER Alert had spread fast and furiously through every medium, spreading the social media butter as thick as possible.

Unfortunately that meant more than a handful of present visitors wanted to get as far as possible from the murder scene even if it'd been on a different floor. The hotel's reputation paled next to a missing child alert.

The desk clerk shuffled pages back and forth as the computer printer coughed out page after page. Harried and overwhelmed he barked into a phone for help while simultaneously handing back a credit card, accepting a handful of hotel keycards and wearing a forced smile.

Molly Callendar had cost them a pretty penny.

"The damned door's going to be locked this time." I studied the red-faced hotel clerk. "We'll need a cardkey to get in."

Bran held up a finger, halting my speech. He pointed at a housekeeping cart down one of the hallways.

"I know they keep their keys on them, hooked to the uniform," I replied, a bit of annoyance in my voice. "We can't strip them down and take the keys."

"Of course not." Bran gave me a broad smile, his public smile. "What do you usually do in a case like this?"

I stifled a growl. He'd gone from delectably hot to annoying in point-two seconds. "I'm not used to breaking into crime scenes. Before you came along I worked divorce cases, runaway kids, that sort of stuff." I gestured at the cart. "I don't do this sort of thing."

"Of course not." Bran kept smiling. "What room was it again?"

"Two hundred twenty-two."

"Go wait up by the room. I'll be along shortly." He rubbed his hands together like a child about to steal candy out of his mother's purse. "Stay out of sight, please."

I scowled and headed for the elevator.

The doors opened to disgorge another group of fleeing guests. They brushed by me, then rushed into the already crowded lobby to do battle with the harried clerk.

I stepped into the empty elevator. As usual I was going against the tide.

The doors slid open on the second floor with a soft hiss. It was like walking into a mausoleum.

I couldn't hear anything other than the low hum of electricity. The other residents had either been relocated to a different floor or left the hotel with the exodus. I couldn't blame them—if I'd been in one of the adjoining rooms, once I'd given my statement to the police about what I had or hadn't heard I'd have headed for the checkout desk.

I spotted the yellow crime tape marking Callendar's room at the end of the hall near the stairwell. As I waited for Bran and his excellent plan I mused on the ironic location of her room.

Word was, this location in any hotel was called the "murder" room, a prime location for murders and suicides. Unfortunately people died in hotels all the time from health issues, suicides and marital conflicts. It'd make life so much easier if we could pull out the "murder" room from circulation and drop the death rate by a fat percentage.

Life, unfortunately, rarely followed the odds.

The elevator let out a soft ding to announce its arrival.

I moved into the stairway, keeping the door open a notch to watch the hall. It didn't take long for Bran to come into view with a giggling hotel maid, a young thing barely old enough to give consent. She wore a generic beige-colored dress with a name tag reading Cindy clipped above her left breast.

His hand was on her shoulder but by the way she was reacting it might as well been on her waist—or lower. You didn't need to be Felis to know she was turned on by the attention Bran was giving her.

He didn't help. He purred something to her in a low tone, easy enough for me to hear. It was nothing more than a compliment on how she made the bland cleaning uniform look lovely but it was enough to have my fingers flex instinctively. I knew he was acting but my blood pressure was skyrocketing.

"So you've heard of me?" Bran murmured as they approached the door.

"I think I've read some of your articles in *Rolling Stone*," she chirped. "You've got my name and number, right?"

Bran beamed, turning on the charm full blast. "Of course. I'll have to say you're an 'inside source' but you'll know who you are and so will your friends."

"'Inside'," Cindy said with a giggle. She pulled out the master cardkey from the fat ring on her belt, the long slender cord keeping it attached.

The green light went off when she slipped the key into the slot. Bran pushed the door open just enough to put his foot through and hold it. The police seal tore easily—they were meant for show. The large X of crime tape would be easy enough to climb under. If we left it intact it'd take a close inspection to see the seal had been broken.

Now all we had to do was get rid of the twitlette.

I considered evisceration.

"A reporter. That's so cool." She giggled, tearing my eardrums with the high-pitched squeal.

"You get to hang out with the stars and all that. Maybe you can invite me to your next party?" She batted long fake eyelashes and for a second I thought she was going to grab his crotch.

I changed my mind. Evisceration was too fast.

Bran took a step back, just out of range. He wagged his finger at her. "Got to work before you play." He held up his cell phone. "I'll snap a few pictures and be out of here." His other hand flashed a pair of fifty-dollar bills, the red ink catching my eye. "Thank you for your cooperation. I'll be in touch."

"Call me." She put her hand up to her cheek, making the international symbol for idiot talking on a phone. A second later she took the bills and slipped them into her cleavage, tittered and trotted off.

I waited until the elevator doors had closed before sliding out from the stairwell. "Bimbo."

"Don't be jealous." Bran reached out and ran his thumb over my lower lip. "You're cute when you sulk."

"I hate seeing women play stupid for cash," I replied. "Besides, you paid her too much. I wouldn't have gone over twenty."

"Probably," he mused. "But she'll stay quiet if the cops come back and ask about us. It's one thing to give up twenty bucks, another to give up a hundred."

I let out a snort. "All about the money." I glanced at his belt buckle. "And bonuses."

"Don't be hating." Bran winked. "Can't help it if I'm irresistible."

"If you pay enough."

He chuckled, his foot holding the door open. "By the hour or by the day, I'm your man." A mischievous look appeared. "Nice place. I liked the last hotel we stayed in." Bran gave a sly wink. "Especially the last night."

My cheeks went hot at the memory. We were lucky we hadn't received a repair bill for the damage we'd done the last night in Penscotta, the night he'd demanded my total commitment to this relationship and allowing my full Felis to come through in all parts of our lives, including lovemaking.

I touched the back of my neck, shivering as I felt the fresh bruise, the skin sensitive to the touch. He'd marked me like a Felis mate and claimed me as his own.

For better or for worse we were together.

This day definitely fell into the "worse" category.

If there wasn't a "deep dog shit horrid hell" one.

Bran looked down the hallway. "I'm sort of disappointed. No guards, nothing. You'd think the cops would leave someone here."

"And make it near-impossible for us to get in. Besides, there's nothing left to guard." I slipped under the tape and held the door. "Nothing left for them, anyway. Once the CSI unit finishes up there's not much left other than telling the hotel when to unleash the cleaning crew."

Bran followed. The door slid shut behind him. "What would you have done if I hadn't been able to convince her to let us in?" He shot me a teasing smile.

"Busted it down." I tapped his shoulder. "What, you think I keep you around just 'cause you're cute?"

"I thought it was because you liked the way I licked—"

"Business before pleasure," I interrupted, feeling my cheeks start to burn. "You start in the bathroom. Look for a brush, tissue, anything that may have some sort of scent. Molly and Liam were here and I can pick them out easily enough—I need to find something the killer used or left behind."

"Your ear." He strode by me with a wide grin.

I bit back my response. "Just search." I dug in

the pocket of my duster and came up with three latex gloves. The fourth had fallen out somewhere.

I threw two at Bran. “Glove up.”

He snapped the latex on his bandaged hand with a grin. “Now this brings back memories.”

I ignored him and tugged the last glove on my right hand. It was unlikely the cops would make another sweep for prints and I’d already been tagged as being in the room but it never hurt to be careful.

The suite looked more or less like I’d seen it last minus the dead body. It was pretty obvious the investigators had done a good job—they’d cleaned the place out. The portable crib was gone, the stuffed lion visiting elsewhere.

They hadn’t done anything with the blood-stained carpet. I could smell the blood soaked into the deep shag. I wondered if the hotel would try to clean it or tear the carpet up.

Or redecorate and put a couch over it.

Bran called out. “Nothing in the bathroom. Looks like they swept everything including the sink and toilet. Garbage can is empty and dry.”

I opened the minifridge. Not even a bottle of water, much less formula. I hoped the killer had at least taken whatever Molly had stored in here for Liam’s sake.

"Techs did a good job." Bran moved around the couch, deftly sidestepping the crimson stain on the carpet. "I want to say it's a good thing but—" he shook his head "—the one time you don't want them to be efficient and they do."

I fought against the rising feelings of depression, hopelessness. It wasn't that I didn't have faith in Attersley's CSI buddies but I wasn't sure Bran could deal with failure. He needed to do something before he exploded with anger and frustration.

I knew the way the police worked. They'd have fingerprinted every surface and compared it to the hotel employees to eliminate some of the prints. They'd have dropped mine out along with Molly's.

Which would still leave them with an overwhelming stack of wild unidentified people who they'd run through the system. Unless, of course, the murderer wore gloves, which made finding a match an exercise in futility.

"Got something." Bran held up a long strand of reddish hair. He frowned and stretched it out between two fingers. "Too long for the baby."

I took it from him and sniffed it. I could smell the hair dye. "Molly's." I crawled around on my knees, squinting at the floor.

Ten minutes later I was cross-eyed and the back of my head was throbbing.

"There's nothing here," Bran said. "They did a good job of cleaning up."

I was beginning to get worried. The longer we stayed here the more likely someone would find us here.

I wasn't willing to put too much trust in the cleaning chippie.

"Let me try something." I closed my eyes and took a deep breath, filling my lungs to capacity.

I gave each scent a color as they floated across my inner eye. Red, yellow, green. Various shades of blue for who I suspected were cops. Hank was here as well—cerulean blue for him.

"Damn." The scents were too mixed and too many. I had a hard time picking out Liam and Molly amid the swarm of police, crime scene technicians and grumpy detectives. Flailing around in the cloud I took another route—elimination.

I got to my feet. My knees throbbed and I hoped it wasn't the first signs of arthritis. It took a second to brush off my jeans and consider adding a permanent supply of painkillers to my pockets.

"I can tell you Brayton and your father weren't here."

"And?"

"That's all."

"That's all?" Bran snapped. "It doesn't mean they weren't involved, it doesn't mean anything." His voice rose. "You can find a fucking clue in a piss-filled, shitty alleyway and you can't find squat in a hotel room?"

A snarl bubbled up in my throat at the reference to Janey Winters. I was tired, terrified and my nerves were jangling like Santa's sleigh bells.

"If you can do better, let's see it." I moved in close, our noses almost touching so I wouldn't feel the need to yell and draw attention to our presence. "It's your goddamn father who got us into this in the first place. He threatened my Pride, he threatened me, he threatened you and he threatened us. Get mad at him but don't take it out on me."

"I'm not mad at you."

I raised an eyebrow. "Not from where I'm standing."

Bran drew back. He drew a hand over his face, brushing away invisible cobwebs. "I'm just..." His fingers twitched. "So fucking annoyed at everyone and everything right now."

"Including me?"

The edge of his mouth twisted up into a sad smile. "Maybe a little bit."

I couldn't help smirking. "Welcome to my world."

His hand shot out and grabbed the back of my neck, a rough, possessive grip.

He pulled me into a heated, breathless kiss. Surprised and shocked, I fell against him without resistance, grabbing his waist for support.

I gasped as he pulled away. My legs were wobbly and not from crawling on the floor. "What's that for?"

"For loving a fool."

"That makes two of us." I relaxed under his touch. "Let me make one last sweep and we'll go. The longer we stay here the more likely someone's going to find us."

Bran moved to the door and leaned on it. He crossed his arms and waited.

I went to the center of the room and closed my eyes, trying to shut out the white noise. A couple making love below us. A car outside, backfiring and burning oil. Bran's heartbeat, fast and increasing with every second.

I wiped out the personal scents in my mental kaleidoscope. Disregard the people, drop the living components. Look at the list of smells from nonhuman sources.

Baby powder. Deodorant. Sour milk.

A dense, acidic taste landed at the back of my throat. Not hair dye, not blood.

Tobacco. Thick, unfiltered cigarette—maybe a Camel.

Molly wasn't a smoker and I knew the cops damned well wouldn't have lit up while processing a crime scene.

I dropped to the ground and inspected the carpet near where the crib had sat. Sure enough there was a scattering of ashes so faint it might have been missed by the techs. The gray residue ground into the shag by multiple shoes, pushed so deep into the carpet it'd be invisible to the naked eye.

But not invisible to a Felis.

I spun the scenario, whispering it loud enough for Bran.

"He came in here via the front door, probably knocked right after I left. Either she opens it without looking, thinking it's me, or he cons his way in saying he's room service or housekeeping or whatever."

I looked at the scarlet stain. "Liam's sleeping in the crib. The killer doesn't make small talk, doesn't bargain with Molly." I lifted my hand and curled my fingers in, index pointing at the stain. "He shoots her using a silencer. One bullet straight to the heart. She hits the ground and he does the follow-up to the back of her head. No one hears the noise."

I turned toward where I'd last seen the crib. "Liam either sleeps through it all or doesn't understand what's going on, God willing. All he knows is this strange man's grabbing his stuff."

Bran nodded, urging me on.

I continued. "He's smoking the entire time, cool and collected. He doesn't panic if Liam makes a noise, doesn't flinch at shooting a woman and stealing her baby." I waved at the almost invisible ash. "Cigarette burns too long while he's here while he's packing the baby up. Ash falls off and he grinds it into the carpet or doesn't worry about it. Not dumb enough to leave the butt behind—he finishes the smoke in here or outside but he keeps the butt with him."

It wasn't what we'd come for but it was something.

Especially if it helped find Liam.

"Well done." Bran smiled.

I tapped my nose. "A powerful thing, this is."

He leaned in and kissed the tip. "I'd say. Wonder how you stand to be with me some mornings, the way I must smell." His voice dipped down. "Especially after a busy night."

I wrinkled my nose, adding in a dramatic sigh.

"I survive. Besides, the shared showers provide a bonus." I went to the door. "Let's move before your sweet little girl decides to sell us out to a higher bidder."

The lobby was clogged with visitors checking out, the frazzled hotel clerk fighting to stem the tide of nervous questions and wary looks. We slipped through the crowd and out onto the street past the doorman who struggled to keep the door open for all the pedestrian traffic.

It was after eight in the evening, late enough for the attire to switch from business suits to jeans and T-shirts. A group of teenagers yelled assorted curses at a fancy sports car cruising slowly down Yonge Street, heading for the end of the road at Lake Ontario. A nearby hot dog vendor flipped over a grilled onion, making my mouth water. The neon signs were coming on with buzzes and hums, lighting up the sky.

It'd be a lovely evening if there wasn't a missing baby out there.

I resisted the urge to start checking every stroller going by. Whoever the killer was, he was long gone.

Didn't mean I wasn't glancing at everyone passing us with a child in their arms.

I tugged at Bran's arm as he went to wave over

a cab from the taxi stand. He frowned and lowered his hand.

"Let's walk for a bit." I wanted him to work off some of the stress and if we talked I wouldn't be worrying about a snooping cab driver.

Bran pulled off the bandages and examined his hands as we walked, the leather duster billowing out behind him as he took long, purposeful strides. I knew it was more from anger than any intent to get away from the hotel.

"I need to talk to my father," he whispered. "I need to get his side in this, find out what he knows or doesn't know." The unspoken question hung between us—whether his father hired Molly's killer or not.

"Do you think he'll tell you the truth?"

His pace increased. "I'll make him tell me. I can't go on not knowing his involvement in this."

I sped up my steps, taking two to his one to try to keep even. "We will." I took his hand, slowing him a fraction. "As soon as Liam's safe."

Bran paused and I saw the inner conflict, the urge to beat the truth out of his father versus the need to find his half brother.

"I've never been a mother but I do know enough about babies to know they're high-maintenance. Whoever wanted Molly dead will be moving to get Liam out of this thug's hands soon enough. I doubt this guy's working as a babysitter on the side and knows much more than how to change a diaper, if that."

Bran licked his lips. "If that," he repeated. "And if Liam doesn't get out of this punk's hands soon enough who knows what could happen."

I didn't pursue that line of thinking.

It would only be a few steps from a hotel or flophouse to a Dumpster to get rid of a baby's body and vanish into the underground if the kidnapping went wrong. The police files were filled with missing children who'd never been found.

My stomach lurched at the idea of Liam joining their ranks. I'd held the wee one for only a few minutes but he'd taken a stranglehold on my heart.

Bran shifted to one side to avoid a gaggle of schoolgirls giggling over something on their cell phones. "I wish you could tell the cops about my father." His right hand waved in the air impotently. "It'd make a big difference."

"It would. But without anything more than my word they won't give your father a second look. He's too powerful and he'll throw up a blockade of lawyers that'll keep everyone out." I shook my head. "It'd take a court order to get a paternity test done and I don't see your father voluntarily agreeing."

"Could we use my DNA?" Bran interrupted. "Check Liam's genes against mine?"

I blinked, a small beam of sunlight chasing away the heavy cloud in my mind. "We could. I think the results would show that. But going from that to your father is a hell of a leap and there'd be a lot of denial flying around." I gestured at the busy street. "Meanwhile Liam's still out there."

Bran stopped and spun around, away from the human migration. He put his back against a stone pillar of some ancient building, masquerading now as an office building. The deep sigh tore at my heart.

"I don't know if I'm screwed up or not." He pressed his palms against his eyes. "I'm pissed off about the affair, I'm pissed off about the baby—but I'm most pissed off because he tried to blackmail you." He held up his fists. "I've never been so angry in my life."

I put my hands over his fists. "I know. And I appreciate it."

"If it were just you and me," he huffed, "I'd be able to deal better. But this is so much more, so many other lives getting messed up because he has to be in control of everything and everyone." Bran looked upward. "If only I'd faced him down before, told him I wasn't taking his shit anymore. Not letting him run my life and my mother's, bribing me to stay silent while he screwed around on her."

"You were a kid when it started. How could you know what was going on? Don't overanalyze it." The cold stone against my back cooled the growing anger against Michael Hanover. "Don't get caught up in the cycle of wondering what if—it'll keep you from seeing straight. I've played the game and once you get started you get twisted up and turned around."

Bran looked at me. "Your parents?"

I studied an empty cardboard box. "I could have been in the car with them. I should have been."

"Why weren't you?"

I rubbed my nose. "I threw a hissy fit about staying back with Ruth and helping her cook pies. It was a holiday. It wasn't supposed to be a permanent visit."

"Except it turned into one."

I swallowed hard. "We rushed to the hospital and the pies burned. Never helped her cook after that. Playing 'what if' can screw you up. Took me a few years to figure it out." I touched Bran's shoulder. "Although I'm happy I'm pretty high up the list of things that mean a lot to you."

He looked at me, deep brown eyes filled with anger and angst. "You're my world, Rebecca. There's no one before I want to remember and there'll be no one after you."

The emotions wrapped around me like a second skin, warm and soothing.

I ran a finger over his lips, choking on my words. There was nothing I could say, nothing would even come close.

His fist uncurled and linked with my hand, fingers intertwining. We stood there for a few minutes, watching the herds of tourists surge back and forth.

I jumped as my cell phone vibrated. It took me a few seconds of fumbling accompanied by swearing before I got it out of my pocket.

Bran tensed up beside me. His jaw tightened to the point of obvious pain.

I stared at the caller identification. "It's Jess," I whispered before opening the connection. Bran ducked in close as I tilted the phone to the side so he could hear.

"Where are you two? I called the house and you weren't there." The disciplinary tone had me wincing.

“We went back to the hotel room to look for clues. Our suspect smokes Camels, no filters.” I could taste the grimy slime on my tongue. “It’s not much, but—”

“Good,” Jess said. “We’ve got a few suspicious hits and that’ll help weed them out. Let me call you back in a few minutes after we dump the chaff.” The line went dead.

SIX

"WHAT DOES THAT mean?" Bran asked.

"It means members of the family are reporting seeing a redheaded baby with someone who's obviously not his father or mother."

"How many of you are there?" Bran asked. "I mean, out there." He waved at the street.

"Hundreds. Maybe thousands. I've never worried about getting an actual count." I rubbed a particularly itchy spot on my back against the rough brick. "You saw how many lived in Penscotta. They work and live normal lives like everyone else."

"Except they're Felis."

"Except for that."

"Now you've got me wondering how many people I pass by every day who are family," Bran said, eyes searching the crowd. "Don't you think about it?"

"No." I couldn't help the bitterness creeping into my speech. "I'm outcast, remember?"

He looked at me. "Not so much now, according to Jess."

I shrugged. "Talk is cheap. All I know is when I was growing up in the foster care system any Felis I met ignored me, turned their backs on me." I scanned the human migration around us. "After a while I stopped looking for them."

The cell phone buzzed for attention.

"Okay," Jess said. "I've got something." A painful silence followed for a few seconds. "Go to Tony's Convenience over at Sterling and McCaster. It's west of Yonge Street by about three blocks."

Bran stepped away, lifting his hand and pointing at the traffic.

"What's the red flag?" I scowled as a pair of cabs sped on by, ignoring us.

"Guy came in to buy diapers and formula bouncing a baby on his hip like a sack of potatoes. Seemed uneasy and didn't look comfortable carrying the baby."

"Pretty thin." I watched Bran flip the bird at another cab charging through the intersection without slowing down.

"Best we got right now. Guy also bought smokes—might be Camels but Tony wasn't sure. We'll check the receipt when we get there but he didn't approve of the guy smoking round the baby. That's what made him even more memorable, puffing like a chimney in the kid's face. Not too many idiots doing it these days, thank God."

"'We'?" I choked on the one syllable.

The chuckle startled me. "Kit, you can't ask me to call a hunt and not expect me to get involved. It's my neck on the line with the Board for getting us all involved and if I'm going to take a hit I'm sure as hell going to bring you along for the ride. See you there."

She cut the connection.

I flashed back to a memory of my first hunt, of Ruth helping me back to the house. Jess had watched us come in, sitting on the porch with her legs swinging back and forth as we limped along the trail coming out of the forest, me hobbling along with a broken ankle and leaning on the older woman for support.

The last Board member waiting for the last hunter to come home.

"You're the last." She looked at her watch. "Late by about eight hours."

I gave a nervous laugh, caught between the pain and the fear. "Having too much fun."

In a flash she was in my face, nose to nose with an angry snarl. "You think I have nothing better to do than take care of you? Your father..." She paused and drew back, the sadness on her face snatching my breath away. “I’ll notify the Board you passed the test.” Jess gave a brisk nod to Ruth before leaving so quickly I had to remind myself she’d been there.

“Rebecca?” Bran’s voice brought me back to the present. He waved at the waiting cab, his tone verging on frantic. “Let’s go.”

The cab driver didn’t mind vague instructions as we zipped through narrow side streets, sliding through traffic and construction with ease until we pulled up in front of the corner store. Bran gave him a handsome tip as we got out, earning us a grateful smile.

Tony’s Convenience was like a hundred other small stores in the city, delivering milk and bread to the desperate at odd hours of the day and night for inflated prices. The postage-stamp-sized shop stood on the corner with neon signs advertising soda and a sandwich board at the entrance announcing the latest lottery jackpot waiting to be won. Various flyers and banners covered the windows to the point of making the glass moot.

Bran pulled on the single door and waited for me. I suspected it was more out of fear of meeting Jess face-on than chivalry.

An electronic jingle signaled our entrance.

The lone man standing behind the small squat counter looked up from his newspaper.

"Anything I can help you with?" The cheerful squeak was forced, the wail of a man who'd imagined a better future and ended up selling lottery tickets and chewing gum.

"We're with Jess," I said.

He folded the newspaper into a tight square before tossing it into a corner.

"I see." He came out from around the counter, giving me a better look at him.

Tony Romano was tall enough to reach my shoulder and reminded me more of a snake than a Felis. Long dark hair pulled back into a ponytail gave his thin face a sharp, feral appearance. He looked like the type of guy who needed a safety line in the shower to make sure he didn't slip down the drain.

His nostrils flared as I approached. He knew I wasn't his usual customer looking for a chocolate fix.

His own scent, thick and oily, assaulted my senses. He was family, all right—the type you didn't introduce your girlfriends to.

Tony glanced at the door. "Jess told me she was on her way." The tone implied he'd be of little help until she arrived.

I surveyed the shelves, trying to slow my racing pulse. Prices were comparable to my own local hole-in-the-wall, which meant they were twice as much as I'd pay at the grocery store. The stacks of noodle cups and potato chip bags reaching to the ceiling gave me a mild case of claustrophobia.

The store of last resort for those late-night munchie runs and desperate men looking for baby supplies. If you bought formula and diapers here you had to be past desperate.

I checked out the formula shelf. The expiration dates weren't all that far away and a ring of disturbed dust showed where the kidnapper's can had come from.

I hoped the kidnapper would at least try to feed him.

Tony watched me stroll around his store, ignoring Bran.

I smiled inside. Big mistake.

Romano's dark eyes narrowed. "You must be the outcast." The last word came out like a curse. "Figured you'd be taller."

I spread my hands, showing off all of my five foot four inches. "Big things, small packages and so forth." I smiled. "But I think you know all about that, eh?"

Romano scowled.

Bran moved up behind me. I felt his body heat scorching my back and I knew he was sizing the Felis up.

Romano looked over my shoulder at Bran, sizing him up. "You must be the human."

"You must be the genius of your family," Bran deadpanned.

The Felis's upper lip curled back.

"And she's no outcast." I felt the soft growl, the heated air on the back of my neck. It was a kit's growl but it was enough to set the middle-aged man back on his heels. This wasn't some dumb human looking to be ripped off by the cunning Felis for some overpriced beef jerky.

"Got a big mouth there, buddy." Romano gave me a fast look before focusing on Bran. "Does she also hold your dick when you pee?"

The challenge flashed between the two men. You didn't have to be Felis to sense that type of unspoken dare.

Bran cocked his head to one side. "Does your boyfriend?"

Romano took a step toward us before freezing in his tracks.

"Damn, human. Makes me wish I was twenty years younger." Jess drawled from her position in the doorway. She leaned on the wooden frame, giving her height as exactly five foot eight inches according to the taped yardstick. "There's something about a man willing to go to the ground for you." She gave a wistful sigh. "If I were younger I'd make you fight for him."

"You couldn't handle him." I wasn't in any mood to dick around with trying to top each other. "Now that we've all massaged our egos let's get down to business and find this baby."

Jess tilted her head to one side and her eyebrows rose. For a horrible second I thought she was going to reprimand me and/or bring up my relationship with Bran. Instead she gave me a short nod and turned her attention to Romano.

Romano shrank perceptibly under her intense stare. It took a second for him to drop his gaze to the tiled floor, scarred by countless shoe heels.

"You don't treat family or their friends like that," Jess warned. "Do it again and you'll answer to me. Is that clear?"

Romano nodded, intensely studying his toes.

"Okay. Over and done with. Now tell us what you saw," Jess said.

Romano cleared his throat before speaking, careful to avoid looking at any of us directly. "He come in here carrying a baby under his arm like the daily newspaper. Puts him down here, wrapped up in a blanket. No car seat, no nothing." He tapped the scratched clear plastic on the counter by the cash register, his anger turned away from us and at the invisible customer. "Baby's crying, fussing, wriggling all over the place. I had to hold him to make sure he didn't fall over the fucking edge." Romano huffed. "Guy runs down the aisle and grabs diapers, canned formula, then lights up a smoke right here, in front of me and the kid." The greasy-haired man shook his head. "That ain't right. You want to screw up your lungs, fine. Ain't right to put that on a kid, not a baby."

Jess waved a hand in the air, encouraging him.

"Guy tosses money at me and grabs the kid and the groceries. Thought for a second he was gonna put the kid in the plastic bag as well. He's puffing up a storm and burns through the smoke like he was on the way to his execution." He shuffled his feet. "I didn't think nothing 'bout it until the alert came in." He gave Jess a halfhearted smile. "That should count for something, eh?"

We all ignored it.

"When?" Jess asked.

"Within the last hour." Romano drew a finger along the counter. "Been nobody in since. You should get a good trail if you work at it."

I sniffed the air. A mixture of bad cologne,

feces, urine and…foul-smelling cigarettes. The scent cloud was here but it was like trying to pick out one specific needle out of a cluster of needles. I could barely identify the cigarettes, much less the smoker.

"Do you recognize him?" Jess's gruff tone brought me out of the mental confusion.

"I can't." I shook my head. "There's too much. Too many."

"Filthy habit, cigarette smoking," Romano scoffed. "I wouldn't even sell them except they make me good money." He rubbed his thumb and index finger together. "Raise the tax, I say."

Bran let out a snort. I didn't even try to figure out what he was thinking.

Romano pointed at a half-smoked butt on the floor. The smashed tobacco was smeared in all directions like an ugly brown flower. "Bastard didn't even blink when he dropped it. Think he was afraid of burning the kid; that's why he dumped it."

Jess snatched it up and held it under my nose. "Try again," she demanded. "Pull it in, breathe it all in." Her words came through in a whisper, the urgency sending a shiver down my spine. "You can do this."

I scrunched my eyes together so tight I felt the pulse against my eyelids.

The tobacco stung my nose. I caught the faintest whiff of a personal scent before it was swallowed up again by mud and dirt and the garbage he'd walked through before stomping on the cigarette.

"Still nothing," I whimpered, the frustration gaining ground.

Bran's hand landed on my shoulder.

"It's okay," he murmured.

I opened my eyes to see Jess shaking her head in disagreement. She reached over and plucked the mashed cigarette from my fingers without comment.

Her thin slender fingers rolled the butt back and forth, dissembling it in her palm. She lifted her hand up to her nose, close enough to snort the shredded tobacco.

Jess inhaled, so deep her white blouse tightened to the point of button-popping. Her eyes closed with a look of intense concentration.

She Changed in a flash, the light brown fur covering her facial features. Her Roman nose shrank down and retreated inward, her eye shifting to pure feline. The ugly scar on the left side of her face became more pronounced, the angry scarlet skin remaining bare.

She took another whiff and I remembered she'd fought her way onto the Board and into a position of power in the Pride—along with terrorizing generations of kits who viewed her with shock and awe.

Bran squeezed my shoulder. The warmth burned through my coat and shirt, soothing the nervousness building in my muscles. His fingers kneaded the leather in a reflexive move to calm me.

Jess didn't notice, focused on her task.

She smiled.

Not a nervous smile, not a smirk, but a true hunter's smile of satisfaction.

"Got him." She tossed the cigarette remains to the surprised store owner and spun on one booted heel. "Let's go." She Changed back within seconds, shifting easily back into full human form.

"Can she track him?" Bran whispered as we fell into step behind her. "Just from that?"

"Damned right I can, kit." Jess stopped shy of the door and shot us a sly grin over her shoulder. "I can track a flea in an animal shelter."

Romano retreated behind the counter in silence

to watch us leave. I resisted the urge to grab something on the way out to push my luck.

Jess paused for a half second on the store's threshold before turning right. "He's within walking distance and working alone," she said, her long legs keeping her ahead of us.

"Based on what?" I tried to keep my tone respectful but a trace of disbelief crept in.

"No place to park here." She swept her arm outward at the busy street. "He wouldn't risk parking and taking the chance of getting noticed, or worse, getting towed."

I glanced up at the prominent NO PARKING signs standing guard every few feet. It was a risk but a calculated risk.

"He would have taken a cab after killing Molly. He wouldn't risk walking through the lobby with a newborn in his arms screaming and crying. Avoid the taxi stand out front and slip out the back, come around to a major street and flag down one of the cabs out of traffic." I ran the argument to ground. "He didn't have time to sit and wait for a parking lot attendant or juggle coins into a meter if he could find one."

Jess spoke. "He brought the baby into the store because he didn't want to or couldn't leave the baby alone. If he had a car and a car seat he'd have left the kid there, less trouble to deal with. He'd already dismissed the cab, otherwise he'd have left the baby with the driver. Same reasoning tells me he's working alone, he's got no one watching his back." She licked her lips. "Good."

She stopped, so suddenly Bran grabbed my arm to avoid me smacking into her back. I missed eating her jean jacket by a fraction of an inch, bouncing back on my heels into Bran's embrace.

"Should use a warning signal or something," he muttered. He knew and I knew Jess could hear but she was too involved to snark back.

She sniffed the air in short, measured pants. Her mouth opened slightly as if she was about to speak but I knew she was gathering even more trace on her prey.

"This way." The tall woman spun ninety degrees on her boots and led us down an alley.

I flinched as we picked our way between Dumpsters overflowing with garbage. A Chinese restaurant, a barbecue place and a sandwich shop spit out enough waste to fill up another whole store.

I could smell the decay, slimy meat turning worse with each second and rotting vegetables in wet cardboard boxes and in dank metal Dumpsters turning into a chemical sludge turning the strongest stomach. The tall narrow walls compressed the stench into a fat wall of smell we waded through. I flinched at the mental image of Liam being carried through this mess.

Bran coughed, a deep from-the-bottom-of-your-belly cough closer to a gag than anything else. "I can't imagine how bad this smells to you."

"Rank doesn't even come close." I huffed through my mouth, trying to cut out the worst of the smell.

Jess strode between stacks of rotting boxes and over half-empty wooden cartons of fermenting cabbage without hesitation, brushing aside the stench and stink. "This way." It was a hunter's run, a light jog I knew she could keep up for miles.

Not so much myself and Bran.

I remembered hearing rumors she'd tracked a wounded stag five miles in the middle of a thunderstorm, breaking its neck when she finally ran it to ground. I hadn't believed it then.

I did now.

We came out onto another side street. Jess turned down another, weaving between the buildings with the two of us in tow. The businesses changed from hole-in-the-wall restaurants to residential. Small apartments wedged into buildings originally intended as single-family dwellings, sliced and diced up in order to make more money renting the rooms and renovated apartments out to anyone who would pay.

The three of us emerged onto a main street. My senses told me we'd come only a block from the convenience store, the mazelike alleys making it a much farther trek.

Jess put her hands on her hips and looked around, finally nodding at a dingy gray building. "He's in there."

"How do you figure?" Bran was brave enough to ask.

She viewed him with a mixture of curiosity and caution before speaking. I knew the tone, master hunter to unblooded kit.

"Look at the buildings." A hand waved at the skyline. "He's looking for a place to hide where no one will care or question what he's doing or what noises he's giving off." The index finger pointed at an old house, the single entrance displaying multiple names on the mailboxes. "Too many nosy neighbors. Couldn't keep a baby there without the neighbors wondering." It shifted to a large single-family residence with a minivan in the narrow driveway. "Definitely not." The hand settled on a hotel and the large sign advertising the rates. "Rooms by the day or week, cash on the barrelhead and no questions asked." She arched an eyebrow at Bran. "Good enough for you?"

He gave her a sheepish smile. "Thanks."

The single word caught Jess unaware. The breath caught in her throat as she looked at Bran then back at me with something almost like approval.

The iron mask fell, cutting us off.

"Don't stand there with your mouths hanging open." She cracked her knuckles. "We haven't gotten Liam back yet."

The moment had passed.

The hotel was a survivor, the stonework marking it as one of the older buildings in the area. The two doors at the top of the steps had been repainted a loud red that shouted discount paint sale. There was no doorman waiting to open the door for us other than a scrawny street cat scampering across the front to disappear into yet another alleyway.

We blew into the lobby like a troop of avenging angels with Jess leading the way.

The decorations consisted of a single beaten-down brown couch and mismatched blue lounger, both of which looked like they'd swallow you if you sat down. A stack of week-old newspapers on the chipped coffee table offered little entertainment. A battered old television set in the far corner bleated the local 24-7 news channel at a whisper.

Jess stopped at the desk.

A teenager worked on his cell phone, fingers flying over the minute keyboard. He wore a T-shirt with a mutilated yellow happy face, the eyes replaced with X's and faux blood drops scattered across the front.

"Youwannaroom?" he grunted, eyes down on the minute screen. "Cashonlynocreditcards."

Jess's right hand slammed down on both of his, smashing the phone and pinning him to the desktop.

I could hear the tiny bones snap.

I didn't care.

Her one good eye caught the kid's gaze, locking it in place. "Man. Baby. Came through here not too long ago." Her lips pulled back, showing bright white teeth. "Room number."

His pupils were dilated, showing recent drug use. He studied Jess's face, noting the scarlet gash on the left cheek with little emotional response.

"Hey. I could charge you with assault," he replied in a monotone drone. He didn't even try to pull free.

"Hey, I could give a shit." The pressure increased, her hand muscles tensing.

The clerk frowned. "Ow." He looked at Jess's hand covering his own. "Ow," he repeated with no anxiety or concern.

I wasn't sure if the kid was stoned or dumb but this wasn't going to end well.

"Dude, just give us the info." I pulled out my wallet and peeled off a twenty. I hoped he'd be cheaper to bribe than Cindy at the last hotel—although they seemed to be sharing the same single brain cell.

His eyes flashed up to follow the bill as I moved it back and forth.

"Room number," Jess repeated. She eased up on the punk's hands but didn't let go.

"Two-oh-eight. End of the corridor." He watched the dyed paper dance in my hand. "Damned baby won't stop crying. Bad for business."

I dropped the money on the desktop at the same time Jess released him. The cell phone let out a pathetic beep as he pushed it to one side and grabbed the cash.

Bran threw down a fifty. "For the phone. And forgetting about all of this."

The kid gave us a slow nod, studying the two bills. He looked down as we passed by the desk.

Jess led the way up the stairs, taking them

two at a time. She didn't say anything and didn't seem to notice we were behind her. Her moves were fluid and quick as if she were twenty years younger.

I'd never seen her so focused, so intently in hunting mode. In her mind she wasn't here in the city—she was in the forest and about to take down a predator almost as dangerous as she was.

She stopped in front of the hotel door. The cheap plastic stickered numbers had been scratched out two or three times with magic marker to the point of being barely visible.

Jess cocked her head to one side, looking at me. "Suggestions on how to do this? This is sort of your area." The low whisper sounded like a gunshot in my ears.

"My area?" I pointed at myself. "I think my area ended when you got the scent off the smoke."

She rocked on her heels, hands in pockets, and wearing a shit-eating grin. "Well if you'd take a bit more time to keep your skills honed you'd have been able to do the same thing."

"Except I work for a living in the city," I replied. "And I don't need to be able to pluck a single scent out of a crowd. In fact it'd drive me crazy if I had to turn it on and off. It's enough I almost go deaf in a group of teenagers, all screaming and yelping."

Jess's scar began to darken, the previous joviality vanishing quick. "It's your heritage, it's who you are. The least you could do is keep it in tune like a fine instrument."

I felt my pulse increase. "You want to talk about keeping in tune…" I took a step back. "You got us this far—feel free to leave." At the back of my mind the warning bells went off. I was tired and stressed out and wandering into dangerous territory.

"You think I'm going to walk away before you, you…" She waved at the door. "You do whatever you're going to do? And what is that exactly?"

A baby's cry came from inside the hotel room, interrupting our argument. It rose and fell in intensity, a continual wail of annoyance and fear.

"Stop it." Bran stepped between us. "Shut up, both of you."

I froze.

Jess gave Bran a curious look but didn't say anything.

"Reb, pick the lock," Bran snapped. He grabbed my arm and pulled me aside, away from Jess. "Do it." He moved beside the door and rolled his shoulders back. "I'll take care of things when we get inside."

I knelt down and pulled the small case of instruments from a pocket. I never left home without them.

Jess stood by and watched, staying silent.

It wasn't much of a challenge even with Liam's crying jangling my nerve endings. The tumbler gave way easily under my assault, a deafening click signaling surrender to my keen Felis ears. I stood back up and nodded to the two adults.

"Now what?" I mouthed.

"Now this." Bran grabbed the doorknob and threw the door open.

He charged in with an angry roar, leaving us behind.

Jess laughed as I gaped before we tumbled in after him.

"I can see why you like him," Jess shouted. "Cut-the-Gordian-knot type of guy."

I didn't answer, focused on assessing the situation as quickly as possible.

The single bare light bulb set in the ceiling illuminated a stark, relatively barren single room. It was a shocking contrast to the clean, comfortable hotel room I'd visited Molly Callendar in a lifetime ago.

The dingy brown couch had more stains on it than a frat house carpet, the fat wide television set practically an antique. The single chair didn't match the couch and had large rips and tears in the dark fabric as if Jazz had gone to town on it.

It also held a man wearing a dark T-shirt and jeans with a baby in his arms. His mouth hung open, long greasy strands of dark hair stuck to his sweaty face.

Liam scrunched up his little red face and screamed at the top of his tiny lungs.

The middle-aged man glanced at the coffee table. To be specific, he focused in on the pistol lying atop a magazine, the silencer extension on the barrel pointed at the far wall. His grip tightened on the bundle lying on his left arm as he estimated his odds of getting to the weapon before we closed the space between the front door and the table.

I leaped at the same time the killer did, letting out a hunter's cry.

He lunged for the pistol, swinging the baby around like a sack of potatoes.

I won.

I swept up the pistol and pointed it at the man's chest. The footlong square coffee table provided a slight barrier between us, stopping my advance.

He stood there and glared at me without any fear.

A tremor ran through my hand as I realized I was most likely holding the weapon that'd killed Molly Callendar. The safety was off on the automatic weapon and I had no doubt there was a round in the chamber, ready to go.

The stranger's left eye twitched. His right hand shot out to grab Liam around the neck, pressing the thin blue baby blanket into the baby's skin.

Liam's cries vanished under the assault.

"One move and he dies," he barked. "You let us both out of here or I'll snap the bastard's neck." The sausagelike fingers almost covered Liam's entire face. "I'll kill him."

"No you won't," Bran said. He lifted his hands and patted the air in a "calm down" move. "You didn't kill him in the hotel room and you won't do it now because someone paid you to take him and keep him alive. We want to know who and why."

"You ain't cops." His lips turned up in a sneer.

"No we ain't," Bran growled in an almost Felis tone. He tilted his head at me. "Which means she can shoot you without anyone giving a shit."

I shifted the weapon down toward his belly. "At this range I can gut shoot you without hitting the baby. Slow, agonizing death." I kept my voice low and steady. "No-win situation here. Let the baby go and we'll sit down and talk about this before someone gets hurt. Whatever you're getting paid it's not enough for this much trouble, is it?"

The baby struggled under the man's iron grasp. I felt, rather than saw, Jess slide away from us.

The thug shook his head. "You ain't getting anything from me." Beads of sweat appeared on his forehead. "I got nothing to say to you."

"Who hired you?" Bran took a step ahead of me—not blocking my line of fire but enough to get the punk's full attention. "Are you holding the kid for ransom? Who's calling the shots?"

His gaze darted from the pistol in my grip to Bran's face, back again to the pistol.

Liam squirmed under the iron grip, a half-hearted flailing against his assailant. The tiny arms thrashed from side to side as he struggled for air.

Moisture dripped from the kidnapper's nose onto the baby-blue blanket.

We were running out of time.

"You're going to kill the baby," I snapped. "Kill him and your negotiating chip is gone."

The baby gave one last shudder, thrashing in his cocoon.

His tiny eyes fluttered one last time and closed.

SEVEN

My finger tightened on the trigger. I'd never killed a man before but I considered this to be a damned good reason.

The thug sneered and increased his grip on Liam.

Suddenly his eyes went wide as if a whole SWAT team had somehow materialized around him.

The thug gasped. He looked through me and his lips fluttered.

I spotted Jess behind the kidnapper, her bloody claws already retracting. She pressed her lips into a tight line.

I lowered the pistol. I wouldn't need it now.

He wavered for a second before letting out a mixture hiccup/cough. Blood drops splattered the blue baby blanket. His fingers trembled against the thin fabric.

The kidnapper arched back, hands dropping away in shock.

He let go of the baby.

The unmoving bundle plummeted toward the floor.

Bran dived forward, right into my line of fire. He pushed the table to one side with a mighty shove and slid on his knees along the bare wooden floor.

His knees smashed into the killer's shins as he reached for Liam.

The man didn't move, too busy gurgling for air. He hadn't stopped looking at me, through me, as if he'd forgotten about the baby.

The baby fell into Bran's arms. Liam didn't move, didn't struggle against the rough treatment.

Nothing.

My heart skipped a beat.

Bran fell back onto the floor, letting out a curse. A second later he rolled upright and bent over the bundle. "I don't think he's breathing." He wrestled the blanket open.

I caught the smell of feces and urine.

The tiny face was pale, too pale.

Bran blew into the tiny button nose, a sharp puff.

A second later Liam gave out a happy gurgle and drew a deep breath. His eyes opened and he looked at Bran, his forehead furrowed with curiosity.

We all exhaled at the same time.

I grabbed the thin T-shirt the punk wore. Blood oozed from one edge of his mouth as he stared at me, his eyes growing duller by the second. His hands fell onto the chair's arms, fingers gripping the shredded fabric.

"Who paid you? Who paid to have Callendar killed?"

He exhaled once, bloody spittle staining his shirt.

"Our Fath—"

His eyes rolled back in his head as he went limp, drowned in his own blood.

"Fuck," I murmured, placing the pistol on the table.

"Mind your language. There's a child present." Jess nudged the body in the chair before her. "Damned fool."

I looked at her. "You okay?"

"Yeah." She swallowed hard. "Just more paperwork."

Inside I flinched. Killing humans was one thing Felis tried explicitly to avoid at all costs due to our superior skills. If and when we did it was an abnormality and had to be reported to the Grand

Council. I had no doubt they'd accept Jess's reasoning but it'd placed another weight on the older woman's shoulders, one she had to carry alone.

I licked my lips, trying to find the words. "Thank you."

"Better me than you," Jess murmured.

"Damned fool." I studied the body. "If he'd listened to me—"

"He was killing the baby and didn't even notice it. Guy was too wired to listen to anyone, much less the woman holding his gun." She gave me a sad smile. "Sometimes you can't talk your way out of situations, kit. Sometimes you got to man up and make the kill."

"Thanks for the pep talk." I pushed the thug to one side and began searching his pockets, praying he wasn't a drug addict and I wasn't about to give myself acupuncture lessons. "But we've lost the chance to find out who hired him."

"I figure that's obvious enough." She jerked a thumb at Bran, who had moved onto the couch, cradling Liam. "His dad."

Bran didn't reply, his full attention on Liam.

"Doesn't add up." I pried a thin wallet from his back pocket, twisting away to avoid getting more blood on my hands. "Why negotiate a settlement if you're going to kill the mother? And why keep the baby alive?"

"Black market?' Jess offered. "Maybe sell the wee one for a few dollars." She held up her hands. "We're in a whole new world of stupid and I can't begin to guess what's going on here."

Liam burbled and curled his tiny finger around Bran's pinky. The baby let out what I assumed to be a happy shout before settling down in his half brother's arms.

Bran didn't say anything.

"Keith Shaw." I held up the driver's license. "Lives on the other side of town." I pawed through the well-worn leather. "A handful of fifties and hundreds. Guess he was saving up for that rainy day." A small business card fell out. "And his probation officer. This guy was doing time for something."

"Good place to recruit someone," Jess said. "Take a special sort to kill a mother and take a newborn."

I went through the rest of the wallet. "Brand-new and squeaky clean. No photographs, nothing to connect him to anything."

"So what was he doing here?" Jess mused. "You pop the mother and take the baby, bring him here for…" She twisted from side to side, waving her arms to encompass the tiny hotel room. "What?"

I looked down at Shaw's body. "Not much now. My guess is he was waiting for instructions from his employer on where to take Liam next."

"Or for his employer to show and pick up the baby," Jess offered.

I shook my head. "If it were me I wouldn't do that. One of two things was going to happen—either Shaw collects his cash and goes on his merry way or Shaw gets killed after he turns over the baby." I stared at the dead man. "You wouldn't want to kill him here for the same reason we're fucked."

"Disposal of the body," Jess said, almost sounding apologetic.

I took a light sniff. "Even in a place like this they're going to search out the stink at some point. And we can't do a *Weekend at Bernie's* and wheel him out through the lobby. So his boss wouldn't kill him here."

"Have him go elsewhere with the baby for an exchange." Jess finished my scenario. "After that Shaw either gets taken out by Hanover or he goes on the run." She pressed her lips together tight before continuing. "Or he has another killer do it. Domino theory to keep as far from the initial crime as possible." She eyed Bran. "Spend a little extra cash to buy more blood."

"Maybe it's not my father," Bran shot back. "Maybe my father pissed off the wrong guy and the bastard killed Molly and grabbed Liam for an extortion plot."

"Maybe it is your father," Jess replied.

I held up my hand, stopping the argument. "We're not going to find out unless you've got a resurrection spell in your pocket, Jess."

"I'm calling it as I see it," she said.

"I hear you. I'm trying to keep an open mind." I bent my head just enough to show my appreciation. "Thank you for the help. I don't know if I'd have been able to shoot him."

"You would have," Jess responded, quicker than I'd have liked. "When it comes to children you do what you have to do."

"So now what?" Bran stood up, cradling the baby in his arms.

"We do this." I walked over and plucked the sleepy child from him. Bran gave a concerned hum when I moved away. A few steps put me in front of Jess.

"Here." I handed Liam over, careful to support the head as I placed the tiny bundle in her arms.

She let out a gasp as she instinctively shifted

to provide more support for the baby. It was one of the few times I'd seen her surprised and I enjoyed it.

"What?" Jess curled her body around the baby as any mother would—she'd raised two of her own and I had no doubt about her nurturing skills.

Mine, well… I tended to kill African violets.

"Take him someplace safe. Keep him there until we call," I said.

Jess frowned. "To the farm?"

"There's no place safer, no one we can trust right now." I pointed at the body sitting in the chair. "We can't leave him in this filth. If I call Attersley and tell him we found Liam he's going to wonder how we tracked Shaw. That's going to open a whole new can of trouble and put me behind bars and out of the game. And we sure as hell can't take Liam home and care for him while working this out."

I kept talking, the words tumbling out in a nervous rush.

"He needs to be someplace safe and I can't worry about him. We don't have time to hire a sitter and I wouldn't trust anyone right now to keep him from harm." I played my trump card. "Except you."

She looked down at Liam. He responded by smacking his lips and making cute baby noises.

"Jess..." I tried not to grumble. "I need this favor."

The knowing smirk made me want to slit my throat. The last thing I needed was to be in more debt to Jess—she'd have no problem calling it in.

"Pass me the diaper bag. There, behind the chair." She wrinkled her nose. "Bastard didn't even have the courtesy to change him after kid-napping him. Little one needs a bath and a whole new wardrobe." She took the brightly colored bag from Bran and flipped it over one shoulder with practiced ease. "You two keep working on this. I'll grab a cab outside."

I frowned. "Where are you parked? Do you even own a baby seat?" I had visions of Liam rid-ing in her lap on the drive to the farm and the po-lice pulling her over. The last thing I needed was trying to explain to Attersley how we kidnapped Liam a second time with an AMBER Alert blar-ing strong.

She gave me a cautious smile. "You do what you do and I'll do what I do best. Plenty of family here in town who can give us shelter—no need to drag him all the way up north." Jess paused, just long enough to scare me. "Be careful, Rebecca.

This isn't your usual hunting ground. These are people who don't care about anything except what they want and how to take it."

She paused for a moment, looking down at the baby before returning her attention to us. Jess sucked on her bottom lip for a second before speaking. "Sanctuary is yours if you want it, Rebecca. For all of you."

I took a step back, absorbing the news. Sanctuary meant Bran and I could disappear into any of the Prides, vanish off the grid and take Liam with us. It wasn't offered lightly and Jess would have to justify it to the Grand Council along with dealing with the consequences of helping us disappear into a new life.

It was an option offered only under the most dangerous of circumstances when total anonymity was needed, a chance to start over with a new life. It was offered to few Felis, a handful within my lifetime.

And to no human, as far as I knew.

Stunned, I couldn't do anything but nod. "Thank you. I'll keep it in mind."

"You do that." She cooed to Liam, who blew bubbles back at her. "Call me when you need the wee one back." Jess strode toward the door. "He is a cutie. Takes after his brother."

Bran shook his head as Jess left. "I have no idea what that woman is thinking from one moment to the next."

"That makes two of us." I tried not to think of all the debts I was accruing with Jess and the Pride.

"He's so small." He looked at his hands. "Hard to believe I was that little once."

"You were." I chuckled, despite the situation. "Don't tell me your mother hasn't told you the story about how she was forty-eight hours in labor without any drugs."

He cocked his head to one side. "How did you know?"

"It's what most mothers say. Can't tell you how many women have ranted to me about how ungrateful their husbands and kids are about all the trouble they went through to give birth." I stopped as a horrible option came clear in my mind. "Could your mother be involved in this?"

Bran took a step back as if I'd punched him in the gut. "My mother?"

"She's a possible suspect." I continued my reasoning despite his pained expression. "If we're considering your father I don't see why we wouldn't have to include your mother."

"No." Bran sliced the air with one hand. "Not

an option. She loves me, adores my father. She's been dedicated to the family for her entire life. Why would she toss it all away for an illegitimate child?"

"Your father—"

"My dad's been a hound dog for years. Why start killing his lovers now? Why Molly Callendar and leaving Liam alive?" Bran gave an emphatic shake of his head. "No. Not my father and not my mother."

I decided not to tell him about Bernadette's threats to me over dinner. Right now I needed us more united than divided.

"Okay." I shrugged. "I don't know. Right now I'm so turned around I couldn't find my way home in my own front yard. I'm not even sure this is the same damned day. Feels like weeks since I got up."

I gave myself a shake and walked around the small room. "Let's search here before we've got to get out. Once we leave we're not coming back." I sniffed the air. "He's going to get ripe soon enough without air-conditioning."

Bran gave me a sideways glance. "You going to be okay with him?"

I wrinkled my nose. "Have to be." I took shallow breaths, trying to cut out the smell of death.

"He's here with no suitcase, no man purse, nothing. Bastard traveled light."

Bran pointed at something lying on the couch. "Not light enough."

I walked into the bathroom and grabbed a handful of toilet paper. "Don't touch it. We've got enough prints around here and I'm out of gloves."

Bran smiled in spite of the situation. "Going to have to teach you to carry more rubbers."

I ignored him and picked up the disposable cell phone. It was slender and looked like a toy.

Bran winced. "Getting smaller and smaller."

"Cheaper and cheaper too." I hit the redial button.

"Hanover Investments." The automated cheerful voice babbled, going through a series of options.

I cut the connection.

Bran let out a heavy sigh. "Is it enough evidence against my father?"

I shook my head. "Not a chance. A good lawyer will make the argument Brayton's an employee of Hanover Investments and it's as likely a call from here was routed to Brayton's office as it was to your father's." I held it up to the light. "But it shows it wasn't a random killing or kidnapping.

Someone set out to kill Molly and kidnap Liam—a definite plan was in place."

"Hardly a relief." Bran stared at the ground. "So we know it's not random."

"It's better than nothing." I placed the phone on the table, careful not to leave any marks on it. "Let's keep looking."

Bran worked on the couch while I yanked on the cheap desk drawers, scowling with each empty box. "No clothing, no toiletries, not even a bottle of water. He wasn't planning to stay here long."

"A pit stop on his way elsewhere." Bran flipped the seat cushions. "Ugh. I think I found Hoffa's body. Or at least the last meal he ate." He withdrew a pen from an inside pocket of his duster and poked at a fossilized French fry. "I hope Liam doesn't have trouble eating."

"Don't worry. If he's a breast man like his big brother Jess'll find a wet nurse in no time." I shot him a sassy wink. "If he's on formula it'll be inside the diaper bag and she'll make it up for him. He's in good hands."

Bran let out a nervous grunt. "I know. I guess I'm still in shock over all this." The weary smile tore at my heart. "Been a hell of a few hours. All I wanted to do is meet you for lunch and maybe a little afternoon delight."

"Keep that in mind." I checked the empty closet. "The day's not over yet."

"Tease." Bran wiped the pen off on the back of the couch.

"I hope Shaw paid for a few days instead of a few hours." I finished my brief search. "He's going to start stinking soon enough."

"Can we find out who he is, where he came from?" Bran asked.

I paused, weighing the options. "I can't call Hank—he'll be on me in a second to find out why I'm asking. A request for a search hours after being at a murder scene is going to get me pulled back into the station for questioning. When we get home I can run a computer search on him but if he's been keeping a low profile there's not going to be much."

Bran kicked the couch with the bottom of his boot. "Fuck."

I didn't try to stop his little temper tantrum. Truth was I felt like screaming.

The system I'd worked in for most of my life, I couldn't access for fear of being caught and accused of murder or at the least, be accused of being an accessory to murder.

The system I'd shunned for most of my life, the

Felis society that had thrown me out, I had to rely on to protect the smallest victim of all.

Irony sucked.

I looked around the hotel room. The dingy brown walls might have been painted a long time in a past life as a real hotel. A cockroach scurried out from a hole in the wall to glare at us before scampering back inside to join his brothers. There was a faint scratching behind the plasterboard as rats and mice made their way back and forth to the garbage bins out back to feed and to breed.

Liam had sat in the middle of all this with Keith Shaw, waiting for an unknown fate. He hadn't asked for his mother to be killed or for his father to be a douchebag. He hadn't done anything other than be born.

Bran motioned for me to hand over Shaw's wallet. "Let's go to the bastard's home. Maybe he left something there saying who he worked for. The cops don't even know he's involved so we won't be tripping over them."

"Good idea." Bran recorded the address on his phone. "We need to find out how he got hooked into Hanover Investments. I don't think he worked there as a temp."

I used my cell phone to take a picture of the driver's license before taking the wallet, and pushed it back into Shaw's pocket. At least they'd be able to identify him when he was found.

Bran studied the pistol on the table. I could almost hear the wheels grinding in his mind.

"No." I picked it up and wiped it down, sure to erase any prints I'd put on the weapon. It took a minute to put it in Shaw's hand and wrap his fingers around the metal grip. I let it fall out of the dead man's hand to the ground.

"It's the weapon that killed Molly Callendar. It has to stay with him." I sounded stronger than I felt. "When they find him they'll be able to track him back to Molly without any problem. We can at least give her parents that much satisfaction, having him dead."

Bran nodded but still eyed the pistol with longing. I couldn't blame him for wanting to pack something more than a smile.

We headed for the door and slipped out the back of the hotel via the emergency stairwell and exit door, climbing over empty beer boxes and puddles of vomit to emerge in the back alley. I wasn't sure how long it'd take for the hotel to find out one of their customers was dead but it didn't hurt to keep a low profile. The kid at the front desk might or might not remember us but the last thing I needed right now was a phone call from Attersley demanding my immediate return to Division 14—or worse, an alert going out to find and bring me in.

"Think Liam is going to be okay?" Bran winced as he stepped over the remains of someone's lunch.

"I think he's going to be spoiled rotten. Doubt Jess is going to hand him over to anyone under the pretense of keeping him in the dark about the Pride." I took a deep breath of clean air as we moved onto the larger and cleaner sidewalk. "He'll be safer than if he were in Fort Knox."

Bran lifted a hand to flag down a cab. "Good."

The first two cabs sped by us as if we were holding up signs saying "We're going to rob you." The next one stopped because Bran held up a fifty.

According to his driver's license Keith Shaw lived in Parkdale, a handful of blocks from my house.

I didn't try to analyze the odds of it happening.

Decades ago the neighborhood had been for the Toronto elite, granting easy access to Lake Ontario and bringing in the rich and their friends to lounge by the lake. Large mansions filled the narrow streets. But times change and the wheel turns and Parkdale had devolved into a lower-class community where prostitutes controlled street corners and if you wanted crack you just needed to put your hand up and wait for a drive-by dealer.

I'd gotten my house cheap and my first task had been the removal of a pair of addicts from the alley right behind me. A firm talk, backed up with a few punches, had convinced the addicts to take their needles elsewhere—I'd pointed out the free needle exchange down the street. Maybe I couldn't stop them from shooting up but I could lessen the chance of stepping on a needle while getting to my car.

Shaw lived in one of the many dilapidated apartment buildings a few streets over where they rented apartments in three-month deals. For new arrivals to Canada it was a great opportunity to save their money and get a fresh start if you could avoid the temptation of the ever-present pimps and drug dealers offering easy money for little work.

"What a dump." Bran stated the obvious as we pulled up. The cab driver shifted in his seat, eager to get moving.

I couldn't blame him. Bran paid the fare and we got out. The cab pulled away and spun around the corner back toward a safer area of Toronto.

Bran gave the tall towers a curious look. "Interesting décor. The shower curtains blocking off the balconies sure make it colorful."

I glanced upward to where a handful of apartments had blocked off open access to the concrete boxes with brightly decorated shower curtains. "Probably pot plants."

He followed me up the chipped cement walkway to the front door. "No kidding?"

I shrugged and pulled the door open, smashing into a scent wall of urine. "Might be. Might be sleeping quarters for a large family who can't afford a second apartment. Around here no one asks."

He looked around. "Hard to believe you only live a few streets away."

"I can walk the same distance from your condo and find the same type of area. All depends on where you go."

The buzzer panel hung off the wall, barely attached by a series of wires. I ignored it and tugged on the locked door.

It opened on the second tug with an annoyed click.

"Ouch." Bran shook his head. "That's not good."

I didn't say anything. Shaw's address put him on the third floor. I stopped inside the empty room masquerading as a lobby and pondered my options.

"Let's try the stairs." I gave the elevators a wary glare. "Wouldn't trust those."

Bran chuckled. "Love you to death but don't want to spend the next six hours waiting for a repairman to show up." He sniffed the air as he pushed the stairwell door open, using his sleeve for some sort of protection. "Smells bad."

"Elevator would smell worse." I drifted by him, taking the steps two at a time.

We'd stepped over a handful of needles and crushed soda cans serving as makeshift crack pipes before we reached the third floor. Bran opened the door and stepped through.

"Do we have a plan?" he asked.

"No." I led him down the hall. "Unless you want to duplicate your last great entrance."

"I was sort of all kinds of awesome."

"Don't start believing your own PR, mister. We're not out of the woods yet."

Bran stopped in front of the apartment door. "Not yet." He smiled. "As long as you're with me I'm fine."

"Good. Let's try the easy way first, 'kay?"

He pouted as I pounded on the door.

"What?" The muffled shout came back.

I kept knocking.

A head stuck out farther down the hallway,

sized us up and disappeared again. The faint smell of marijuana drifted over us.

"What?" The door opened a fraction of an inch. A bleary bloodshot eyeball glared at me. "Whattauwant?"

"You know Keith Shaw?" I asked.

The eye narrowed. "Who wants to know?"

Bran pulled out a wad of cash from his pocket. "We owe him some cash. Looking to pay up." He glanced left and right. "Let us in and we'll talk about it. Don't want to be chatting out here in the hallway.

I glared at Bran. The last thing we needed was to be mugged on our way out.

The cheap gold-colored chain serving as a barrier jingled as the eyeball studied the thick pile of bills for a few seconds.

The door closed.

The door opened.

The rank smell of body odor was overwhelming as we entered the dimly lit apartment. It took a second to adjust and realize what I was seeing.

The apartment was decorated in post-garage-sale décor with nothing matching but the mold on the walls. An odd water stain looking something like a happy face spotted the far wall and I could smell beer and urine, each trying to top the other.

"And you are?" Bran extended his hand to Shaw's roommate.

The sliver of a man smiled, then rubbed his palm on his dark blue T-shirt before taking hold. "Frank Yupp. Two P's." He gave me a nod. "So you got something for Keith?"

Yupp had to be in his sixties, maybe seventies judging by the scattering of thin white hair on his head. A scattering of homemade tattoos on his hands identified him as a longtime criminal.

Bran put the wad back in his pocket and withdrew a slender leather case. He flipped it open to show his Toronto *Inquisitor* identification.

I scowled and bit my tongue.

"We're doing a story on female guards sexually harassing male inmates." The words poured like warm honey off his tongue. "Keith was supposed to meet us earlier today for a meeting but he didn't show." Bran tilted his head to one side. "Any idea where he is?"

"The *Inquisitor*? Oh, wow." Frank scratched the back of his neck. "I read your stuff all the time. Best thing inside, if you know what I mean."

Bran beamed. "Thank you." He looked around the sparsely decorated apartment. "Since Keith kinda stood us up, I was wondering if I could interview you." He patted his pocket. "We pay very well for informants." His free hand dug into a pocket and came up with a notebook and pencil.

The old man grinned. "Sure." He jabbed a thumb at me. "Who's she?"

"Rookie learning the ropes," Bran replied. "Say hello, rookie."

"Hello, rookie."

"She's the silent type. Now let's get down to it."

I loved seeing Bran at work. He knew when to talk and when to listen, when to push for more information and when to sit back and let his target babble.

Like right now.

The chatter went from bawdy prison stories during which Yupp revealed he'd been in for breaking and entering (but totally not legit, he was set up by the cops donchaknow) to how he'd met Keith Shaw in a prerelease program and accepted his offer to room together. They also shared the same probation officer.

"So what are you doing now?" Bran asked.

Yupp shrugged. "Working in a soup kitchen/food bank. Only thing I can get right now and they pay shit." He grunted. "But it keeps me in the clear and looks good on the resume."

"Which kitchen?" Bran drawled. His tone was so seductive I wanted to answer.

"Second Chance, Second Life. Off of Yonge Street and Charles."

I brought up a mental map of downtown. It was a pretty rough area, prime spot to help the street people.

"Did Keith work there as well?" Bran prompted. He glanced at me, intercepting my question.

"Keith? Sure. He worked out on the loading bay—when he wasn't posing for the cameras. Pretty boy there got picked to be a model for some photo ops. Happened a few weeks ago and he got all excited over it." Yupp let out something between a cough and a snort. "He musta cut a deal with someone for some work on the side 'cause suddenly he's got extra cash and pays me up his half of the rent on time."

Bran didn't falter. "He say where he got this extra cash from? Maybe some sugar mama from the inside calling him for a booty call?"

Yupp frowned. "Don't think so. He never said. I figured he was getting a job, you know—" he waggled his fingers "—under the table."

"As in going back to jail if he got caught?" I asked.

Yupp looked at me as if I'd somehow materialized from another dimension. "Didn't say yes, didn't say no. And I ain't gonna badmouth my roomie."

"What was Keith in for?"

The ex-con shrugged. "Something hard-core. He didn't say what exactly but I wasn't gonna ask." He frowned. "What you want to know that for?"

Bran peeled off three bills from the wad. "Background details. Thanks for the chat."

Yupp escorted us to the door, fondling the money. "Come on back if you want more stuff. Don't know where Keith is but we're paid up for another month so it's cool."

The door shut behind us.

"Better?" Bran asked.

"Best." I led the way back to the stairs. "So Keith Shaw suddenly comes into a lot of cash while working a loading dock at the soup kitchen."

Bran hopped over a hypodermic needle. "After a photo shoot. Good place to find someone to do your dirty work."

We headed out into the lobby and back onto the street. I pointed to the left.

"Queen's that way. Not a chance of finding a cab along this street."

I didn't mention I needed the time to clear my

mind and senses. It was getting close to midnight and I'd burned through all of my energy reserves.

Bran pulled out his cell.

"Who are you calling?" I asked.

"I want to see if this soup kitchen is one of our charities." He tapped on the tiny numbers. "I've still got some pull at the office. Let me see if—"

I put my hand atop his, killing the connection. "It's close to midnight. You're going to get the same recording Shaw's phone got. We'll have to wait until morning."

As we walked I kept glancing around us. The odds were good no one saw Bran and his obscene amount of money but it never hurt to be cautious.

"Brayton could have met Shaw at one of the charity functions," Bran said.

"So could your father. Or mother, or one of your father's friends/enemies," I countered, hating to play the bad guy. "No one's in the clear, not yet." I steered us under the streetlights. "Tomorrow we head for the soup kitchen, start stirring up some trouble. Someone knows something. Shaw didn't trip into this job—he was recruited to kill Molly Callendar."

He cut me off. "And then what? We can't take this to the cops. We can't tell them any of this." He rubbed his eyes. "We can't even tell them we've got Liam."

"What do you want?" I asked, keeping my voice low. We'd come up on the side of a 7-Eleven, the convenience store doing brisk business with people rushing in and out for munchies and cigarettes. "What do you want to do?"

Bran leaned against a bright placard advertising lottery numbers. "I'm not sure." He let out a painful sigh. "I don't know. I really, honestly, don't know."

I shifted my weight from one foot to the other, unsure of what to say. This was far beyond anything I'd dealt with.

There was only one more option I could offer.

I exhaled, closed my eyes and drew on what little calm I had left before speaking.

"Say the word and I'll forget it all."

"What?"

"The only thing connecting Liam to your father is this." I tapped my nose. "Say the word and I'll forget I ever picked up the scent. We'll have Jess drop Liam off at a hospital anonymously. They won't be able to trace him back to any of us. They'll take care of him, probably put him with Brayton or the grandparents."

Bran stared at me.

"Your father already thinks I'm bonkers. I'll apologize to him and that'll be that." I had to force the words out. "As long as he doesn't do any more investigation we'll be fine. You talk to him, you tell him I'm a wee bit nuts and tell him to back off or I'll have a breakdown. Or something like that. He'll probably stop anyway if Liam shows up again. He'll be busy covering his tracks."

Bran stared at me.

"Say something." I stamped my foot. "Say something, damn you."

He pulled me into a hug, a hug so tight I felt the air escaping my lungs.

"I love you," he whispered.

I didn't say anything. I couldn't say anything.

Bran pulled back just enough to kiss me, a deep searching kiss that left me dizzy and glad he was holding on to me with both hands.

"Eep."

"Eep?"

"Eep. Don't let go." I wobbled in his grip. "So was that a yes or no?"

Bran shook his head. "I can't let my family get away with this, whether it's my mother or my father. God knows what else they've done over the years. And I can't let them get away with threatening you and your family. If my father does this once he'll do it again and again. I know how he thinks—if he knows it's your weak spot he'll dig at it until it bleeds."

"There'll be more blood than he's prepared for."

"I know. Which is why we have to stop him."

EIGHT

WE WALKED BACK to the house in silence, holding hands. I was caught between wanting to sleep for a day and a half and wanting to tear Michael Hanover's throat out.

Bran sighed as I unlocked the front door. He didn't say anything as Jazz trilled and maneuvered between our legs.

"Shower. Bed." I wasn't sure what else to offer.

He tossed his coat on the sofa as I locked the door, double-checking the locks. The last thing we needed right now was unwelcome visitors.

Jazz hummed as I dumped another cupful of food in her bowl. I patted her on the head before heading for the stairs.

A trail of clothing led up to the bathroom. I held my tongue and picked up them up before depositing them in a heap in the far corner of the bedroom.

I stripped down, taking my time. My eyelids

were already drooping and I needed to stay awake long enough to not drown.

Bran had his back to me when I entered.

I tugged the shower curtain across to make sure we didn't flood the bathroom. We'd already had a few near misses due to some sexual escapades.

Bran didn't say anything. His right hand was flattened against the white tiles, his left hanging at his side as the hot water splashed down over us. He didn't move as I touched his back and ran my fingers down the small scars and scratches dotting his skin.

He began to shake, keeping his head down.

I wrapped my arms around him, pressing my face against his slick skin, and tried not to listen to his sobs.

I WOKE IN bed, alone.

My heart went into double beats as I scrambled to find something to wear, slowing when I smelled fresh tea from downstairs and heard Bran muttering to Jazz, who was begging for more food even though her bowl was already full.

He'd pulled on a clean white T-shirt from the collection in his single drawer in my bedroom but hadn't gotten to socks and shoes, padding around barefoot in his jeans.

I paused in the doorway, unsure of how to proceed after last night.

Bran gave me a wide smile and offered me a mug of tea. "Got confirmation from my father's personal assistant that Second Chance, Second Life is one of Hanover Investments' smaller charities." He gestured at the table. "I made up bacon and eggs. You've got to be famished."

I tried not to give a sigh of relief. We were good, at least for the time being.

I dived on the food with unladylike manners, shoving strips of bacon into my mouth until my stomach stopped growling.

Bran chuckled and sat down across from me with a cup of tea. "I see I was correct."

"Aren't you eating?" I mumbled as I speared another forkful of eggs.

"Already did." He pointed to the dishes in the sink. "I thought I'd let you sleep in a bit."

I glanced at the clock. "Eight-thirty? Holy..." I grabbed my mug and slurped hot tea. "We've got to get going."

"I saw Liam's picture on the morning news," Bran murmured. "The Callendars did a live interview. They were crying, both of them."

"He's safe." It wasn't much but all I could offer. "Let me check in with Jess."

I dug out my phone from my jean pocket and dialed.

"What?" She answered on the first ring, her tone impatient.

I put the phone on speaker so Bran could hear. "Hi, Jess." I kept shoveling food into my mouth. "How's it going today?"

"The little one likes cats."

I almost spewed eggs and bacon across the table. "What?"

"Don't panic. He was fussing a bit last night and I thought I'd give him something to look at."

Bran's mouth fell open. He looked at me as if I'd been the one who had Changed.

"He did have a little stuffed lion in his crib." I reached for my tea to try to avoid choking. The mental image of Jess Changed and cooing to Liam was almost too much to bear without laughing. "Aside from that, he's fine?"

A disgruntled huff came across the line. "I was taking care of babies long before you came along. Just call me when you need him back."

She cut the connection before I could respond.

"Would you think less of me if I said I found that both reassuring and terrifying at the same time? If he grows up with some sort of fur fetish..." Bran stole the last piece of bacon from my near-empty plate.

"Don't even start." I got up and dumped the plate in the sink. It took me another minute to finish off the tea, during which I tried to not giggle at the mental image of Jess and Liam.

"I figure we'll start with the soup kitchen," Bran said. "See who Shaw met." He lifted a finger before I could speak. "Not necessarily my father. There's a lot of bigwigs who go on these outings, you know."

"Duly noted. Think they'll tell you who showed up? Isn't there some sort of secrecy pledge on this sort of work?"

"Doesn't matter." He pointed to his chest. "Hanover, remember?"

"And then what?" I turned the water on as he walked into the living room.

"Then we take it from there."

The answer didn't make me feel any more confident. I wagged my finger at Jazz, who immediately hopped up on the kitchen counter and spread out next to the Brown Betty.

"Don't ever have kittens. I couldn't deal with it."

She trilled and rolled onto her back with a snort.

We caught a streetcar most of the way to the soup kitchen, hopping off a block early. Bran had given me an odd look when I rang the bell requesting a stop.

"I don't want to step off right in front of the place," I offered by way of explanation. "Gives us a chance to see what's going on around the building before we walk in and start rocking the boat."

"It's a soup kitchen. Maybe stirring the pot?"

I ignored him and studied a trio of homeless men sitting on a nearby bench, graciously donated by some corporation that advertised their charity with a large metal plate screwed into the front of the seat. The blank-eyed stares at the pigeons gathering around their feet told a thousand stories.

This area of Toronto hadn't undergone the deconstruction so popular these days, shredding old buildings in favor of high-priced condominiums with views of other condominiums.

"There's the place." Bran pointed at a storefront that had seen better days, the chipped pale yellow paint barely holding the wood together. He frowned, taking in the dingy façade. "You'd think it'd look better given the amount of money we pour into it."

"They put up a fancy neon sign and it'd be broken within the week. Around here it pays to be quiet and discreet."

No cheerful bell jingled when we walked in to announce our arrival. The large room held over twenty plastic tables covered with red-and-white paper tablecloths. Vases held artificial flowers on some of them.

At the back sat the serving area, with orange trays already cleaned and stacked for the lunch crowd. A lone woman looked through the stainless-steel windows and frowned.

"We're not open for lunch until noon."

Bran strode the length of the room with long, leisurely strides that hid his impatience. "I'm here to see Stacy Hampton."

The elderly woman looked him over, pursing her lips. I couldn't blame her trying to figure out who this man was; I had no doubt emergency buttons lay within easy reach for all of the staff.

She turned away from us and adjusted her hairnet. "Stacy? Some man up front here wants to talk to you."

I could imagine her fingers creeping toward the red button.

I tugged on Bran's arm, pulling him to a stop a proper distance from the serving windows. "Give them a minute."

He looked at me and frowned.

"They're prepared for trouble. Give them a minute to assess the situation."

A door opened beside the stacked trays and a woman walked through. Young, blonde and in her twenties, she smiled as she approached us. Wearing jeans and a pink T-shirt with the charity title emblazoned across the front in bright yellow letters, she latched on to Bran automatically as the leader.

"Can I help you?"

Bran extended his hand. "Brandon Hanover. I'd like to talk to you about your work here."

I could see the wheels spinning behind her eyes. Hanover. Family. Grovel. Start.

"Of course, Mr. Hanover. A pleasure to meet you." I got a half-assed nod. "And your friend. How can I help you today?"

"I'm working on a story about some of your employees." He gave her a thousand-dollar smile. "Keeping it all in the family, as it were."

"I see. Come on back to my office and we can talk." She waved at the open door with a wary glance toward the front.

Stacy Hampton was a smart, street-savvy woman.

We followed her through the kitchen to a series of small offices carved out of the back loading dock area. Skids of canned vegetables sat near a forklift.

Stacy pointed at three men sitting at a folding table and playing cards. "When your break's over, get this unpacked. The lunch crowd's going to arrive soon enough."

The three men got to their feet as one and nodded. They were all older men and looked like they'd been doing hard time before they'd hit puberty, their skin leathery and scarred with more than prison tattoos. She had their respect. Hampton wasn't a woman to be taken lightly.

The office was as generic as they come, the appropriate motivational posters on the walls with whales and dolphins and penguins delivering their pep talks. I noticed a framed print advertising a benefit dinner for the soup kitchen, held last year and prominently displaying Hanover Investments as their sponsor.

Stacy motioned for us to sit in the two folding chairs while she maneuvered her way behind the desk, gingerly shifting stacks of folders so they wouldn't fall on her.

"Can I see your identification, Mr. Hanover?" She wasn't a fool.

Bran handed over his driver's license without

comment. She studied it for a minute before handing it back.

"Thank you. I don't mean to be impolite but Hanover isn't such an uncommon a name."

"And my father's assistant told you I'd be coming," Bran added.

The thin smile didn't falter. "She did. We tend to be cautious where the media's involved even if it is, ah, family."

It didn't take a genius to see between the lines. She was worried about bad press, be it justified or not. I'd see too many good causes curl up and die like slugs on salt licks when the press got it wrong and the fallout killed a good group. A retraction on page 87 didn't undo the damage when it came to asking for public support and money.

"I understand." Bran beamed. "I'm working on a freelance article regarding the rehabilitation and reintegration of criminals back into society and thought, well—" He spread his hands. "Where better to start than at one of my family's good works?"

Her nose twitched. She wasn't buying it.

I hid a smile. That would keep Bran humble.

Bran's lips pressed together in a thin line as he realized Stacy Hampton wasn't going to be as easily hustled as his other pseudo-journalistic targets.

"We're here about Keith Shaw." His tone shifted from friendly to hard-core steel. "We know he worked here on the loading dock."

Stacy studied him for a second before responding. "Who told you that?"

"Frank Yupp." I leaped in, unwilling to sit back and let Bran do all the heavy lifting. "He told us Keith was flashing some cash, more than he should have been holding." I pulled out my private investigator's license and tossed it on the table. "We're investigating a theft and think he might be involved."

It was a half lie. I didn't want to say the word "kidnapping."

Stacy's eyes went wide as she saw the official identification. "I didn't think we had private investigators in Canada."

I sighed. "Yes, we do. And we're wondering how Keith Shaw goes from unloading veggies on your dock to waving around hundred-dollar bills."

"I didn't know about that." She gestured at the sparsely decorated office. "I can tell you he didn't get it from here. We never keep more than a hundred dollars on hand including personal wallets. We believe it's best to avoid temptation."

"Understandable." Bran leaned forward. "Keith

Shaw only came into this cash after some sort of photo shoot, some publicity stunt. Tell us about it."

Stacy frowned. "It was a meeting with some of our sponsors. Hanover Investments is at the top when it comes to donations, as you know. Some of the board members showed up to take pictures with the workers for newsletters, the usual fluff they send out to let their people know where the money's going." She shook her head. "No one got paid for it."

She dug for a folder at the bottom of a stack to her left. "I have the photographs here. We were discussing how to use them at the last meeting."

She flipped the plain brown folder open to reveal a series of black-and-white images of the men from the loading dock, the three we'd passed on the way in. They perched on the lone forklift, Keith Shaw among them. He glared at the camera and I imagined he wasn't the top choice for a poster boy.

Behind the forklift stood a line of dignitaries, local government flunkies making time with the press. Bernadette beamed at the camera while Michael scowled, obviously eager to get out of the spotlight and back to work.

"Keith hasn't been in for two days. He called in sick yesterday and hasn't shown up today so far." She cleared her throat. "As long as he reports to his probation officer there's no problem but if there's more—" She let the sentence hang. "Should we be calling the police?"

I resisted the urge to wave my hands frantically in the air. The last thing we needed was to have the police on our trail or worse, doubling back on our tracks. If they found Shaw's body they'd be searching for his killer and not necessarily connecting it to Liam's kidnapping. If we told them it was connected Hank would have my ass back in jail faster than I could blink for withholding evidence and I'd be trying to explain why I hadn't handed Liam over to the authorities.

I still hadn't figured out how I was going to dodge that bullet.

"No." Bran waved her off. "My father, he thinks someone picked his pocket. We always carry spare cash, you see." He displayed his own thick bundle of cash, ignoring my eye roll.

Stacy let out something akin to a peep.

He gave her another killer smile. "You'll understand we want to handle this as quietly as possible."

"Oh, yes," Stacy agreed.

"My apologies for the deception," Bran said. "I didn't want to cast aspersions on Mr. Shaw until we verified he was the actual criminal." He gave a noncommittal shrug. "For all we know he won a lottery."

"But you can't find him." Stacy looked from one of us to the other. "Doesn't it confirm he's the thief?"

"Not really." I leaped in to try to save the conversation. "He could be on a bender drinking away his winnings. You understand we don't want to make any accusations until we have more than just vague theories to go on. Not to mention the embarrassment to the center here if we wrongly accused him and it got leaked to the press."

A flash of panic in her eyes told me I'd said the right thing.

"We've got to get going." I slipped my business card across the top of the photographs. "Please call us if you hear anything about Mr. Shaw."

Like, say, his death.

She added the card to the folder before closing it up and placing it back atop the precariously teetering stack. "I can't believe Keith would steal someone's wallet."

"Why?" Bran asked as we stood up.

"Because he's a paroled murderer. This would put him back in jail for the rest of his term." Stacy covered her mouth. "I'm sorry, I'm not sure I should have said that."

"I think it's okay," I said.

BRAN LOOKED OVER at the shippers as we made our way to the front of the kitchen. They were busy emptying a truck that had arrived while we were in Hampton's office. The forklift spun around, neatly depositing a half-full skid of plastic boxes in a corner. The other men stripped the shrink-wrap away and sorted through the canned vegetables.

"Think they know anything?" Bran asked.

I hesitated. "I don't think Shaw was into sharing—if he brought one of these guys in they'd demand a share and wouldn't be here." I winced as the forklift tines screeched for oil.

Bran led me through the front eating area. I could almost hear his teeth grinding.

It wasn't proof either way but it was a link between Shaw and the Hanovers. Brayton was nothing but a sheep being led to slaughter on the Hanover altar.

"Now where to?" Bran put his hands on his hips. A homeless man started to approach us, hand out, but spotted Bran's annoyed expression and paused, unsure what to do.

"I don't know," I admitted. "The important thing is that Liam's safe." I dug in my pocket for some spare change, finding a few gold-colored dollar coins. I flipped them toward the man with a wan grin. He scooped them up and scampered into a nearby alley.

"For how long?" Bran kicked at a stone. It bounced into the street and off a moving car, causing a dent or at the least, a scratch. "Jess can't keep him forever."

I chewed on my bottom lip, running through our options.

They ranged from few to none.

Bran's cell phone rang.

We both jumped.

Bran dug his phone out of a pocket. He looked at the caller ID and went pale.

"My father."

I drew a deep breath. "Your call. You don't have to talk to him if you don't want to."

His fingers hovered over the small screen. "I don't know what to say to him."

"Don't say anything," I prompted. "Let him lead the conversation. Let him call the shots."

He touched the clear surface and laid the phone down on his palm so we both could hear.

"Dad." His tone was calm and steady. "What's up?"

I moved in and touched Bran's shoulder. There was no way I could imagine the emotions rushing through his system right now and I wasn't sure I wanted to. It was one thing to be told you had a half brother and quite another to hold him in your arms and know there was another connection to your lifeline, another link in your family chain.

"Good morning." Michael's tone was low and calm. "How are you and Rebecca doing today?"

"Fine, thank you." Bran glanced at me and shrugged.

"My assistant told me you called her regarding a charity front. What's that all about?"

Bran hesitated, long enough for his father to pick up on it. Michael Hanover hadn't made his money by being dim. "A story idea. You know how these things go."

"I see. Did you meet Rebecca yesterday?" Smooth as silk and sweet as cotton candy. Now I knew where Bran got his charm.

Bran threw me a look. "Yes, I did. We've been chatting."

"Really." The calmness made my skin crawl. "What about?"

A streetcar rumbled by, the long extended body

painted in red and white. It came to a shuddering stop not far from us and discharged a pair of shabbily dressed men who quickly walked away from us. One cast a glance over his shoulder, assessing our potential for future interaction.

I scowled at him.

Bran didn't notice or didn't care. "About you blackmailing her into doing some work for you."

Michael snorted. "Blackmail is a very strong word, son. I wouldn't toss it around unless you have something to back it up." His voice deepened. "Or something to hide."

"She's not hiding anything from me."

"Are you sure?" Michael purred like a lion playing with a mouse. "How well do you know Rebecca Desjardin?"

"Well enough," Bran snapped back. "I want you to stay out of my personal business."

"Your business is my business. As long as you take my money."

I winced. I knew Bran wasn't financially independent—his reputation as a serious journalist was growing but a freelance writer only got paid per story, nothing guaranteed from week to week, month to month. He'd managed to snag some good paychecks as of late but it didn't cover the amount of money he'd been tossing around since we'd been together.

I wasn't the only one being blackmailed here.

"Where are you right now?" Michael asked.

"We're hanging at a diner on Queen Street. Got some great steak and eggs," Bran lied without missing a beat. "Talking things over. She's upset with the way things went yesterday."

"I understand. And believe me, I didn't mean for it to get so…complicated for her. I can't imagine the shock of finding a dead body and then having to deal with the police." I could imagine him wrinkling his nose in disgust. "I hope she's coping."

"She's doing as well as can be expected."

"Good. I hope she's had a chance to consider and can see things from my point of view," Michael said. "I understand it's rough with her, coming from such a disadvantaged family, to understand how things work for us."

"What do you mean?" Bran asked.

I could imagine Michael Hanover sitting behind the oak desk, studying the photographs on his wall. "I understand it's her job to be suspicious but I hope she's not going to be silly and take her wild theories to the authorities."

"What wild theories?" Bran asked.

I heard the hitch in Michael's voice. He didn't want to bring Bran into this but if he wanted to secure my total silence he had to.

"That I'm somehow more involved with this than I already am. I told the police everything—about how Brayton needed a discreet courier and I connected the two. Nothing more."

Michael wasn't stupid. He was worried about his line being tapped. A bit paranoid, but he hadn't gotten to where he was by trusting people to stay silent.

"So she's told me," Bran replied coolly.

"I assume you don't agree with her."

"Reb has a different way of seeing things." He reached out and tapped the edge of my nose. I responded with a smile despite the situation.

"She's got to understand how things work in our family, Bran." Michael's tone grew harder. "If you expect us to accept her fully you're going to have to keep her under control. She's got to learn to know what to say in public and what stays behind closed doors."

"Like Mom does?" Bran barked. "Letting you screw around behind her back, doing any woman who's stupid enough to spread her legs for you?"

The men on the bench shuffled away at hearing his raised voice.

"Bran—"

"No. No no no." Bran punched an invisible speed bag. "We are not going to do this over the phone. Come over to Reb's place and we can talk about this."

My stomach lurched. I didn't want to be standing between Bran and his father. Having lost my own at a young age I couldn't bear to be the reason their relationship fractured.

"Rebecca's place?" Michael asked. "Why there?"

"Because I said so. We need to talk and I'm sure you don't want me tearing up your office in front of all your employees."

I couldn't fault his logic. His father wouldn't be at ease in public and definitely not at work. At least if he came to the house he'd be on my turf and we'd be able to deal with him without outside intervention.

"Okay. I'll be there within the hour." He hesitated. "It goes without saying I expect no tomfoolery from you."

Tomfoolery? I mouthed the word.

Bran snorted. "Like what? Having the cops hide in the closet like some cheap detective novel?"

I bit my tongue. It wasn't all that bad an idea. Except Hank would kill me for asking.

"Don't be an idiot," Michael replied. "All I'm asking is that you allow me to present my view of the situation."

Bran shook his head. "See you then." He cut the connection.

"What are you going to do?"

"I want to hear the truth. I'm not letting him threaten you. We're no closer to getting any answers and I'm fucking tired of getting to the party a day late and a dollar short. He'll tell me what we need to know about Liam and about Molly Callendar."

"And what happens if you don't like what you hear?" I said softly.

He gave a halfhearted shrug. "Won't be the first time." He looked around. "Where's the streetcar stop?"

"Let's walk out to Yonge Street." I waited until we were well away from the soup kitchen before venturing into dangerous territory. "What are you going to say to your father?"

"I don't know," Bran admitted. His hands curled up into fists and uncurled, curled and uncurled. "I want to smack the shit out of him but it won't change anything. Especially if he's responsible for what happened to Molly." He rubbed his palms on his jeans. "I don't know what to do. I'd say for you to call Attersley but there's nothing we can give him that won't put you in jeopardy." He shook his head, lips pressed together in a thin line. "I won't let that happen."

I took one of his hands and held it. "Just think before you act."

"You're one to talk."

"One little incident and you've got me all figured out, eh?"

Bran swooped in for a kiss, soft and sweet. "Not a chance. And I hope to spend many more years trying to figure you out." The loving tone was tempered with sadness. He'd lost something today and I had no idea how he'd cope or recover.

This love thing was tough.

NINE

THE STREETCAR RIDE was fast enough—we'd caught a straggling rush hour car and it surged along the tracks, dropping us near the house within the half hour.

"How fast can your father drive?" I wheezed as I trotted along, trying to keep up with Bran's long strides.

"He has a driver. Probably sitting on the Gardiner in traffic." He turned into the small yard. The rosebushes struggling to survive at the front jabbed out at us with fresh thorns as we brushed by and headed for the front door.

I worked on the deadbolt. Not that it stopped certain people from gaining access but I had to put up at least a façade of home security.

"What do you want me to do?" Bran asked.

I gave him a blank look. "What?"

"What do you want me to do?"

"I want you to do whatever you feel is right for

you and for Liam." I pushed the door open. "We'll make do with the rest."

Jazz strolled by us and hopped up on the couch, oblivious to the drama happening around her.

Bran let his breath out slowly. "Sometimes I envy that cat."

I chuckled. "You'd like to be coughing up hairballs?"

"Not so much."

"Do you want me to try and tape this?" I had an ancient cassette recorder in the bottom of my desk. I wasn't even sure if it still worked.

Bran shook his head. "Not admissible in court unless both parties know they're being taped. And I can promise you my father won't give permission." He smiled and held up his cell phone. "If I wanted to I could do it with this. But it'd still be inadmissible."

I resisted the urge to slap my forehead. I hadn't figured out all the bits and pieces of this new phone.

"I'll make some tea." I headed for the kitchen, grateful to keep my hands busy. There was no way this meeting was going to end well.

All I could hope for was that the damage wasn't permanent.

I heard the limo before Bran did, the low hum of the finely tuned engine a distinct sound in this area.

I listened. One set of footsteps coming toward the house.

Inside I breathed a sigh of relief. I wouldn't have put it past Michael to bring a whole troop of security thugs to make his point. I wasn't prepared for a fight but I'd make them all bleed for it.

"He's here." I headed for the door. "Alone."

"Good," Bran answered. He rubbed his palms on his jeans.

I put on my neutral face and opened the door.

Michael Hanover stood there, his attention everywhere but on me. His eyes kept darting around the front yard as if zombies were about to rise up and eat him.

He should be so lucky.

Behind him the elderly white-haired driver leaned on the hood of the black stretch limousine reading a magazine.

"Rebecca. Brandon." Michael wore another power suit, gray with a white shirt and salmon-colored tie. His hair was perfect, the gray spots at his temples carefully brushed into the short red strands. "May I come in?"

For a second I thought about slamming the door

in his face with a laugh. That, or punching him in the face, laughing and *then* slamming the door.

"Rebecca," Bran said behind me.

I put away the fantasies and stepped back to let him enter.

Michael Hanover moved to the center of the living room. His body language told me he didn't want to be here.

I left the door unlocked. If we needed police or an ambulance I didn't need the extra trouble of having to release the deadbolts again.

As far as I was concerned the danger was inside right now, not outside.

Michael looked around the living room with a nervous glance.

"Just us," Bran said, guessing at the reason.

"Good."

I headed for the couch and sat down.

The two men stayed silent. This wasn't going to be easy or quick.

Jazz trilled, then nudged my hand and lay down beside me, letting out a demanding merp. I patted her head and reached for the ever-present packet of cat treats on the unbroken side table.

Bran didn't look over.

It was like watching a young lion and an old lion jousting for leadership. Bran rubbed his chin, unwilling or unable to sit down while Michael took up a position in the center of the living room, arms crossed, waiting for something.

Michael loosened his tie and cleared his throat with something close to a cough.

Jazz, sensing the tension, scooted up the stairs with a last nudge of her cold clammy nose on my hand.

"I'm not sure where to start," the elder Hanover mumbled.

Bran stayed silent.

I got up and perched myself on the edge of the sofa and spun an imaginary wheel with my fingers. "Let's begin with you blackmailing me last night."

Michael glared at me. "I don't like that word."

"I don't like being threatened. So now we're equal."

The elder Hanover eyeballed me, searching for a weakness. I knew he was looking for a way to break through my armor and make me bend to his will.

"Don't even try. You don't have enough mojo to get out of this." I let a snarl creep into my voice. I was tired of parents and family. "At the start you pulled me into this because you wanted to have no paper trail leading back to you and your associates. The sad thing is I might have done it for nothing if you'd asked nicely. Instead you threaten to fuck me over by digging up my family tree," I rumbled. "And trust me—you wouldn't be happy with the results of your excavation. Some roots are better left unearthed."

Michael crossed his arms. "Maybe I should send in the diggers regardless of what happens here."

I wagged my finger in the air. "I wouldn't. Not unless you want to be responsible for more deaths."

That earned me a frown and a cautious look before the stoic mask returned.

I didn't flinch. I already felt partially responsible for Callendar's death—I couldn't allow myself to get wrapped up in emotional bondage again.

"Who is Molly Callendar?" Bran growled. I heard the anger and sadness in his voice battling for control.

Michael looked over. "A woman." The dismissive tone sent my pulse skyrocketing. "A temp who worked in my office, doing paperwork and the like." He waved his hand to the side. "No one special."

Bran slapped his hand down on the remaining

side table, making me jump. It sounded like a rifle going off. “She’s the fucking mother of your son.”

Michael’s response didn’t change. He didn’t break into tears or start raging. I could almost see the computer inside his mind weighing what to say and how to look while saying it.

He was a pro at keeping secrets.

“Says who? You? The police?” His tone shifted to dismissive. “Rebecca here, of the mysterious past and less than reputable employment?” He scowled at Bran. “Who says the baby’s mine?”

“Is he?” Bran stopped pacing and faced his father. “Is Liam your son?”

“Where did you get such a crazy idea?” Michael nodded in my direction. “Did she put you up to this?” He gave Bran a predatory look. “What’s your game here?”

“Is Liam your son?”

“Looks to me like you’ve already made up your mind,” Michael shot back. “What wild theories are spinning around in that brain of yours? What crazed, warped worlds are you wandering through right now?” He gave me a sideways glance. “Did she give you some sort of drug? Are you drinking too much?”

Bran wasn’t going to be diverted from his mission. “Molly Callendar’s baby. Is he your son?”

Michael glared at me, hoping for a better reaction. "What have you put into his head?"

"Nothing but the truth," I replied in as calm a voice as I could muster. Part of me wanted to jump up and claw his face to shreds, pound that smug smile into snail snot for what he was putting my mate through.

The other, saner part, reminded me this wasn't my fight. I couldn't fight Bran's battles and he couldn't fight mine.

Didn't mean I couldn't be ready to jump in if needed.

"Is he your son?" Bran repeated through clenched teeth.

Michael let out a sigh. "Brandon, don't be such a drama queen." He studied his well-manicured fingernails. "You make it sound like it's something important."

Bran moved in on his father, charging into his personal space. "Molly Callendar is dead and I think you're responsible."

Michael tucked his hands in his pockets and rocked on his heels, ignoring the challenge. "Oh, do you?" He sneered at me. "And why would I have your girlfriend run papers back and forth if I were going to kill Molly Callendar?"

I noted he'd already placed himself at the center

of the murder conspiracy. "You had David Brayton play the role of Callendar's ex-lover to keep you out of the picture." I kept spinning the scenario. "You asked him to pretend to be the father and arrange for the payoff to Molly and Liam."

"Liam," Michael Hanover repeated, rolling the word out far longer than he should have. "Nice name."

I ignored him. "Brayton negotiated a good deal for her and she agreed to keep everything secret. But maybe sometime between me returning to Brayton's office and going back with new terms she changed her mind. Perhaps she decided she wasn't happy with the idea of leaving town and starting a new life elsewhere." I tried to keep the snarl out of my voice, only partially succeeding. "Maybe Molly flinched, didn't want to leave her family and friends in order to live a lie out west. Possibly she called you up direct and asked for more money, maybe she asked for official recognition for Liam and inclusion in your family tree, something you weren't prepared to deliver." I paused, breathless from running down the theories.

"Maybe dwarves came up from their underground caves and killed her for not agreeing to marry their evil king," Michael drawled.

I looked at Bran. We were spinning our wheels and going nowhere fast.

"Such a wild theory." Michael crossed his arms, feet anchored to the floor. "And your proof is..." His eyes bored into mine like a diamond drill. Here was a man who'd withstood legal questioning on financial affairs and had dozens of expensive lawyers on speed dial. He wasn't going to break down on my watch.

Mentally I stuttered, smashing into the invisible wall.

Bran moved in to save me. "You don't have to be a rocket scientist to see the resemblance, Dad." He held up his hands, his voice suddenly soft and gentle. "I held him. He's adorable and has red hair and the cutest wee eyes."

Michael drew a sharp breath, something almost like a gasp.

Bran's voice went up a notch. "Did you ever see him? Did you ever hold him?"

The mask fell back into place. Michael's features hardened. "Of course not. Why would I?"

Bran stuttered through the reply, shocked. "Because he's your son. My brother."

"Technically he would be your half brother," Michael corrected him. "And what makes you think he's even that?"

I resisted the urge to squirm off the edge of the sofa. We were wandering into the danger zone.

"He looks like you. Like me," Bran said.

Michael huffed. "Bullshit. You looked like a turnip when you were born. Didn't make me think your mother banged a farm wagon."

Bran glanced at me. It was enough to redirect his father to a new target.

"Rebecca." Michael turned away from Bran, zeroing in on me. "What makes you think he's my son?"

"Brayton's a bad liar. So was Molly." I gestured at Bran. "Ask him—I can smell a lie a mile away. It's my job." I kept talking, waiting for signs the story was taking hold. "Let me lay it out for you. You ask for a favor, albeit blackmailing me for it. I trot over to Brayton's office and he spins a tale for me about his wife and a secret lover and a baby." I glared at the older man. "You don't think I've seen someone lie for a friend before? He blusters and blathers and flaps his arms like he's about to take flight. I've seen—" I coughed.

I was about to say crib brothers.

I doubted he'd understand a Felis reference.

"I've seen family lie for family and friends lie for friends. I don't know what you've got on Brayton but he's not as good a liar as you are."

His eyes narrowed. He was buying some of it but not all.

I bit my tongue to keep the urge to tell him it'd taken seconds to scent his paternity on Liam's wee little body. My theory would have to be enough to convince him—one Hanover knowing about the Felis was enough. I couldn't afford to say more and at this point I didn't give a rat's ass if he believed me or not.

I sneaked a glance at Bran. You could bounce a coin off his shoulders, the tension pulling the shirt so tight across his frame.

"But it's all gone belly-up and now the question you have to ask yourself now is, will Brayton take the fall for you? It's one thing to play the jilted lover, the single father sending monthly checks to his son. Quite another to go down on a murder rap for killing Molly Callendar. Maybe he's your best friend, maybe you've got dirt on him. Maybe he owes you a big favor for all those years of making money and squirreling it away in offshore accounts. But is it enough to keep him quiet through a murder trial and prison? Or is he going to jump at the chance to cut a deal and throw you to the wolves to save his own skin?"

Michael's face armor faltered for a second before hardening again. But it was enough to let me see the cracks.

I stayed on the offensive.

"Brayton's going to get one of the best defense lawyers and those men and women don't flinch at digging up bodies to save their clients. She's going to ask questions and check schedules and use all her resources to establish an alibi for Brayton and throw the jury off his trail. Question is, what will the hunters find when they start following the trail back through Hanover Investments?"

Michael cleared his throat. It sounded like a rifle shot in the silence.

I kept going. "I can tell you what they'll find. They'll find whoever was paid to kill Molly. People talk, people gossip—and when there's a baby missing people tend to throw everyone under the bus to keep a child safe. When they find Molly's killer is he going to point the finger at you or at Brayton? Did you pay him enough to keep quiet through a murder and kidnapping rap or is he going to roll for a few years off his sentence?"

I knew Shaw was dead but he didn't. Easier to let him believe Shaw could be found and flipped for a plea deal.

"When they drag the guy you paid into the station, can you count on him not to talk? Follow the money—right back to your office." I smiled and spread my hands. "And if he doesn't spill everything the cops will still be throwing charges around. They'll get one of you for the murder and the other for assisting. They don't care which name goes on the arrest warrant as long as it sticks."

Now it was my turn to circle Michael and Bran, taking soft silent steps around my living room. Michael stared straight ahead while Bran watched me with a mixture of fear and sadness. I was shredding his father in front of him and it had to be done.

I continued. "Now here's how I would play it if I were your lawyer. You might have told the thug to take Liam from Molly and leave her behind but it goes all wrong. Molly puts up a fight and won't give her baby up. She throws something at him, threatens to call the cops, maybe she starts to scream hoping to draw attention to herself. Guy panics and shoots her. Now he's fucked—this isn't what he wanted, what he was paid for. He takes the baby as agreed to but now there's a problem—instead of a kidnapping you've got a dead woman, something you can't make go away with your money. He runs and now things are a lot more complicated. He calls Brayton and now it's spiraling out of control. Brayton didn't sign on for this."

A slight tic appeared on the elder Hanover's left cheek.

I went in for the kill.

"If you go to the cops now and explain what's going on you might save your ass. I know we don't have the death penalty in Canada but a full confession would help Molly's family to begin to move on and allow you to cut some sort of deal," I offered. "A good lawyer can work out a plea deal, maybe a few years on lighter charges and probation. You didn't pull the trigger." I played the final card. "Liam's got to start life without a mother. Let's not make it worse by putting his father in prison."

Michael looked at me intently for a long minute, studying me.

I didn't move.

His eyes locked with mine as he tried to assess how serious I was.

I glared back.

His lips split apart into a wide smile.

He clapped, the hollow sound echoing through the living room.

"Bravo." He glanced at Bran. "She's got a great

imagination. I can only wonder what you two get up to in bed."

Bran scowled, his fists at his side.

"I've read some good detective stories. Sherlock Holmes, the usual. Loved the Spenser series. Can't say the same for the television series—I think Ellery Queen was the best." Michael sauntered back and forth in front of us, hands clasped behind his back. "If I recall correctly in all of these stories the bad guys have a motive, a raison d'être for committing the crime." He paused for effect. "So what's my motive in killing Molly Callendar?"

I winced inside.

"Ah." He wagged a finger at me. "And there's the rub. If I wanted Molly killed I'd have done it before she had the baby, perhaps when she announced she was pregnant."

My stomach twisted into knots. "When Molly told you she was expecting what was the work situation? Did you let her go?"

Michael stopped and shot me a puzzled look. "What sort of man do you think I am?"

I swallowed back my response.

"She worked up until her ninth month, as long as the doctor said she could." He lowered his chin and let out a chuckle. "Brayton told her she could leave whenever she wanted but she asked to finish out her contract. Have to appreciate that sort of work ethic."

I resisted the urge to grin. I loved it when people forgot to compare notes.

Made it easier to catch him/her in a blatant lie.

"So Brayton knew about the pregnancy from the start?" I asked.

Michael nodded.

"Strange. He told me he didn't know anything about Liam until she showed up with him in her arms asking for child support."

Michael's lips slipped into a tight thin line.

It wasn't a smoking gun but it was a definite crack in the wall.

I didn't spend any time enjoying my victory. "Who did you tell about Molly other than Brayton?"

Silence.

"I'm not asking you for your credit card number. I'm asking who else knew Molly was pregnant."

Bran interjected. "Brayton's assistant? His receptionist?"

Michael's nostrils flared. "When she began showing she requested a transfer to another area so she could sit down more. It was the least we could do for her."

I noted he hadn't confessed yet to fathering Liam.

"Where did you send her?" I asked.

"Down to the charities and foundation floors." He gave a little shrug. "Put her to work pushing papers until she left to give birth." Michael smiled. "Even had a goodbye card and collection going around on the floor if I recall correctly. I tucked a twenty into the envelope." His tongue flicked out to wet his lips. "Least I could do."

Bran shook his head. "You bastard."

Michael took three short steps, stopped in front of Bran and slapped him.

Hard. This wasn't a love tap. It was the sort of slap men shot each other over.

I charged toward the two men, skidding to a stop on the hardwood floor inches from them as the reality hit me.

This wasn't something I could fix. This wasn't anything I should be trying to fix.

This was between them.

Father and son.

Betrayer and betrayed.

Bran glared at his father as his right cheek

flared an angry scarlet. He didn't move away, didn't give an inch.

"You bastard," he repeated. "You get her pregnant and then shove her out of your life with a few dollars. Like anyone else who didn't want to play by your rules."

Michael sighed. "Don't be such a drama queen, Bran. If, for the sake of argument, I did have an affair with Molly Callendar and she got pregnant I would have offered to pay for an abortion if she wanted it. And if she didn't I'd support her carrying the child to term and consider making arrangements for both of them to have a good life elsewhere." He pulled out a white handkerchief and mopped his forehead.

Bran's mouth fell open as if someone had stolen his speech.

I couldn't think of anything to say. Nothing that wouldn't involve swear words.

There was a faintly sour taste at the back of my mouth, as if I'd drunk vinegar. I swallowed and licked my lips, trying to identify the source. I inhaled once, a sharp puff that laid down the scents around me.

The overlying sweet scent of male cologne drifted in.

I wrinkled my nose. Bran had given up putting

anything other than deodorant on after our first few days together resulted in major migraines for yours truly. I liked my men au naturel—as much as possible.

This wasn't the cheap stuff you gave your father and grandfather for Father's Day either. This was pricey stuff, the liquid gold selling for hundreds of dollars per tiny bottle.

I located the source and smiled inwardly as I forced the scent out of my mind.

Michael's expensive cologne had turned, the delicately balanced mixture warping and twisting under the sweat and pheromones coming off the businessman.

He was nervous. This situation was far beyond anything he'd dealt with before.

He was terrified.

Michael took a deep breath, the air stuttering out of his lungs as he steadied himself. His eyes closed.

I looked at Bran. He stared at his father intensely as if his gaze alone could pull the confession out.

"Dad," Bran said, his voice starting strong but trailing down into a whisper as it went on. "Tell me the truth. For the love of God, tell me what your part is in all of this. He's my half brother. I need to know."

"Why?" Michael countered. "Why in God's name do you care about any of this?" He swept his hand around, encompassing the two of us. "I asked her to help me out, that's all there is to it. Whether or not this baby is my child is none of your business."

"It is my business." Bran thumped his chest with a closed fist. "Because I held him and I know he's ours. You tell me the truth right now or I'm calling the cops and letting them deal with it." He scowled. "And the press. Let's see how you handle a roomful of hungry reporters. We'll start with the *Inquisitor* and let it go from there."

I held my breath. It was a hell of a bluff.

"I am your son. Liam is your son." Bran pressed on. "For my sake and his, tell me the truth."

"I..." Michael paused and closed his eyes.

I held my breath.

"I asked David Brayton to negotiate the deal with Molly, send her out of the city with the baby and out of my life. I asked him to make sure she'd never return in exchange for being fully provided for, her and the baby." He drew a shallow, strangled breath. "I did not kill Molly. I did not arrange to have her killed." His dark eyes snapped open. "I did not mean for any of this to happen."

I felt dizzy. There was truth in his words. Maybe not what we wanted to hear but it was a confession of sorts.

Michael Hanover was scared—but he wasn't lying.

Bran looked at me. I nodded, so slight only he could read it.

The unspoken question reverberated between us. If Michael Hanover hadn't arranged for Keith Shaw to kill Molly Callendar and kidnap Liam—who did?

"Speaking of this baby…where is he?" Michael blustered. "You said you saw him, held him." He spun around on Bran, eyes blazing as he zeroed in on his son. Fear twisted to anger in a split second, taking over. "But you never met her. You never knew she existed until this entire damned thing got started. So you've seen Liam after the murder, after she was killed."

Michael sounded proud as if he'd finished a tough word puzzle. "So where is he?" His voice rose into attack mode, the tone he used with his underlings and his son. "Where is Liam?"

Bran didn't flinch.

I cleared my throat.

Michael turned away from his son. "Where is he?"

"Safe," I replied. "Until we figure this whole thing out."

He glared at me. "With who?"

"He's safe," I repeated. "And he's not going anywhere until Bran and I decide it's time to bring him back."

Michael looked at me, sizing me up. I wasn't one of his employees who would bob and grovel to stay in his good graces. I didn't pull a paycheck from any of his companies and I sure as hell wasn't a recipient of any of his charities.

"I could call the police. Tell them you've got the baby," Michael threatened.

I rolled my shoulders back. "You could. But we'll have to start talking about all those other little nasty details." I cocked my head to one side. "You want to start this roller-coaster ride right now?"

He turned back to Bran. "Son…" he started.

"No."

Michael peered at his son. "You could at least let me finish my sentence."

"I know what you're going to say and I'm saying no." He sliced the air from side to side with his right hand. "I'm not going to tell you where Liam is so you can send your flunkies to get him. I'm not going to make her tell you either."

Bran looked at me and I almost melted. The love and respect rushing from him almost knocked me off my feet. It didn't matter what happened with his father. He'd already chosen a side and it was beside me.

"I didn't kill Molly Callendar," Michael repeated. "What sort of person do you think I am?" He directed this at Bran. "What sort of person kills an ex-lover in this day and age?"

"You'd be surprised. I see it on the news every day." I glanced at Jazz, who was peeking at us from the top of the stairs. Her little red nose twitched as she watched us. The tip of her long white tail wove around her feet. "Usually before the weather forecast as they go to jail for a long, long time."

Michael's nostrils flared.

I continued my questioning. "But if it wasn't you or Brayton, then who? Someone looking for payback, someone trying to destroy your reputation? You've got to have some idea of who else would want to do something as horrible as this." I couldn't help pricking him with that needle—his pride. "Because when this breaks, and it will, your name won't be worth the ink to write it with."

Michael lifted his head. "You'd be surprised what the business world will tolerate. Has tolerated." A smile tugged at his lips as if we'd missed a private joke. "I won't lie. I've made plenty of enemies. But I can't see any of them going to this degree to get back at me." He gave an angry shake of his head. "Not when there's a child involved."

"Was your affair with Callendar well-known? Aside from Brayton, did anyone else in the office know about you two?" I found myself leaning forward against the mental battering from Michael Hanover. The man dominated a room as much as Jess, if not more. "Secretaries, personal assistants, limo drivers?"

He gave a halfhearted shrug. "People in our world tend to see what they're told to see—nothing else." His lips curled into a wry smile. "You write the check, you write the reality."

I wasn't one to actively hate anyone but Michael Hanover was beginning to work his way up the ladder.

"We didn't fool around in the office. I knew better. Met in hotel rooms away from her apartment, used private transportation, the usual options open to men in this type of situation." He eyed Bran. "I know how to keep secrets. She learned how to. Molly knew there was nothing more to our relationship than pure physical attraction. I never promised her marriage or anything more than total carnal satisfaction." A wolfish leer appeared. "But I'm sure you know about that, son."

He looked at me. "Did he tell you about all the women he screwed before you crawled into his bed? All the debauched games he used to play? The man's a chip off the old block."

I fought back the urge to yawn. I wasn't going to be diverted from the matter at hand. A quick glance at Bran confirmed he wasn't falling for it either.

Bran pressed his lips together, showing the strain this questioning was putting on him. He wasn't going to rise to his father's baiting to get away from the topic at hand. But I could tell he was getting tired and annoyed and about to lose his temper in a horrible explosion of anger.

I wanted to hug Bran, tell him everything was going to be okay.

I couldn't lie. Everything was definitely not going to be okay, not for a long, long while.

Silence wrapped around us like a death shroud, sucking the energy away.

"Enough." I broke the standoff and stepped forward, taking the attention away from Bran. I dug out my cell phone and brought up the image of Shaw's license. I shoved it in Michael's face. "Do you know this man? Have you ever seen him before?"

Michael peered at the standard ugly government-issue image. "Can't say that I do." He swallowed hard. His tongue darted out, wetting his lips as he studied the picture. "Is he the one who killed Molly?" The sadness in his voice startled me, the sense of loss almost overwhelming his steely confidence.

It was the first sign of honest emotion I'd seen in the man since we'd met. The wavering in his voice, the sudden tenderness when he said her name, it showed the real Michael Hanover under all the smoke and mirrors.

"We think so." I glanced toward the kitchen, desperately needing a drink. The Brown Betty held cold tea but I knew we had more beer in the refrigerator.

Unfortunately this wasn't the right time for a good drunk. That'd come later.

I continued digging. "Do you have a specific nemesis, business or personal, someone who would do something like this? A reporter sniffing around for a story, a dubious business connection your radar told you would be trouble. A former friend out for revenge, a former lover."

Michael stood for a minute in thought, his forehead creased with worry.

I stole a glance at Bran, who was staring at the floor.

"No," Michael finally confessed. "Don't get me wrong. I've had my share of dealings bordering on illegal." His halfhearted smirk pissed me off. "On the razor's edge and barely this side of the law. But not enough to warrant this sort of response. Besides, an illegitimate child isn't big news these days. Maybe ten, twenty years ago it'd break your reputation. Now it's a footnote at the bottom of the newspaper, a commentary in the financial section." He spread his hands. "No offense but they'd have to try harder to wipe me out. Bigger fish to fry and so forth. It'd be a blip on the business radar if it'd show up at all. After all, it's only a baby."

I couldn't figure Michael Hanover out. His tone fluctuated back and forth between his love for Molly and his disdain for Liam and vice versa. Whatever else the man might be, he rode the emotional hurricane on a minute-to-minute basis.

"It's my brother," Bran repeated.

"Your half brother. Remember that."

I winced inside. Words were power and whatever happened here wouldn't be easily forgotten by either side.

Bran crossed his arms in front of him. "You don't tell me what to remember. Okay let's take this from the top. If we believe you—" Bran held up a finger, forestalling any reply from his father. "If we believe you didn't have her killed, who did?"

Michael shrugged. "I don't particularly care if you believe me or not. The fact is I didn't kill Molly or have her killed. And if you had any proof to the contrary I'm sure your fine friend on the police force would have already arrested me or, at the least, taken me in for further questioning."

I must have made some sort of sound, because Michael stared at me.

"Oh, yes," he purred. "Don't forget I've already been to the station and spoken to your friend Detective Attersley. I told him about how I asked you to do this favor for me—a little thing considering you're sleeping with my son and trying to move up in the world."

Michael pointed at me. "I was part of your damned alibi, Rebecca. I told them about sending you to Brayton and took you off the suspect list. I didn't like it and my lawyers told me not to do it but I figured it was the right thing to do.

Keep your name clean." He glanced over at his son. "But I could call them back. I could weave a different tale if I wanted to. Tell them about the baby being your half brother and lay the foundation for them to suspect you and Rebecca here." A sneer touched his lips. "Wouldn't it be a story for the *Inquisitor*—eh, son? About how you found out Liam was your half brother and you arranged for him to be kidnapped and killed to keep him from his part of the Hanover fortune?"

I resisted the urge to punch him in the face.

The balls would be a much better target.

I drew back, ready to deliver the mother of all kicks to the family jewels, when a breeze brought me more than Michael's nervous sweat and Bran's natural musk.

Another scent—one I'd recognize anywhere.

TEN

A SOFT SOUND came from behind us, accompanied by a sickening-sweet whiff of perfume. I closed my eyes and berated myself for not locking the front door.

"What about the Hanover fortune?"

Bernadette Hanover stood in the doorway.

At the back of my mind came the quiet fact I'd been taught on the farm—always have an exit strategy. I'd instinctively left the front door open for a quick exit in case things got ugly.

Except now things were about to get very, very messy. *Exploding cans of spaghetti in a pure-white room* messy.

She wore a long black coat over her overpriced jeans, a wisp of white ruffle sticking out at her neck. A small black handbag swung from her left elbow.

"What about the fortune?" she repeated.

Michael crossed the room with a handful of long, quick strides to stand in front of her. He took hold of her arms as if she were a porcelain doll teetering on the edge of a cliff.

"You shouldn't be here. How did you get here?"

"I asked Andrea where you were. She said you were meeting with Bran." She smiled, artificially whitened teeth almost blinding me. "I called your driver and he told me the address."

"Ah. Yes." Michael turned toward Bran and me. "We were just talking about…ah…" His face went blank.

He might have been a practiced liar but not a good one when it came to improvising excuses for discussing murder.

I stepped in, seeing his confusion—not to rescue him but to try to minimize the damage from friendly fire.

"We were talking about making a donation to help find the missing child. You remember when we met at the police station?" I tried to make my tone light, fluffy like cotton candy. "The AMBER Alert and all."

Bernadette frowned for a second and looked up to one side, accessing her memory file. "Yes, I remember. Horrible thing." She pushed by Michael and approached me, ignoring her husband. "A reward would be a great idea." Her voice slipped from soft putty to hardened steel. "But that's not what you were talking about."

I looked at Bran, not sure how to handle this.

"Don't worry about it." Michael stepped up beside her. "I thought you'd be at the board meeting and I didn't want to bother you." He touched her arm. "Now that you're here, let's go out to a nice café and relax; let these two crazy kids have some time together. I can call Armando's and get us a table for dinner."

Bernadette looked at him. "I'm fine, dear." The coolness in her words screamed frostbite. "Do you know how boring those meetings are?"

Michael grinned. "I know. But you enjoy helping out people." He looked at Bran. "We all do." The hardness in his words warned his son to not reveal anything, to leave it to him.

I wasn't sure if it was the best option. From where I stood Michael had made nothing but bad decisions from the start where Molly Callendar was involved.

The sweat poured off the elder Hanover's forehead, dripping from the edge of his nose. The sour smell increased to the point of threatening to choke me out.

"I don't. Not anymore." Bernadette took a few steps away from her husband. "Do you know what goes on at those meetings? They're nothing but gossip central. Women nattering about this and that, about what's happening with their husbands, their boyfriends." She stared at Michael. "Their husbands' lovers."

Both men moved toward her at once. I hung back, unsure what to do. I'd seen husband/wife confrontations before in this very place, in my office usually due to something I'd discovered on the urging of one or the other. Usually I was able to push one party out the door with the threat of calling the police or, if all else failed, showing off my Taser.

But this was family and I didn't know what to say or do.

Being neutral didn't seem to be enough.

"What are you talking about?" Michael tried to bluff, the pasted-on smile beginning to weaken around the edges.

Bernadette's face hardened into a scowl, the words grinding through clenched teeth. "I know about you and Molly. And all the others." She looked at Bran, her deep blue eyes wide and sad. "If I had a dime for every woman your father's screwed I'd be independently wealthy."

Despite the situation I choked back a laugh.

"She was just a diversion, a flavor of the

month." Michael walked toward her, his arms outstretched. "It wasn't anything serious."

"They never are." She glanced over Michael's shoulder. "You deal with this sort of stuff all the time, Rebecca. Do men ever just have one affair?"

I swallowed hard. This was not the conversation I wanted to have with my possible in-laws.

"It depends on the relationship between the husband and wife." I fumbled through the verbal minefield. "Some men regret having an affair and spend the rest of their lives making up for it. Some women never forgive them no matter what they say or do." I tried hard not to look at Michael. "Some men can't handle a monogamous relationship, period."

"And some women put up with it—" Bernadette waved a hand in front of her as if brushing away a fly "—because of the perks, to be rather crude. Dip your wick anywhere you want but keep the bills paid." Her voice dropped a level. "And never, never look over the credit card bills and ask what this charge or that charge was for."

"Bernadette..." Michael's voice shifted to low and threatening. "Let's go home and discuss this over a drink or two. We don't need to bring Bran into this."

"Yes, yes, we do." She smiled at Bran. "You

grew up to be a smart man." There was a waver in her voice, scratching nails across my inner chalkboard.

Bran gave me a sideways glance before nodding. "Yes, Mom. I'm pretty smart."

"Smarter than your father." She looked at me for a second before returning her attention to Bran. "At least you've been careful. You don't have any little bastards out there waiting to come knocking on our front door years from now to demand their inheritance."

We all froze in place.

Michael stayed silent.

Bran took short, measured breaths.

A stabbing pain erupted behind my left eye.

"A child, Michael." The sharp reprimand in her voice reminded me of Jess. "You idiot. I knew you were screwing around on me, but a child? What were you thinking? Haven't you ever heard of a condom?" She brushed one hand across her face as if pushing a curtain aside. "You haven't touched me in years and I never complained once even though you know I wanted another child."

She shook her head. "You sent her down to the charity floor where everyone could see her, see the results of your infidelity." Her voice broke on the last word, the sob tearing down the last barrier. "She complained about having to take off her ankle bracelet because of the swelling. The silly bitch showed it to a coworker as I was walking by."

Bernadette took a deep breath before continuing. "She told her friend it was from a weekend trip, a visit to a little boutique in Montreal. Les Deux Amant. I may not be a private investigator but I'm not stupid. She couldn't afford to go there, not on a temp's salary. And she sure as hell couldn't afford an ankle bracelet from an exclusive boutique you've taken me to a handful of times. I checked the credit card receipts and there it was, bright as day." Her voice rose. "When I heard she'd transferred in from Brayton's office I knew you were involved—Brayton's an idiot at the best of times and wouldn't buy jewelry for his own wife, much less a mistress."

The headache blossomed into a full-fledged migraine with a nausea chaser.

Michael Hanover had sent Molly Callendar to her doom with a simple office transfer.

Bran stepped between his parents, caught between the pair. He lifted both hands, palms out between the two as if he could raise a wall between them with his mind.

"It was an accident," Michael answered calmly.

"She was going to leave us alone, take the child and go as far away as she could. It was the best solution under the circumstances."

Bernadette gave a dainty snort.

"The best under the circumstances. Do you have any idea what that means?"

A single tear broke free and ran down her left cheek. The streak of dark mascara reminded me of war paint. "Do you know how hard I work to keep this company going? All the damned glad-handing, all the stupid board meetings, all the bloody charity balls and dinners and crap I have to deal with while you prance off with your business buddies to play golf and smoke cigars?"

Michael shook his head, frowning. "I don't understand."

"The best solution would have been for you to get legal custody from her, use the legal resources at our disposal and take the child." Bernadette shook her head. "That child has your blood, Hanover blood. Despite your moral failings he deserves a better life than being raised in a trailer park by some trashy woman who'll probably end up popping out baby after baby with anyone who wanders by. He deserves the same sort of upbringing our son received."

Bran blinked. "Like me?"

I moved closer to Bran. His right hand moved toward me, finding and grabbing on to me like a drowning man to a life preserver.

"You had the best." Bernadette looked at him. "You had the private tutors, the proper schools and the best university. Everything you deserved."

"Because of my name," Bran said.

"Because of the Hanover name," Bernadette corrected him. She turned her attention back to Michael. "I was not about to let this baby roam through the public school system and become another dropout, another failed statistic of the educational system." She shuddered. "What sort of man would he become? What sort of future would he have with that sort of handicapped start to life?"

I knew the truth but had to say it out loud. "You did it. You arranged for Molly Callendar to be killed."

Bernadette nodded as if I'd asked her if she liked milk or cream with her coffee. There was no remorse in her eyes and more than a little crazy leaking out.

"It was the only thing to do. I couldn't allow Michael to let this little baby go off into the world. A check arriving every few months for his mother to spend on cigarettes and beer? What could that silly bitch offer him?"

"She was his mother," I replied.

Bernadette shrugged. "An accident of genetics." She eyed Michael. "Your father and grandfather worked hard to make Hanover Investments a success; my family gave you what you wanted to move to the next level, including me. I couldn't let you throw it all away with an uneducated, untrained illegitimate child showing up in a few decades to take it from us."

"You followed me to the hotel. Or to be more precise your paid killer did." I spoke calmly and slowly as if to a child. I wasn't sure where to go with this or what to do. The situation was spinning out of control and all I could do was hang on for the ride.

"I knew Michael was talking to you about something sleazy, something your type would be dealing in." Her upper lip curled away from brilliant white teeth. "It didn't take a genius to figure out he wanted you to help Brayton finish out this little charade. It was easy to have someone follow you and find the woman." She tilted her head to one side. "You're not so bright when it comes down to it."

I ignored the slight. "How did you find someone to do the job?"

"If you give to enough charities you can always

find someone willing to take out the garbage." She giggled. "He was shocked at first but we got down to negotiations soon enough."

"Keith Shaw," I added. "You met him when you were at Second Chance, Second Life. He was on parole for murder and you knew he'd be easy to buy." I knew now why I'd had an odd feeling on the street, the feeling of being watched. "You told him to follow me the second I left the offices and he tracked me to the hotel and Molly's room."

Bernadette glared at me. "You're not as incompetent as you look."

Her right hand ducked inside the purse and returned with a small silver-plated automatic, a ladies' weapon. She swung her arm out to one side, sweeping it around. "Now all of you listen to me." Her voice hardened.

I took a deep breath. This was going from bad to worse to deadly at warp speed.

ELEVEN

I STUDIED THE weapon. It was a small caliber, most likely a .22. It wasn't likely to kill you unless you placed a lucky shot right into the head or a vital organ. But a bullet was a bullet and I'd rather no one got shot in my house today.

Michael glared at her. "What are you doing?"

I winced at his tone. If he was hoping to intimidate her into giving up her weapon and her advantage it wasn't going to happen. This was a woman who'd gleefully ordered the death of another human being without any sign of remorse—she wasn't going to weep because her hubby grew a pair.

"Keeping our future secure." She waved the light weapon around. "The baby's better off with me, with us. We'll give him everything he needs, everything he deserves."

"So you're going to show up with Liam at the next charity ball?" I brought her attention back to me, keeping my eye on where the pistol was pointed. "How are you going to explain him away?" I gestured at her slim form. "You don't look pregnant. Going to be tough explaining a year-old child away as a newborn if you're planning the 'taking a year abroad for my health' scenario and returning with him in your arms."

She let out an annoyed sigh. "Don't be an idiot. It's a classic scenario. A distant relative's child brought to us after an unfortunate accident overseas. We adopt the baby as our own and no one cares as long as the proper paperwork gets filed. If you have enough money you can make anything happen." Her warped smile grated on my eyes. "Hanover Investments will have a future."

"What?" Bran interrupted. "What about me?" His grip tightened on my fingers.

"You're still our son. But you've never shown any interest in the business. This fascination with journalism—we thought you'd outgrow it in time and consider your responsibilities to us, to your heritage."

I frowned. We were slipping down the rabbit hole fast and furiously. "He's a respected journalist. What do you want from him?"

Bernadette smiled. "I wanted him to step up and be a man, claim his place. Instead he persists in writing these stories for pennies, scrabbling out a living when he could be working beside his father."

"I like what I'm doing. It's my life," Bran replied.

"But you could do so much better," Bernadette whined. The pistol waved in my direction. "You just need to expand your vision." Her upper lip curled up. "If you came back to the family business you couldn't bring her to the dances, to the parties. The Knights have a lovely daughter and the Bentlesons have two. Good families, good reputations. They'd kill to marry into the Hanover line."

I bit my tongue at the unfortunate phrasing.

"But I don't want to," Bran interrupted. He raised our entwined hands. "I love her."

"Love," Bernadette scoffed. "Love won't keep a roof over your head or food on the table. Money does. You should know that. You're living in the condo, the one we bought. You're cashing those monthly checks. So don't tell me how important love is to you when you have your fingers in your father's pocket."

My pulse hammered in my ears. I couldn't even begin to imagine what Bran was thinking, what he was going through. Within the last twenty-four hours he'd discovered his father was an adulterer and his mother was a murderess, along with the existence of a half brother. I wondered why his head hadn't exploded.

To say this was a lose-lose situation was a major understatement. The least that could come out of this was someone going to prison for a long time. The worse would be more dead bodies. Judging from the wild look in Bernadette's eyes it was a viable possibility.

Her hand shook, not from the weight of the tiny weapon. Her master plan was unraveling and I wasn't sure how far she'd go to keep it alive. I kept watching the pistol barrel as it jumped up and down, left and right on her emotional wild ride.

I might be able to get out of the way of a bullet with my Felis reflexes but I knew Bran wouldn't and I was darned sure Michael couldn't.

"So you hired Keith Shaw to follow me to the hotel and find Molly Callendar. You told him to kill her and take the baby back to his own hotel room until you could meet him." I kept talking, hoping to find some way to bring her back to earth and ground her in reality. Maybe if she realized the depth of what she'd done, the enormity of her bad decisions, she might come around and let us settle this as best we could.

She stared at me.

I didn't see a high-society woman trying to do what she thought was best for her family.

All I saw was madness.

My heart went into overdrive.

Any hunter will tell you the most dangerous animal isn't necessarily the one that's injured or cornered.

The rabid ones are right up there, because when you don't fear anything you might do anything.

I continued talking, trying to predict her next move. "He sat there in his dirty, grungy little hotel room waiting for your phone call to arrange to drop off the baby or for you to show up and finish the deal."

The small pistol moved between the three of us, shifting targets. "The woman left her apartment weeks ago, not long after the baby was born. I didn't know where she was." She scowled at Michael. "She didn't leave anything behind, nothing to track her with."

Michael didn't say anything.

"I paid for her parents to be followed. I figured they'd go visit their daughter at least once before she left town. Nothing." The spittle flew from her lips. "Damned woman thought she had it all figured out—don't let anyone know where you're going, and cover your tracks. I had nothing and Shaw was waiting."

Her eyes tracked to her husband. "Until we had dinner and you asked to talk to Rebecca alone. I knew you didn't like her any more than I did. I told Shaw to be there when you had your meeting with her and she trotted off like a good little courier girl to go to where the bitch was holed up." Her voice broke. "Nice fucking hotel. Keeping your whore in high style."

Bran's grip tightened.

"I told Shaw to follow Rebecca and as soon as she was gone to take care of the woman. I knew the cops would look at Brayton. As far as I can tell they still are. The sole ones who know who Liam is are right here. I went to the hotel where Shaw agreed to meet me and saw you walking in, you and Rebecca with some other woman. I waited until I thought it was safe and went to Shaw's room. He was dead and the baby gone." The edges of her mouth twitched. "Killing Shaw saved me a bit of cash—I assumed he'd ask for more when he had the baby in hand. Thank you for that much." The icy stare returned. "But that means you've got Liam. Where is he?"

The pistol swept the room, her gaze following.

I anticipated her next move. "He's not here.

He's with a friend. Safe and sound and out of danger." Now it was my turn to sound menacing. "From both of you."

"Shaw struck me as a pretty tough character. How did you get the jump on him, stab him like that?" Fear entered her voice for the first time since I'd met her.

My stomach jumped at the memory of Shaw's dead body. But this wasn't the time or place to get sensitive about death.

I curled up my fingers, squeezing them into a fist. "What do you think?" I sounded as nasty as I dared, given the circumstances. If she were afraid of Bran and myself so much the better.

I left out the part where it was Jess who delivered the killing blow, not myself. The devil might be in the details but right now the devil pointed a pistol.

"He was smothering Liam," Bran offered by way of explanation. "We had to do something to save the baby."

"What? Why would he do that?" The pistol wavered in her grip, enough to tempt me. I might make it across the floor to knock the gun free but I wasn't willing to play those odds with Bran's life.

"The asshole was freaking out because we found him," Bran growled. I sensed the tension in his voice, in the way he held himself. He couldn't take much more of this. "He was killing Liam. Drop the gun, Mom. Drop the gun and we'll sit down and talk about this."

"We'll do no such thing. We'll call the fucking cops," Michael snapped.

Bernadette's stare slashed the air around her husband. "You'd hand me over to the police?" The disbelief in her voice rose. "You bastard. You go around screwing anything with a vagina for decades and now I'm the bad guy?"

I felt sorry for her, despite the situation. In a society where men were considered studs and women whores if they took multiple lovers I couldn't help but agree with Bernadette on one level.

That, however, wasn't the level where killing and kidnapping were acceptable actions.

"Put the gun down and we'll talk," Bran repeated. He shot his father a warning glance—*don't piss off the woman with the weapon.*

Michael Hanover might be a business genius but you could put everything he knew about women in a thimble and have room left for more.

Michael opened his mouth as if to respond to Bernadette's accusations and then closed it.

It might have been his best decision in days.

“Put the gun down, Mom. Please.”

Bernadette looked at him as if he’d asked for a second serving of pie. “You don’t understand. I get it—you’ve been writing your little stories and doing your little trips around the country. I understand how you don’t get what I’m talking about.” She drew a ragged breath as if she was running a marathon. “When I married your father your grandfather was adamant about us keeping the family strong, keeping the business strong. We can’t let just anyone take over the family business. We need to guide them, nurture them.” She tilted her head toward Michael. “All of his hard work can’t be wasted on someone who won’t know what to do with it. We need a Hanover at the helm, someone to carry the business into the future.” She sneered at her husband. “If Bran decides not to take it, who will? Your cousin Eric? The idiot who keeps getting caught cheating on his income tax?”

“What, you’re going to take the kid and spend twenty years raising him to take over the business?” Michael snapped. “That’s insane.”

I bit the inside of my cheek. He wasn’t helping.

“If Bran doesn’t take it, then who?” Bernadette replied.

Bran shook his head. “There’s plenty of good

friends, good relatives you can hand it over to." His eyes narrowed. "I'm not going to take a business steeped in blood."

She shook her head. "I'm tired of this. I want the baby and I want him now." Bernadette directed her comments to me, ignoring her husband and son. "You call whoever has him and tell him to bring the baby here."

"No," I replied.

The acidic sting tore at my senses as if I'd inhaled a full shot of lemon juice. I spun around, yanking my hand free from Bran's grasp.

Bran stared at me.

Michael squinted, looking past me at his wife.

She looked down at the barrel of the pistol with a confused expression as if it'd jumped up and bit her.

A light puff of smoke rose from the tip.

TWELVE

MY LEFT ARM itched.

The itch turned warm, burning hot.

I looked down to see the ragged three-inch gash in my skin, just below the shoulder. It oozed as the jagged pain shot up my arm.

"Reb!" Bran caught me as I fell to the ground.

"Where is the baby?" Bernadette asked, her voice trembling.

"You bitch," Bran cried as he cradled me in his arms. I babbled something incoherent.

"You will not talk to me like that. I am your mother." She waved the pistol again. "Where is the baby?"

"With a friend," Bran answered.

Michael stood helpless to one side, paralyzed.

I gasped, clawing at Bran's arms. He looked down at me.

"You're going to be okay," he murmured.

"No I won't," I whispered.

The world around me shifted and warped, changing enough to both scare and thrill me.

I was Changing.

The burning in my arm dimmed as my senses came into full focus. I could smell Bernadette's fear, hear the loud pounding of her heart. Michael's sweat dripping off him like small grenades, exploding when they hit the hardwood floor.

My claws shot out, digging into Bran's duster. The sharp edges tangled in the dark leather and pulled him closer.

Bran pulled me close, hiding me as best he could from his parents.

I drew in short huffs. I couldn't afford to Change—not here, not now.

"Stop it," Bran whispered, lips pressed to my ear. "You know how to do it." His words took on a commanding, dominating tone. "Stop it."

I squeezed my eyes shut, trying to push away the overwhelming rush of information attacking my senses.

The irony didn't escape me. After being unable to Change at will for decades I was now trying to stop myself from Changing. The secret I'd had to keep from his parents was right in front of them if Bran shifted his position even a few inches to either side.

Bran sucked in his breath over clenched teeth. I knew what he was seeing—blond fur covering my face with dark brown horizontal streaks. My mother had once called them war paint, invoking a long speech from my father about political correctness.

The last time he'd seen me Changed he'd cut and run.

This time it was different. His eyes were soft, tears threatening to break free as he gazed at me.

"Damn, you're beautiful," Bran murmured.

I didn't know whether to laugh or cry. Instead I burrowed into his chest.

The pounding in my ears began slowing as I forced myself to draw long, deep breaths. All I needed to do was take control again.

I might as well be trying to control a runaway train with a shoelace held in my teeth.

"What's wrong with her?" Bernadette snapped.

"She's in shock," Bran responded. "You shot her." He swept his duster over my shoulders as I ducked my head down.

The thick musk of alpha male swallowed me up, cutting out some of the outside influences smashing into my senses. It was a blessing and a curse, the shredding pain in my arm mixing with the inherent urge to protect my mate and lash out at those who had hurt me, hurt us.

I ran through mental exercises I hadn't thought about for years, going back to the start to stop the Change. A powerful Felis like Jess could Change back and forth in seconds.

I might take a wee bit longer.

"Where's the baby?" Bernadette repeated. "Get me the baby and you can call the ambulance, take her to get help."

Michael's voice cut through the pain. "Bernie—what are you doing?" The sadness in his voice tore at my heart. "Why are you doing this?"

"I'll call her," Bran said, surprisingly calm. "I need to get my phone out of my pocket. Don't shoot me."

"Smart-ass," Bernadette shot back. "She'll live. Just get me the baby."

I suppressed a growl.

He shifted behind me and pressed his knee against my side, holding me in his shadow. "Keep chilling," he murmured. "I got this."

His right hand slipped into a pocket and extracted the cell phone. He held it up over us.

My arm burned, the pulsing running from my fingertips right into my shoulder and back.

"Put it on speakerphone," Bernadette barked. "No funny stuff. I don't trust you." She gave a light giggle, the phony type reserved for the public. "No offense."

"None taken." Bran leaned in. "What's Jess's number?"

I choked the numbers out between clenched teeth. I peered at my arm trying to see the jagged tear but couldn't.

It was, in all likelihood, a good thing. Between trying to control the Change and being in shock I was pretty well mentally screwed right now.

Jess answered on the first ring. "Reb. What's happening?"

"Jessica. It's Brandon." His tone was clipped and professional. "Sorry to bother you but Rebecca and I wondered if you could bring Liam over? We've decided to take care of him ourselves and take him off your hands." He looked down at me. "You know Rebecca's always been a soft touch for babies."

She didn't miss a beat. "Sure. Everything okay with Rebecca? Can I talk to her?"

"No," I heard Bernadette whisper. "No talking."

I wasn't going to argue with her. I was in no condition to verbally joust with anyone.

"She's having a bit of an allergic reaction right now to Jazz. You know, the usual. Too wheezy to chat. Took her meds, but I'm afraid she's going to cough up a hairball."

"Tell her to stay calm. I'm on my way." The phone line went dead.

"Where is she?" Bernadette asked.

"I don't know," Bran admitted. "She's in the city with friends. I don't know how long it'll take for her to get here." He glanced down at me. "She'll get here soon enough."

I wasn't sure if it was going to be a good thing or not. If I knew Jess she wasn't going to hand Liam over to a pistol-packing insane woman without the mother of all catfights.

"Better hope she doesn't take too long," Bernadette snarled. She waved the pistol at us. "How badly is she hurt?"

Bran smiled in spite of the situation and brushed his lips over the top of my ear. "She's good for now."

I held my breath, fighting back the urge to toss him off and break free. My claws dug into the floor and scratched the varnish. My arm hurt and I wanted to return the favor with interest.

"Breathe, Reb," Bran said, low and soft. "Take control. I know you can do it."

I glared at him through Felis eyes. I could smell him, all of him, from the addictive musk he always gave off to the sweet, tangy sweat under his shirt that never failed to arouse me.

I wanted to rip it off him and have him right there, roar my domination over my mate and to hell with a simple injury.

Right after I shredded his parents into bloody meat ribbons.

"Reb." The warning tone reminded me of Ruth, chastising me after a temper tantrum. "Take it down. Take back control."

I inhaled and tried to calm down despite the spikes of pain in my arm. I couldn't help him like this, I couldn't help Jess and I sure as hell couldn't help Liam. After what seemed like a lifetime I felt the edges start to disappear, my enhanced senses slowing down and diminishing as the cold, drab world I was used to returned. My claws receded and slipped back under my skin with a stab of pain, taking my mind for the second off the angry gash in my upper arm.

I wasn't sure whether to be relieved or heartbroken. After losing my ability to Change at fifteen I'd never expected to get it back. Now it'd shown up at the worst time possible and I had to banish it, put it back in the box and slam the lid.

I didn't know if I'd be able to unlock it ever again.

"Where did you get that?" Michael snapped. "It's not one of mine."

"You don't remember, darling?" Bernadette purred. "You bought it for me a few years ago at some silly charity auction to support the police. A dainty lady's weapon—I believe that's how it was described."

Michael made a noise, something between a grumble and a gargle.

"Isn't it darling?" she asked.

Bran gave me a nod. "Good. Good."

I could feel the Change drifting away, the pain of losing it almost as bad as the gunshot.

The rage dribbled away and I felt the pain surge in my arm, the natural painkillers dying with my anger.

I looked at my hands. The claws were gone with only thin bloody slits showing I'd ever been normal, ever been Felis.

I felt like crying.

Bran kissed my forehead again. "Good to have you back," he whispered. "Can you stand?"

"Watch me." I pushed him off and levered myself with my good arm to get to my feet.

Bernadette glared at me as I staggered upright. "You're a tough one. Not much of a crier."

Michael Hanover gave me a curious look. Maybe he saw something, maybe not.

Right now it was the least of my worries. Jess was going to be walking into an ambush with Liam in her arms.

I studied Bernadette. She rocked from side to side, the pasted-on smile fraying at the edges. This was beyond what she'd imagined what would happen when she first saw Molly Callendar, pregnant with her husband's child, sitting at a desk stuffing envelopes.

"You were going to kill Shaw, weren't you?"

She gave me a sly look. "Maybe."

"Come on." I motioned at the pistol. "You couldn't afford to have anyone know the truth—you were going to shoot him as soon as you got into the hotel room."

She shrugged. "I considered it. Depending on how bitchy Shaw got and if he got too greedy."

"Ever think about how all this might affect Liam?" I was trying to draw her attention away from the two men. "Seeing his mother gunned down in front of him?"

"He won't remember anything," Bernadette answered. "All he'll know is his mother loves him and he's got a wonderful heritage to grow into."

"His mother's dead," I replied.

Her lips tightened. She glared at me.

"What are you going to do when Jess gets here? Kill her, kill me, kill all of us?" My arm was numb. I wasn't going to be able to go much longer on guts and adrenaline.

Bernadette gave me the skunk eye. "There's no need for further violence. Once we get the baby we'll be on our way."

"We who? Way to where?" Michael asked. "Where do you think we're going to go?" His voice rose to a shout. "You killed Molly."

She shook her head. "Shaw killed the woman. Bran and Rebecca killed Shaw. There's nothing to connect us to the crime. We leave here, get on the private jet and go on our merry way to raise our new child."

"And us?" Bran asked.

Bernadette continued. "You shut up and stay quiet about all of this. You're already in it deep with killing Shaw; you'll have as much to lose by speaking up as we do."

"Bernie..." Michael took a step toward her. "We can't do this."

"Sure we can. All it takes is a little money to

hide everything." She pointed at the open door. "The police have nothing to link me with Shaw other than wild theories and conjecture." She smiled. "David Brayton won't talk and if he does no one will believe him. All the evidence points to Brayton and to Brayton alone."

"A paternity test will prove Liam's not his child," Michael said. "And what about Shaw? They're going to find him at some point."

Bernadette let out an exasperated sigh. "Who's going to make the connection between Shaw and Brayton? And who's going to point the finger at us?" She began to speak louder and faster. "And who's going to ask for a DNA test? I am getting tired of this. We'll make it all go away. We have the money and we have the power." She waved the pistol in the air.

I couldn't fault her logic. Unless someone had the bright idea of doing a paternity test with Liam and Michael there'd be no reason to suspect Bernadette. Brayton would be the only one who could or would bring his friend into the story and I wasn't sure if he'd crack under Attersley's interrogation or not. Even if he confessed it'd take a lot to hook this on to Michael Hanover, much less his wife. If she'd covered her tracks with Shaw there'd be no easy evidence linking her to any of this. It looked suspicious having him at one of the Hanover charities but a good lawyer would tear it to shreds with a wide smile and testimony on how many other people were helped by the same program.

For my part I couldn't testify to anything other than I'd run the package around and found Molly's body. Revealing Liam's parentage would reveal the Felis and that wasn't an option.

Jess sure as hell would go to ground before going into a courtroom and saying she clawed Shaw to death to save Liam's life. Not because she regretted it but because it violated our secrecy and would open a whole new world of fear and persecution for our Felis family. She'd go to jail or die before giving up the secret.

We were, collectively and individually, screwed.

"No." Michael Hanover walked toward her, his right hand outstretched. "This ends now, Bernie. Give me the pistol and I'll call Danny. He'll meet us at the police station." He whispered, "Let's stop this now before someone else gets hurt."

She shook her head like a petulant child. "I'm not going to let this family be destroyed because you can't keep your dick in your pants. You started all this with letting her become pregnant. Don't you dare think you can start calling the shots now."

I couldn't help grinning at the last few words despite my pain.

"All this," Bran snarled, "all this death and destruction because Dad screwed up?" He took a step closer. "You're both so fucking messed up." He lifted his fists, visibly shaking with anger. "So fucking messed up."

"Do not use that language with me. All families have secrets, Brandon. Some have small white lies that choke the life out of people, some have larger ones that suck you dry over time. But the good ones know the net worth of keeping them." Bernadette giggled, an almost maniacal sound. "I'm sure Rebecca knows that."

I froze.

"What are you talking about?" I forced the words out.

"I saw the investigator's report on your parents. Dead in a car accident." She chuckled. "How wonderful you had family to take you in and raise you. Family like Jess Hammersmythe." Bernadette gave me a beatific smile. "What secrets does Jess have, hmm? How about her family and friends? We could dig so much deeper if we tried. What do you have in your past that you want to keep hidden?" She laughed. "You'll toe the line and like it or we'll set the dogs on all of them. How would you like that, hmm?"

My breath caught in my throat. The woman was signing her own death warrant and she didn't know it.

"Bernie, give me the gun," Michael repeated. He advanced on her.

I saw the wildness in her eyes, the fear of being proven wrong mixed with a mad sense of destiny. Logic had no place in her universe—it was all about appearances and devotion to family, no matter what the cost.

"Bernie." Michael's voice dropped to a low, authoritative tone. "Give me the gun."

"Not a chance," Bernadette snapped. "I'm getting the baby and raising it with or without you."

"No," Bran shouted.

Michael kept walking toward her, hands outstretched.

Bernadette let out a whimper, taking a step back to avoid her husband.

Bran leaped toward her, pushing his father aside as he reached out for the weapon.

Her hand jerked—whether out of fear or self-preservation I couldn't tell. The pistol flew upward even as it fired again, a wild shot toward the two men.

Bernadette stood and gaped at them, the pistol dangling from her fingers.

The two men crashed to the floor, skidding across the varnished wood in silence. Neither of them moved.

I smelled Bran's blood.

I went mad.

The world narrowed for me into a crimson tunnel with Bernadette right at the center of it.

I attacked, hissing like a wildcat. I didn't care if I Changed or not, didn't care if she knew I wasn't human, didn't care if I killed her with or without claws.

Her bright blue eyes widened as I rammed into her, sending us both down. The pistol bounced out of her hands and clattered away, out of sight.

I rolled away before pouncing again, landing on her chest and pinning her to the floor. Her arms were splayed out to each side, fingers fluttering.

My left hand went around her throat to hold her in place. The pain blossomed again from the gunshot wound, spiraling down my arm and up into my jaw. I felt the skin leap under my touch, her pulse hammering against my fingers.

I jammed my right fist under Bernadette's jaw and pressed hard on the delicate ivory skin.

She gasped for air. Her hands flew up, clutching at my arms. The delicately manicured fingers clawed at my shirt.

Out of the corner of my eye I spotted Bran trying to sit up. Blood gushed from his nose, smearing across his face and hands. He burbled and spit onto the floor with an incoherent curse.

Michael rolled onto his back, breathing heavily as he watched his son. I couldn't smell his blood, only fear.

She'd missed.

The bullet had gone wide, embedding itself somewhere in my ceiling.

I didn't care.

Bernadette let out a whimper. I increased the pressure, cutting off most of her air. Her eyes bulged out and she drew short, wheezy hiccups.

I held my breath and reached for what I'd lost, stretching out to grab any trace of the Change left.

I didn't need much.

Just my claws.

THIRTEEN

"REB." THE FAMILIAR female voice came out of nowhere, a sharp whisper.

It sounded like my mother.

I shook my head, clearing the cobwebs.

A hand landed on the back of my neck.

"Rebecca," Jess murmured.

I didn't turn to look, focused on the woman under my hands.

"Reb." It was Bran this time. "I'm okay." I heard him gurgle for a moment before spitting. "Rebecca, I'm going to be fine." He coughed. "Maybe a broken nose."

"I don't care. I'm done with this, all of this." I felt my claws edge forward, slipping toward the open air.

Jess's grip intensified, tugging on a sensitive spot Bran's latest love bite had created. "Don't do it."

"She killed Molly. She wanted to kill us," I hissed. "She's a threat to our family."

"Yes, she is," Jess said. "But she's the mother of your mate. You can't kill her."

The first jagged edge burst through the bloody slits between my knuckles, the second break-through more painful than the first.

"She shot me." The throbbing in my arm intensified. "The stupid bitch shot me."

"I know. It'll heal, though—the wounds always heal," Jess whispered. Her mouth was near my ear as her grip intensified on the back of my neck, now a painful pinch. "Don't do something you'll regret."

Bernadette's eyes went wide as she felt the pointed nails press against her delicate pale skin. Another few millimeters and her blood would gush out, splashing against my shirt. She'd bleed out in minutes, her lifeblood pooling around us as she shuddered and shook, her body shutting down within minutes.

"Don't." It was a request, not an order.

"She wants me to keep her secrets. My secrets, her secrets," I whimpered, feeling the claws shift. "I can't keep so many secrets."

"You don't have to," Jess said softly, so low I could barely hear her. "You've kept enough. We've kept enough. Let her go."

I drew a shallow breath, reaching out to tweak the mental string again.

The invisible thread in my mind twitched once, twice—then went slack.

I felt the claws slip back under my skin. The coolness on my flesh went to hot burning as the minute openings were exposed to the open air. They'd heal in time but it'd hurt like a bitch for now.

"Reb." Bran appeared at Jess's side. "It's okay. We're going to be okay."

"I don't think any of us ever will be." I released my grip on Bernadette's throat and got to my feet.

She rolled to one side, gasping for air. Her palms slapped the floor. Drool spilled from her lips onto the hardwood. Tears rolled down her face, leaving dark smudges under her eyes and streak marks on her cheeks.

Bran grabbed my arms and helped me up. I sagged into his arms, my knees weak. I felt a thousand years old and almost too tired to breathe. Between being shot, Changing, Changing back and trying to Change one more time, I had all the strength of a weak waterlogged kitten.

My vision cleared enough to take in the terrified woman at my feet, Michael off to my left, still on his back, and Jess on my right.

"You got her?" Jess asked.

Bran nodded. He gave me a weak smile, blood dribbling out of his nose.

"Good. Don't move, you two." She glared at Bran. "Don't. Move."

He didn't say anything as Jess dropped to one knee beside Bernadette.

Bernadette looked at Jess. "Thank you," she rasped.

"Don't thank me." Jess's fist shot out and smashed into Bernadette's right cheek. Her head whipped to one side before bouncing back. Before the woman could recover Jess grabbed the limp white ruffles and pulled her up. "You don't mess with my family. Ever." She looked over at Bran. "I'm putting him under my protection right now. You mess with him, you mess with me."

"I'm his mother," Bernadette burbled through a mouthful of blood.

"That's the only reason why you're still alive." Jess's grip tightened. "Threaten either of them ever again and you'll answer to me. Understand?" Her lips drew back, showing bare teeth. "And I never touched you."

Bernadette nodded, staying silent.

Jess released her.

Bernadette began to weep, deep throaty sobs punctuated with short choking sounds.

Michael pulled himself into a sitting position, wheezing. He made no move to go to his wife.

Jess pointed at Michael. "Make yourself useful for once. Call 9-1-1."

He pulled out his cell phone and dialed, unable to look away from the mewling woman.

Jess stood beside me and inspected the bloody gash in my upper arm. "Need a few stitches but you'll be fine."

I winced at her examination. "Fucking burns."

"No shit." Jess placed her hand on the sore spot she'd caused on the back of my neck. She rubbed it gently, trying to ease the ache.

I groaned.

"You did the right thing," she whispered. "It's a horrible thing to have someone's blood on your hands."

I nodded, unable to speak. The knotted muscles under her touch loosened.

"I'll keep an eye on her until the cops arrive." Jess nudged me to one side. "You two go sit down."

Bran pulled me toward the couch. He didn't say anything to his father, who lay a few feet away, cradling his cell phone in both hands.

"Damn," he said, gingerly touching his swollen and bloodied nose. "There go my ruggedly handsome looks."

"You'll survive."

"We both will." He started to lean in for a kiss, hesitating at the last second to see my reaction. I knew it was from his bloody lips and chin—an instinctive fear.

I met him halfway, using my good hand to pull him close. I'd tasted him before.

He chuckled and licked his lips. "Thanks."

I met him halfway before lowering him to the ground. "Don't thank me yet." I heard the sirens in the distance. "We've got a long way to go before this ride comes to a complete stop."

ATTERSLEY SHOOK HIS head, balancing his bulk against the corner of my sofa. I hadn't seen him so confused since giving him a sudoku book for Christmas.

Around us strode paramedics and police, the first group taking care of Bernadette, Bran and myself—the second bunch collecting the pistol and mapping out the shootings.

The female medic tending to me finished bandaging my arm. "We'll need to do X-rays to make sure no bones got hit but I'd say off the top of my head you got lucky." The older woman clucked. "Going to have a nasty scar, though."

"I'll live with it." I turned to one side as she made notes on her clipboard. Hank stood over Bran, who sat on the floor.

"So you claim your mother had Molly Callendar killed in order to get custody of the baby." He scratched his chin.

I guessed it was Hank's body language for "explain, please."

"Having him kidnapped and delivered to her later provided the opportunity for her to declare Liam a distant relative and new adoptive son without having any direct connection back to her," Bran said from where he sat on the floor, surrounded by discarded gauze and bandages. The paramedics had done a fine job of bandaging his nose but insisted he go to the hospital.

Hank waved his hand in the air, urging him on. A good cop knows when to listen and when to talk.

"If Liam was left behind he'd go into foster care and be released to the Callendars as the closest living relatives. Odds are they'd ask for a paternity test before agreeing to joint custody with Brayton and the jig would be up."

"The jig?" Hank asked.

“David Brayton isn’t Liam’s father. Michael Hanover is.”

Hank didn’t react. No twitch, no shocked expression. But I knew inside he was falling-down drunk over this revelation.

“How do you know this?” he asked.

Bran gestured at me. “She’s the one who put the pieces together. Look at Liam and look at me, look at my father. He doesn’t look like Brayton—doesn’t take a genius to put it together. And I think my mother’s actions bear it out, don’t you?”

It was thin, damned thin. But it was better than trying to explain Felis scenting.

Hank grunted. The pen danced over his open notebook. He didn’t look at me. I was in trouble and it wasn’t the type a bottle of whiskey could make right.

“So you and her went sniffing around looking for the baby on your own.” The note of disapproval was loud and clear.

“We knew you were covering Brayton and Callendar.” Bran shrugged. “Figured we’d try something different.”

“Why didn’t you tell me?” This was more for me than Bran.

“No concrete proof, just a theory.” Bran stood up. “You were busy trying to find a missing baby and a killer. We didn't want to distract you when there could be nothing there." He nodded in my direction. "Limited resources—no need to send your men on a wild-goose chase and waste your time. And we didn't need my father's name spread all over the papers as a possible suspect—I don't have to tell you how fast a man's reputation can be trashed on rumors and innuendo."

Hank pursed his lips. It wasn't forgiveness but it was a start.

"So you're saying you found the kidnapper. And he is..." The detective's eyes fell on me, harsh and unyielding.

He'd get along with Jess just fine.

"Dead." I gave him the address of the cheap hotel. "He was dead when we arrived."

"How did you track him?"

I didn't even want to begin to describe that connection. I pointed at my feet. "Old school is still the best school. Got a tip through my sources. Convenience store close by told us a guy with a newborn came in looking for supplies. Followed up the tip and found him in a nearby hotel. Punk who's uncomfortable with a newborn and buying diapers tends to stand out." Tony Romano would back us up—he feared Jess more than the police.

"You found him dead." Hank made it sound like more of a question than a statement.

I nodded. "We picked up Liam and put him someplace safe."

"Someplace being with your friend." Hank gestured toward Jess, who hovered a few feet away, leaning on the kitchen doorway.

She didn't scowl, didn't glare. Her face was a mask, hiding her feelings from everyone around us. I knew she was watching and studying and cataloguing things in her mind.

Jess never forgot her friends and enemies. I hoped Hank would make it on the friends list.

"We didn't know who to trust." It sounded lame, even to my own ears. "We hadn't ruled out Bran's father as a suspect. Michael Hanover is a pretty powerful man with police connections. We were worried the baby would disappear before we could get the full story."

The senior detective studied me for a long minute. I could tell he believed half of it—which half was the question. And the difference between spending quality time in jail or walking free.

"Should I ask what your next move was going to be?"

I pointed toward the two Hanovers at opposite sides of the room, being questioned by uniforms.

"We got a call from his father that he wanted to talk. We met him here and went over the situation, talked it all out. Until his wife showed up."

That at least was the honest truth.

"Sorry." I couldn't add anything else.

Attersley sighed and turned away to make a phone call. I visualized the kid at the hotel's front desk freaking out as police swarmed over the cheap flop and he had to stop texting.

I could tell by the detective's frantic gesturing that he was coming in for quite a bit of heat himself from his superiors. This was a public relations nightmare and it could only get worse before it got better.

Attersley's attention came back to me, scathing and unyielding as he hung up. "Uniforms are on the way to verify your statement." He gave a weary sigh. "Did you ever think about calling it in? Never thought we might want to know this little bit of information? We've got men and women running around trying to find this baby and sucking up time and money that could have been rerouted elsewhere."

"Sorry." It sounded weaker the second time.

"You could be charged with kidnapping," Attersley snapped. "All the good works and wishes might not be enough to keep you out of trouble this time."

"I think not." A pudgy, slightly overweight woman emerged from the crowd. She wore a light blue blouse and jeans, a laminated identification card hanging from the lanyard around her neck. The clipboard in her hands held a good inch's worth of paperwork.

"And you are?" Attersley spit out. I couldn't blame the man for being short-tempered, he'd had a hell of a past few days.

"Denise Farnsworth." She stuck her hand out. "Social Services."

I risked a glance at Jess. She didn't look at me.

"And you are here because—"

"Liam Callendar was placed in our care early this morning and the AMBER Alert canceled." Her face was a perfect mask of innocence. "I guess you didn't get the memo."

If Hank could have snorted smoke, he would have.

"What?"

Denise gave him a wide smile. "The baby was registered as a ward of the court today. Thus, no kidnapping and/or violation of the law."

I sniffed the air.

Family.

Hank rolled his eyes. "Of course. Anything else I should be informed of?"

"No." Denise looked at her clipboard and tore off a page from the pile. "Here's the paperwork. Whatever else you may find to charge Ms. Desjardin with, it won't be kidnapping."

I felt dizzy and not just from the rip in my arm.

My family was curling around me, covering for me.

I couldn't even claim it was because of Felis business. The only Felis involved in this mess was me, an outcast.

I bit the inside of my cheek. Crying wasn't an option, not here and now.

"Okay." Hank scanned the pink carbon copy before tucking it into his pocket. "Thank you."

Denise nodded at me before walking over to Jess. The two women exchanged a fast look before falling silent.

"Who killed Keith Shaw?" Attersley asked.

"I killed him," Bernadette uttered from where she sat on the couch. She hadn't said a word since Attersley had arrived with the uniforms and paramedics. Her right eye was swollen and bruised from Jess's punch. The scratches on her throat didn't require bandages but the black-and-blue marks weren't going to disappear quickly.

"You." The disbelief in Attersley's voice matched my own feelings.

"I paid Shaw to kill Molly Callendar. I killed him afterward to cover my tracks."

Attersley put up a finger. "Do you want a lawyer? I've already given you your notice and you have the right to stay silent. You don't have to say another word about this matter until we get to the station and you have legal representation."

Bernadette nodded. "I understand completely and wish to continue my statement. Shaw called me and told me where he was staying. I stabbed him."

"With what?" Attersley pressed on.

"A knife." A wan smile appeared. "I threw it away. You'll never find it."

My head was spinning. There was no way for the prosecution to prove she did it and no way for her high-priced lawyer to prove she didn't do it, thanks to these statements.

"Why didn't you take the baby right there? Why did you leave Liam alone?" Attersley pressed onward.

Bernadette paused and I could almost see the internal wheels spinning to create a story. "I left the room to dispose of the knife. I was worried about carrying the baby and the diaper bag and the knife all together and I needed to get rid of it right away." She smiled. "I took it outside and threw it into the sewer."

She was weaving the perfect story and I couldn't stop her.

"When I came back into the hotel I saw Brandon and Rebecca in the lobby. I couldn't approach them and instead watched them go into Shaw's room and find Liam. When I saw them leave with the baby I had no reason to stay there. So I went home and got my weapon." She bowed her head. "I asked where my husband was and his assistant told me he was here, meeting Rebecca and Brandon. I came here in order to force them to give me the baby." Her gaze flickered around the room, unfocused and wild. "I thought he'd be here. All they had to do was hand him over." She rolled her attention back to the detective. "I didn't mean to hurt anyone. I just wanted my baby."

I bit down on my lower lip. The only way she'd know about Shaw being killed would be if she came to the hotel after we'd left—and now she was taking the blame because she was worried about Bran taking the hit for the murder.

She wanted to protect her son, save his reputation.

I was pretty sure she didn't care about mine.

Attersley looked at me. He wasn't buying this any more than I was but he was bound by the law to follow procedure and her confession would stand at least for the time being.

"Where did you meet Keith Shaw?"

Bernadette smiled. "I met him at Second Chance, Second Life—one of our charities. He is—was quite photogenic." A wistful look came into her eyes. "I hated having to kill him. So hard to get good help these days."

For a second I believed she'd actually killed Shaw. She had, at least in her mind.

Attersley shot me a warning look. Whether he believed her or not was irrelevant. She would be in for psychiatric assessment the minute she got to the station.

"Bernadette Hanover, I'm placing you under arrest for assault..." he droned on as he gestured for her to stand up, pulling handcuffs free from one pocket.

Michael Hanover didn't look at his wife as the detective repeated his previous warning and went through the litany of offenses.

Attersley pointed at each of us in turn. "Mr. Hanover, I need you to go with me to the station. You," he barked at Bran, "I'll see at the hospital along with Rebecca. After you receive the medical all-clear you'll be going back to the station for further questioning." The unspoken question of arresting us before, after or during the hospital visit hung in the air.

His eyes lingered on Jess for a second. "I don't believe we've properly been introduced. You are..."

"Jess Hammersmythe." She shook his hand with the usual bone-crushing grip. I had to give it to Hank, he never flinched. "I'm a family friend of Reb's."

"Ah. Funny she never mentioned you before." The wariness in his voice was tempered with exhaustion.

"Guess it never came up," she replied.

The two of them ignored me, busy with their own private joust.

"And how did you get involved with this mess?" Attersley swept his hand outward, encompassing the living room filled with medics, cops and suspects.

"Reb asked me to take care of the little one here while she continued to search for Callendar's killer. I called Ms. Farnsworth and dropped off the child early this morning."

"How do you know Ms. Farnsworth?" Hank asked.

"Bingo." Jess didn't miss a beat. "Every Thursday night at the Roadhouse Bingo Hall over on Sherbourne Street."

I tried not to smile.

"Bran called and asked me to come over and bring the baby. He didn't know Liam was already safe with Social Services."

Hank didn't give ground easily. "And you didn't call the police."

Jess shrugged. "Why would I? I didn't know all this craziness was going on." She gestured at Bernadette. "When I got here she was on the floor, Reb was shot and I told Michael to call 9-1-1."

Hank continued his not so gentle questioning. "You saw Liam yesterday, took him from these two." He tilted his head in my general direction. "Where did you pick him up?"

"At Yonge and Dundas, right on the street corner," she replied.

"They brought the baby out to you."

"Yes, they did." Jess smiled, hands tucked in her pockets. "I met them at the corner, took Liam and went home. I called Denise and she said to bring him over the next morning." The underlying steel in her voice spoke volumes.

"Of course," Attersley said with a defeated sigh. He wasn't up to verbally jousting with Jess—I'd yet to see anyone who could.

Jess looked at me. "I'll have a lawyer meet you at the station. Take your time sorting through the mess. Don't say anything else until he meets with you. I'll be here when you get back."

"You haven't needed a lawyer before, Reb," Attersley said.

"Never got into this much trouble before." I gave a respectful nod to Jess. "I appreciate it."

"We take care of our own. Call me if you need anything else." Jess locked eyes with me. "Anything," she repeated.

I got to my feet and watched Bran walk out the door, Michael behind him with two policemen escorting Bernadette, and Hank waiting to accompany me. "How about a time machine?"

FOURTEEN

It was well past midnight when I stumbled up the short walk to my front door. It was unlocked and I wasn't worried in the least. Anyone who thought they'd be able to rob a house with Jess inside deserved whatever he or she got.

I shut the door behind me, feeling the tension begin to ease out of my body. I was home and I was safe—for the time being at least.

My arm ached. The prescription painkillers had taken the edge off but it hurt like hell, even resting in the simple sling. I wouldn't be doing much for the next few weeks while it healed.

The doctor at the hospital had mumbled something about a nasty scar while he put in the handful of stitches needed. He'd suggested a plastic surgeon, clucking his tongue at having such an ugly line on my fair skin.

I'd resisted the urge to show off the claw marks on my back.

The widescreen television Bran had recently

bought blared some science-fiction movie, the spaceships chasing each other with bad special effects.

Jess looked up from petting Jazz, the two of them sprawled the length of the sofa. Jazz let out an annoyed trill and rolled off to land on the floor with a thump.

I wagged a finger at the fat white cat. "Tell me you at least played hard to get for a few seconds."

Jazz lifted her nose into the air and strutted off toward the stairs.

Jess turned the television off and stood up. "Rolled over for a few cat treats and told me where the silver was." She looked me over, her lips twisting into a sad smile. "I'll start some tea. You look like you need some." Jess headed for the kitchen, humming a hunting song I'd forgotten the words to.

I felt like I'd fallen down a rabbit hole instead of coming home.

"Don't even think about pressing your luck on that wound. Remember Johnny Ladder?"

I didn't but wasn't ready to get into a conversation about Felis I'd met and forgotten years ago.

She continued, ignoring my nonresponse. "He got himself shot by a hunting party who mistook him for a deer."

I sat down on the still-warm cushions. "A deer?"

"Damned fool was running out at the farm and went off our territory. He limped back to Ruth with the same sort of gunshot wound." I heard the sound of water running. "He figured he'd get back to work at the warehouse before the doctor cleared him. Idiot ended up with an infection and laid up even longer."

"I'll keep it in mind." I grimaced as I spotted bloodstains on the hardwood floor.

It'd take a lot of scrubbing to get them out.

Or a well-placed throw rug.

I made a note to scour the local yard sales for a good hunk of carpet.

"Can I ask how Liam is? Or is he in some weird witness protection program?"

"He's safe with a foster family." She poked her head out of the kitchen and held up a palm before I could speak. "Not ours, before you ask. He'll be treated like a king until the courts determine who gets custody—the grandparents or his father."

"His father." I rolled the words off my tongue like a piece of sour candy.

"Like it or not, Michael Hanover is his father. DNA test'll prove it quick enough." The voice drifted to me as I looked around the living room.

It looked the same but so different in my mind. I couldn't get the images of Bernadette holding us at bay and of my being shot out of my mind.

It'd be a long time before I could relax on this couch again.

The tangled wreck of the table Bran had destroyed lay in a neat pile. She'd swept the mess together but hadn't disposed of the warped, splintered wood. "The Callendars will likely get full visitation rights so don't worry about that. But they're the grandparents and the courts usually rule for the biological parent to get full custody." She paused. "And Hanover has the money to buy enough legal beagles to either tie the Callendars up forever in court or bankrupt them."

My stomach twisted into knots. "Even if he doesn't want the child?"

"Ah." Jess held up a finger. "There's the money question. Will he pay support to the Callendars and let them raise Liam or buy himself a nanny and be an absentee father?"

I shook my head. "He didn't want the baby in the first place. Why would he want him now?"

"Appearances." I heard the ceramic mugs clink against each other. "He may want to look good for the social papers. Right now the barbarians are at the gates and he's going to want to spin this to look good."

"Even if his wife is bat-shit nuts."

"Even if." Jess chuckled. "I'm no lawyer but I'm willing to bet that unless the cops can prove the father had previous knowledge of the attack on Molly Callendar he's going to end up with the child. It helps that Bernadette is confessing to everything and everyone." She let out a sigh. "Not the best outcome but it'll have to do."

I rolled my head back and forth on the cushions. It was a lovely feeling after hours of sitting alone on hard wooden chairs.

Bran had disappeared into the depths of the hospital as soon as we'd arrived, a classic case of splitting us up so we couldn't chitchat and get our stories to match. It'd taken a few hours to get stitched up and cleared medically—afterward I'd stayed silent the entire way to the police station as per Jess's instructions.

My lawyer had been waiting for me, clutching a stack of paperwork to his chest under a plaid bow tie. The elderly man was a classic image of the country lawyer, patting my good shoulder and murmuring reassurances in my ear that it'd be okay, it'd be all fine.

I didn't have the heart to tell him it'd never be okay. Never again.

"Bill Watts says hello and thanks for the work," I told Jess.

He'd been a godsend, cutting through the police red tape with ease and efficiency. It didn't hurt that he knew most of the prosecutors in a nonprofessional capacity and argued my side with enthusiasm. The Felis even had a packet of beef jerky in his pocket he slipped to me, knowing I'd be ravenous after the long day.

Watts had made a good enough argument with the result of a lot of the more serious charges being dropped. I might end up with a fine and probation for not reporting Shaw's death but even that was a long shot due to what they called the "extenuating circumstances," meaning my concern for the baby.

The family had enough connections to win me the lowest possible punishment since I had no previous convictions or even a hint of a run-in with the law before now. Watts was a lawyer but I knew we had friends and family at higher levels who would work deals to keep me on the outside.

Jess's voice came through the thin walls. "He's a good fellow. Dated him a thousand years ago. He'll make it right."

I tried not to think about Jess dating. It was

like imagining your parents having sex and I'd had enough trauma for a day.

The kettle screamed for attention. I stayed on the couch. Jazz hopped up and head-butted my hip, demanding attention.

"Aren't you a fickle one?" I stroked her automatically, relishing the cool, sleek fur under my fingers. It was a constant in the sandstorm I'd been riding recently.

Jess came out of the kitchen carrying my Brown Betty teapot on a tray along with two mugs. She placed it down on the table between us and sat in the chair.

I rubbed my eyes with the palm of my good hand.

Jess cleared her throat.

I waited.

She licked her lips, watching the teapot. Her one good eye didn't waver from the fat brown ceramic pot.

"Family is difficult. Our family is difficult."

"Our family is insane."

A smile tugged at her lips. "At times, yes. But don't forget you only see a slice of the entire pie, a wedge of our reality." She swept a hand around. "There are Prides around the world, Felis in almost every occupation you can think of, all family interconnected by our shifting ability."

My stomach growled.

Jess chuckled and got up. "I believe you've got a package of scones in the breadbox."

I took advantage of her departure to pour out the tea before it got too strong. There was already a splash of milk in each mug, enough to take the edge off.

She returned with a pyramid of blueberry scones, the tiny triangles covered with a thin sugar glaze. I grabbed three of them and gobbled them down before she could reach her mug.

"Napkin." She handed over a paper towel. "Let's pretend you know your manners."

I swiped at my mouth. "Yeahsureyoubetcha." The hot tea burned my throat but it felt so good, so regular, so comforting after the last twenty-four hours.

"Family," Jess started again. She shook her head. "Fuck."

I chuckled.

"You're worried about how Bran's going to deal with this." She cradled the mug in both hands, leaning forward.

"Yes," I confessed. "I'm partially responsible for his mother going to jail and his father, ah…"

"Being an adulterous idiot?"

I scowled. "That, not so much."

Jess looked down into her mug. "He's a good man. His parents, however, are a piece of work. The father blackmails you into doing errands for him and the mother holds further investigation over your head to try and buy your silence."

I flinched at the truth. It sounded even worse when she put it like that. "How did you know?"

"I heard Bernadette shrieking before I came in. I knew there was trouble inside and I wasn't going to walk in without doing a bit of recon first." She reached out and broke off the edge of one scone. "Am I wrong?"

"No." I sat back and sighed, my initial burst of hunger sated for the moment. "She threatened to let the investigators loose, let them go wild digging up my family tree."

Jess sipped her tea. "She'd have found a handful and a half. And you know how we'd have reacted."

"Which is why I agreed to all this in the first place." I let out a weary grunt. "And why I'm worried about Bran. I didn't kill his parents physically but I sure as hell gave them some mortal wounds emotionally."

"They did this to themselves." She snapped another edge off. "You just got caught in the final mutual murder-suicide."

I studied the little glazed crumbs in my palm. "When I was finished at the station I went looking for him. The cops told me Bran was gone with his father—trying to figure out what to do about Bernadette and how to handle it. Watts told me they're not charging Bran with anything at this point and he's got a high-powered Hanover-authorized lawyer watching his back." I rubbed the back of my neck. "I don't know how he's going to handle this. His father's adultery, his mother's insanity, the little half brother."

"He's a strong man. He'll survive." Jess popped the last bit of the scone into her mouth. "Don't underestimate the mettle of that one."

"His mother's going to jail for some time. His father's got a new baby to deal with and his reputation is trashed. The family name is tarnished." I shook my head. "They had everything. How did it all go so bad?"

Jess took a deep breath before speaking. "I can understand where Bernadette's coming from."

My heart began to hammer in my chest.

Jess kept talking. "Sometimes we do what's right for the family, not what's right for us as an individual. That thing about needs of the many outweighing the needs of the few."

I felt nauseated. The scone and tea curdled in my belly.

Her fingers tangled and untangled in her lap. "I think it's time for me to talk to you about something."

"Oh God." I clutched at my chest, half-serious. "You're not my mother, are you?"

"No." Jess chuckled. "Isn't that a relief, eh?"

I didn't say anything.

She chewed on her lower lip before continuing. "Did you ever wonder how I got this?" She gestured at the deep scarlet scar marring the left side of her face.

"Figured it was a challenge. Some kit taking you on."

Jess shook her head. "Not exactly. It was a woman, believe it or not."

I wasn't surprised. Challenges in the Pride could come at any time. We'd been brawling with each other almost from birth, rolling in the dirt with our crib brothers and sisters in mock battles. True challenges were heavy-duty, with both fighters usually ending up bloody and marked—not something to be entered into lightly.

Jess tapped her lips. "I was dating a young man. I loved him and I thought he loved me."

"Ah." I tried to sound knowledgeable but inside I was floundering around like a drowning kitten. This was unfamiliar ground.

"He cared for me but I don't know if he ever truly loved me. There's a difference." She sipped her tea before continuing. "We were teenagers. Hormones in flux and all that. We were dating and it was pretty serious for about one year." She smiled into her mug. "I thought he was going to ask my father for my hand."

I shoved another scone in my mouth to avoid thinking too loudly.

"There was another girl who had her eye on him. He liked her too—not enough to drop me but enough to make me wonder about the depth of his love, his dedication to me."

I shifted on the couch. This was not something I needed to hear.

"She told Eddy she loved him and knew he loved her more than he loved me. Eddy, God bless him, wasn't sure what to do. He wanted to make us both happy but since Felis don't have polygamous relationships he knew he'd have to pick one."

"He didn't pick." I could see where this was

going. “He didn’t want to hurt either one of you so he didn’t pick.”

Jess nodded. “She challenged me, figuring it would settle the situation once and for all.” She gestured at her scar. “I underestimated her badly, underestimated how much she cared for Eddy.” Jess stared at me. “Edward Desjardin. Your father.”

I almost fell off the couch. Jazz trilled and bumped my hip again, sensing my confusion.

“My mom did that?” I didn’t know whether to laugh or cry.

“One helluva fighter.” Jess traced the narrow gouge. “She fought for your father. She didn’t mean to do this. This was an accident. A slip, a fall, and this happened.” A sad smile appeared. “I never held it against Grace. Not when I saw how happy they were together. On my best days with Eddy we were never that happy together. He and Grace were a perfect match, perfect mates.”

“You and my dad.” I wasn’t sure whether to be revolted, terrified or just confused.

“Afterwards we became close pals, the three of us.” She wagged a finger in the air. “Not that way, before your dirty little mind goes there. Grace and Eddy knew they could count on me to be there.”

“Then why...” I coughed on the words clogging

my throat. The scars across my back throbbed as if they'd been reopened. "This." I waved over my shoulder with my one good hand, unable to speak the words.

Jess looked down, fumbling with the half-empty mug of tea. "I thought you had more of your mother in you, the fighting spirit I saw when she challenged me for your father. I thought if I attacked you, forced you into a corner, your Felis nature would come out."

A single tear broke free from her right eye. It slowly dribbled down her cheek, curling up under her chin.

She swallowed hard before speaking. "I was wrong."

I wasn't sure what to say in response, if anything.

"When your parents died I promised myself I'd take care of you, guide you into a power position in the Pride." Jess sniffled, making a halfhearted swipe at her nose with one hand. "I figured your… disability was a mental thing, something we could work through. After their accident, when you stopped being able to Change, the doctors couldn't find anything physically wrong with you so…" She stopped speaking.

"So you thought you'd beat it out of me." The

words came out harsher than I meant and I regretted them as soon as they escaped my mouth.

"Yes." The whispered response ripped the healed wounds open as easily as if she'd clawed me again. "And I'm sorry about it. I was wrong." She drew a stuttering breath. "We were wrong. The Board made the decision but I went along with it. I thought if it was me it'd be different, it'd call up your mother's blood..." She looked down, shaking her head and falling silent.

I couldn't begin to sort through the emotions swirling around in my mind and heart, thoughts bashing and crashing into each other as I looked back on the decades I'd spent exiled from my home and family.

And yet...

I closed my eyes, trying to figure out what I thought and felt after the first surge of rage and sadness.

Where I was, what I was, existed solely because of my past. All the missteps and all the decisions from both the Felis and me had led to my being here.

With Bran.

I put my mug down and reached across the tray to take Jess's free hand.

"I understand."

Her fingers tightened on mine for a long minute, her gaze riveted on the floor.

I swallowed hard. "You did what you thought was right—like Bernadette."

Her head shot up and I saw a flash of anger in her good eye before it dimmed to a sad nod. "That's why I had to tell you this. Family secrets. Some of them don't deserve to be kept."

I shifted, feeling the tightness across my back. "I'm not going to thank you for it but things worked out okay." I looked around the living room. "I'm here. And I have Bran. Wouldn't have any of that if I'd stayed on the farm."

"Be a lot easier if you stayed out of trouble," she growled.

I resisted the urge to smile. There was the Jess I loved and feared.

I also knew I wouldn't be able to turn down the next request for help from Jess, not with a clear conscience. I'd racked up a shitload of IOUs with the family and it'd take time to pay them all off.

"Thanks for the help with Liam." I shifted the conversation into safe ground. "I felt better knowing he was safe."

"Glad to do it. Been a while since I held a baby. Sort of missed it." She stood up and put the cup on the tray. Her nose wrinkled. "Except for the diapers. That I definitely did not miss."

I couldn't help laughing. A full diaper smelled bad enough for me—I couldn't imagine how much stinkier it smelled with Jess's heightened senses.

Jess cleared her throat, once again the badass Felis Board member. "Now that you're back I'm going to head to the farm. Too much excitement for one day for this old lioness."

"You're welcome to stay here for the night." The words were out of my mouth before I realized it. It'd been the politest thing I'd said to her in months.

The scars on my back didn't ache.

She smiled. "Thanks, but your mate's going to be home soon and I don't want to interfere in the discussion you two are going to have. I'm no dummy—I know when to get out of the way." She snatched up her leather jacket from the coat rack standing near the front door. "Besides, I'm a light sleeper. Be too uncomfortable to stay awake all night listening to the two of you making up."

Jess trotted out before I could come up with a snappy retort.

I stood up, every bone and muscle aching from the mental and physical abuse I'd endured over the past day. Jazz mewed before rolling into the warm spot I'd vacated.

The front door was unlocked. I headed toward it, planning to barricade myself in the house for at least a few hours until dawn. It'd been a long strange day and I wanted to climb into a hot shower and scrub all the strange off.

A familiar scent drifted in, replacing Jess's.

I inhaled deeply, feeling the aches and pains starting to be replaced by a calmness, a steadiness only one person could create. I walked out the front door.

Bran stood in the front yard. He had his back to me and stared up at the night sky. On good nights you could actually spot stars through the ever-present city haze.

It was a good night.

A full moon helped illuminate the grass and rosebushes lining the small patch of dirt, giving them an otherworldly look.

He stood there, his hands in his pockets, looking up. I walked up beside him and glanced subtly at his left side. A small bandage ran across the top of his nose. The blood was gone and I caught the smell of antiseptic wipes.

"Not broken," Bran said to the night sky.

"Oh." I didn't know what to say. There was

so much ground to cover and I didn't even have a map.

"Jess just passed through." A wide grin split his face. "Gave me a hug."

I blinked. "A hug?"

"Yeah. Can't figure that woman out."

"Tell me about it." I stood beside him and looked up into the darkness. "I've been trying for years. I want to say she's mellowing in her old age but I'm afraid she'll rip my throat out for even thinking it."

Bran laughed. "I can see that."

I swallowed hard, not knowing where to start. "Bran, I'm—" I shook my head. "I'm so sorry."

He frowned. "For what?"

"For all of this." I couldn't stop the tears from flowing. "This is all my fault."

"What?" He turned me toward him. "What are you talking about?"

"I should have walked away from it all," I mumbled. "All I had to do was tell Hank what I saw and leave. If I hadn't scented Liam, if I hadn't found out who his real father was..."

"Because it would have been so much better for my mother to get away with murder." The ironic tone slapped me across the face. "Because it would have been preferable for Liam to grow up living a lie and my mother denying him the truth about his family. Because the Callendars wouldn't mind burying their daughter and wondering where in the world their grandson is and if he's even alive."

I sniffled. "I should have just not been..." I flapped my hands, knowing I looked like an idiot and not caring. "Not a Felis."

"Don't you say that," he growled. "Don't you ever say that."

"If I hadn't—"

He cut me off with a slash of his hand, moving in on me. "Molly Callendar's death would have gone down as a horrible crime with no one answering for it. Mike Hancock's murderer would still be running the police force down in Penscotta and doing God knows what under the Board's noses. And Janey Winter's family would still be wondering who the hell killed their mother and wife." He huffed. "Don't you ever, ever say that you don't want to be Felis again."

"But your mother—"

"My mother's been messed up for years. If she'd gotten away with this, God knows what would be next."

He grabbed my shoulders and pulled me close. "If you weren't who you are, my life would suck. I'd be writing crappy tabloid filler and sleeping alone every night, drinking myself to sleep and wondering if there was something better out there." His voice dropped to a heated whisper. "I love ending every day with you wrapped in my arms. I live to wake up every morning curled around you in bed." Bran cupped my face in his hands, tears now running down his cheeks. "You've changed me forever. And I wouldn't trade it for anything in the world." His thumb rubbed against my lips. "My ferocious little Felis."

The light kiss tasted of tears, both of ours.

I hiccupped and slumped in his arms, dizzy with emotion.

Bran grunted. "How long for the arm?"

I winced and looked at the bandage. "Too long."

"Oh, well." He gave me a soft smile. "I think I'll have to be on top for a bit. Just to make sure you don't fall off and pull those stitches out."

"Sure." It was time to get serious. "Did, ah, did you get an update on your mother?"

He looked down and dug the toe of his running shoe into the half-dead grass. "Mom might make bail tomorrow. Lawyer's doing his best to make it happen. There's talk of going for diminished capacity."

"Mental illness. Do you think she'll go for it?"

He shrugged. "I don't honestly know. It won't

keep her out of jail forever but she'll at least be able to get some help to deal with things." He shook his head. "The society papers are going to have a good run at this. Liam's existence, his mother's murder at my mother's command and my father's infidelity, all out in the public for everyone to see."

"Spice up those tea parties." I fumbled for something proper to say. "Might even make some of them have more than one cucumber sandwich."

"Just might." He let out a pained sigh. "I saw Dad. He, well…he wants what's best for Liam. I overheard his lawyers talking about going to the Callendars, working out some sort of deal. He's a bit long in the tooth to take care of a newborn."

I touched his shoulder. "Liam deserves a family."

"I'm not sure Dad is the right type of family. Look how I turned out." He spread his hands palm-up. "Fucked up five ways to Sunday."

"You're not so bad." I gave him a gentle nudge with my hip. "Except when you scratch and bite."

"Thought that was what you liked."

A hot surge of lust burned through my veins. Ever since our foray into the Pennsylvanian wilderness our lovemaking had been a bit rougher, a bit more frantic. I'd been able to let my Felis side out and Bran liked it—returning my efforts with interest.

It was a flash of the old Bran. I felt a bit better.

His left hand uncurled from his pocket and slipped into my right. "I told my father I'm done with the Hanovers. The family, the company, all of it."

I frowned. "What?"

His grip tightened. "I've lived off their money for years. The condo, the credit cards—all backed by Daddy's money. It never bothered me, because I made myself believe the cash I got from writing was enough to live on. Now I realize it was a payoff, a way of buying my silence. About his affairs, about everything. The problems we never spoke about, the secrets we kept." He lifted our entwined hands. "I wonder if it would have turned out this way if my family chatted more around the breakfast table like regular folk instead of rushing off to work or to charity meetings or photo ops."

"Maybe, maybe not." I smiled. "You've never been much of a morning person."

"I'm giving it all up. The condo's going up for sale and I already shredded the credit cards."

I felt like I'd been punched in the stomach. "Everything?"

"Everything. No more steaks, no more tailored

suits, no more fancy restaurants." His free hand swept over the yard. "I don't want any economic links to either of them. I might be blood kin and I can't do anything about that, but I'm not going to take their money and be expected to keep their dirty little secrets." The words rolled out as if he were afraid to keep them inside for a second longer. "I'll do what's right by Liam. He's my half brother and I want to have a relationship with him, if and when the Callendars will let me. But that's all."

"Whuf." I couldn't think of anything more appropriate to say. A part of me whimpered at the loss of those fabulous rare steaks. The other part was relieved Jazz wouldn't get any fatter on fancy leftovers.

The third part wondered where he was going to go now.

"Problem is, now I'm homeless. And I'm a wee bit too old to go sleep in the park with the other kids."

"Oh well." I gave a dramatic sigh. "I guess I'll go get your spare underwear and socks and stuff them into a plastic bag. I think there's a park over by the lake that's got a few empty benches at this time of night."

"What?"

I couldn't sustain the seriousness needed to pull the joke off.

"Would you like to move in with me?"

Bran rubbed his chin. "This is a big step forward in a relationship. I mean, what if you find your perfect mate next w—"

I cut him off with a growl, pressing my lips to his.

His teeth closed on my bottom lip and tugged, almost painfully.

I pulled back first, breathless and smiling.

"We are one screwed-up couple," Bran said.

"Yep." I took his hand and led him inside. "It's a good place to start."

* * * * *